MAROONED

BEN CHALFIN

Cover Design by Michael Pickard
Distributed by Simon & Schuster

ISBN: 978-1-998672-24-0
Ebook: 978-1-998672-25-7

FIC027330 - Romance/Sports
FIC133020 - Performing Arts/Film, Television & Radio
FIC027190 - Romance/LGBTQ+/Gay

#Marooned

Follow Rising Action on our socials!
Twitter: @RAPubCollective
Instagram: @risingactionpublishingco
Tiktok: @risingactionpublishingco

To Eli, my fiancé and forever beta reader: I love you, and I can't wait to marry you

MAROONED

CHAPTER 1

DAY 1

The motorboat bounces and heaves as it skips over the waves. The ocean is a deep, sapphire blue, the clearest I've ever seen, and emerald-green islands surrounded by pristine beaches dot the horizon. It was raining earlier, but now the sun is shining, obscured only occasionally by giant cotton ball-like clouds speckled across the sky. I was expecting Samoa to be beautiful, and so far, it hasn't disappointed.

If only I could actually sit back and *enjoy* the beauty, that would be great. Instead, I'm trying my best not to throw up, and not just from seasickness. In a few hours I'll be stranded on one of these deceptively harmless-looking islands with seventeen strangers, with little in the way of food or shelter, all of us competing to be the last one standing and claim a million-dollar prize.

Five of those strangers—namely, my competition—are on the boat with me, along with the captain. We all just met this morning, but we were instructed not to talk to each other yet, so we sit in relative silence. I knew this was coming. The producers don't want us to do any strategizing before we're on camera, because they might miss something and the show might not make sense. But how much strategy can you really get from a simple *Excuse me* or *Hi, nice to meet you*?

So instead of chatting with the others, I silently analyze them while trying to look like I'm doing anything else. There are three men, including me, and three women. One of the women is Black and older than I am, probably in her forties or fifties, with long brown hair that whips in the wind as she gazes around with wide eyes, a tiny smile on her lips. The other two women are younger and could probably both be models. For all I know, they *are* models. One is Asian, with high cheekbones and shoulder-length jet-black hair, while the other is white and blonde, and looks like she probably grew up on a farm somewhere smack dab in the Midwest. The former is smiling too, but the latter looks grim, as though she's about to throw up, either from motion sickness or nervousness.

In between the two maybe-models sits one of the men, who lets out the occasional *whoop* when the boat speeds up or bounces on a particularly large wave. He looks to be in his late thirties or early forties—so, about a decade or two older than me—and his attire is that of a quintessential redneck: a dirty-blond mullet, goatee, and creased green baseball cap. He probably sells tractors and tractor accessories for a living. Or, at least, that's what he wants us to think. I've seen every episode of all eighteen seasons of this show, and if there's one thing I've learned, it's that appearances can be deceiving.

Sitting next to Green Hat is a muscle-bound Hispanic man with quite a few tattoos and a thick mustache, who looks like he's about to throw up, too. He's deeply tanned, and his face looks weathered, so I'm guessing he works outdoors, but I obviously don't know for sure.

One of the models glances in my direction before quickly looking away, and that makes mee wonder what conclusions the other five are drawing about *me*. They can probably guess from my pale skin that I don't get outside very much, and I'd bet that my short, dark hair and clean-shaven look probably give that same impression. I doubt they'll see me as a physical threat since I probably weigh half of what Mustache does, even though I'm the tallest one on the boat. That could be a good thing or a bad thing—or, more likely, both.

In truth, I probably won't find out if my wild guesses are correct anytime soon. If this season is anything like previous ones, we'll be split into two tribes to start, and I doubt all six of us will be together. Realistically, I'll get to know two or three of them soon, and the rest later, assuming they're still in the game by then. Assuming *I'm* still in the game by then.

But I don't know who will fall into each category, so I try

my best to evaluate all of them as best I can without actually speaking. The game is about to start, and I need to have as much information as I possibly can if I want to win.

And I don't just want to win, I *need* to win.

A gasp from the Black woman draws my attention, and I look up to see a ship, a real-life wooden ship, with sails and everything, in the distance. As we draw closer, I can see that it's a replica of a pirate vessel, albeit painted with bright colors that I assume are to make it look better on TV screens, and it sits in front of the prettiest, most jewel-like island I've ever seen. I can't deny a bit of a stirring feeling in my chest; if I'm going to starve and get rained on and sleep in a poorly-built shelter every night, at least I'll get to enjoy the view.

We continue to speed towards the ship, quickly getting close enough to see people walking around the top deck, holding cameras or adding finishing touches to the decor. One woman waves at our motorboat and speaks into a walkie-talkie, and her voice crackles from the captain's side. I can't make out what she's saying over the sound of the engine, but the captain nods and responds with, "Understood. Coming around to starboard. Over."

Slowing as we approach, we circle around to the other side of the pirate ship, so we're between the ship itself and the island. Two other motorboats like the one I'm on are waiting; we're too far away to make out the occupants, but they must be the other contestants. In truth, I only spare them a glance, because my attention is drawn to the pirate ship. A wide hole gapes in the island-facing side of the ship, as though it's been shot by a cannon, with wooden beams sheared off to expose the interior. The effect is striking, and I could almost believe that this is a real pirate ship that the producers somehow discovered and refurbished to look like new.

After a few minutes of waiting, we draw up to the side of the ship far from the gaping hole, and one of the walkie-talkie people lowers a rope ladder for us to climb up. The six of us on the boat line up, with Green Hat in the front and me sandwiched between Model One and Model Two. Once it's my turn, I scramble up the ladder, the rope rough against my hands.

Once I've reached the top and clambered onto the ship, a producer points me towards a large open area on the deck with two mats on the ground, one purple and one sky blue. "Stand on one of the mats—doesn't matter which one—and we'll get started quickly," he says, his tone bored, like he does this every day. "Remember, no talking until we've started filming."

I follow his instructions and stand on the purple mat, remaining silent despite the fact that it feels incredibly strange not to say a single word to the people I'm standing with.

As I'm standing there waiting, it finally hits me that I'm *here*, about to play the game that I've loved watching on TV since I was ten years old. I applied for the first time as soon as I turned eighteen, and kept applying every year after that, at first because I *knew* I could win, and because I was sure the journey would be more than worth it even if I lost.

But two years ago, everything changed. By the time I finally got the call from the casting department a few months back, all I could think was that I *have* to win, no matter what. Living on a beach with no shelter or food or water may not be the most alluring prospect, but it's a small price to pay to be able to finally do something for the one person who's always been there for me.

I'm so caught up in my own thoughts that I don't pay attention to the last group of contestants coming on board, only coming out of my mini-trance when one of the producers, the same one who directed us to the mats, stands in front of us and waves his hands. "Okay, everybody, if I could have your attention for a moment," he says. He looks old enough to be my father—I push down a slight pang of pain at the thought—and he has deeply tanned skin, a bald head, and a gray goatee the same color as his T-shirt. "My name is Steve, and I'm an executive producer. In a few moments, we'll get started. First, the host will do an intro with all of you in the background. Then you'll be split into tribes. You may quickly introduce yourselves to each other during that brief period, but other than that we ask that you please continue to remain silent until we explicitly say otherwise. Finally, we'll do a brief outro.

"Once that's all done, we'll send you off to your tribe beaches, where you'll be living for the next thirty-three days. Does anyone have any questions? If so, please raise your hand." He pauses for a moment, but nobody moves, and he nods. "Excellent. In that case, just hold tight and—"

He's interrupted by a squawk from his walkie-talkie. Once again, the voice coming from it is inaudible, but Steve just nods and says, "Alright, sounds good. We're ready whenever he is." He puts the walkie-talkie away and turns back to us, a hint of a smile gracing his face. "Perfect timing," he says, waving to one of the cameramen, who hoists up his camera on his shoulder and aims it at us. "If you could all just look off to your right—yes, just like that, perfect—you should be able to see it any moment now …"

I do as he requested. At first, I'm not quite sure what I'm looking for, but then I spot another motorboat in the distance, heading our way. In my peripheral vision, I see Steve wave to yet another worker, who commands a camera-loaded drone to fly straight up into the air and hover overhead. There are only two people on the boat, one driving and one standing in the center. The latter looks imperious even from a distance, as though it's a battleship and he's the captain. *Could it be …?*

The motorboat rapidly closes the distance, and it's not long before a tall Black man with close-cropped hair and an easygoing smile—Alex Crawford, a man I've seen a million times on TV but never in person—steps onto the boat. He's the one mainstay of this show, the host since the very first season, pretty much an institution unto himself.

Alex walks towards us, his stride powerful, still looking every inch the captain, the man in charge, the intermediary between the eighteen of us and the millions who will watch the show at home. He pauses so someone can clip a small mic to his white shirt, then moves to stand on a small red X painted onto the deck. Finally, he looks at Steve, who gives him the thumbs up.

Only then does Alex turn to us, his shoulders back and his chin held high. "Contestants," he says, gracing us with a professional smile. "Welcome to season nineteen of *Marooned*."

CHAPTER 2

DAY 1

Alex pauses to let his words sink in, but before I can really feel their impact—*I'm really here, this is it, don't mess up, please don't mess this up*—he's talking again. "There are eighteen of you standing before me, but only one can win the million-dollar prize," he says, his voice perfectly intoned. "Over the next thirty-three days, you'll compete in challenges, build a shelter to keep you dry, forage for food and water, and live off these islands as best you can. Eventually, you'll get to know each other, become friends and allies … and stab each other in the back. Unless, that is, you get betrayed first." He pauses again, his expression momentarily serious before his smile returns in full force. "But first things first: let's get you separated into your tribes, so you know who you'll be living with for the first portion of the game."

Alex waits as a young woman steps forward and hands him a silver plate with several wrapped parcels on it. "On this platter, there are eighteen packets, labeled with your names. Each packet contains a tribal insignia that you must wear at all times. Once everyone has taken their packet, I'll tell you to open them. Make sure you take the correct packet, and please do *not* open yours before I instruct you to. Understand?" He waits for us to nod. "Once you've all gotten a chance see what color your insignia is, I'll ask you to please move to the matching mat, if you're not already on it."

He steps forward, starting at his left. When he gets to me, I take the packet labeled with my name and hold it. It's hard to tell exactly what's inside just by feel. In previous seasons, it's always been something small that we can all wear, like a bracelet or a headband. Nothing fancy, just a way to remind the viewers what tribe we're on. The producers surely determined who would be on what tribe long ago, so it's not like wishing for luck will change anything, but I do so all the same. It would be nice to be on a tribe that can win challenges, one that has at least a few people I can work with, and maybe a few easy targets too. But most of all, I need whatever will get me to the end and win, even if I don't know exactly what that is yet.

Alex hands the last packet to the final person in line—Model Two, who handles it gingerly, as though it might bite her—and moves back to where he was standing before. "Okay, contestants," he says. "Go ahead and open your packets, put on your insignias, and move to the correct mat."

My hands trembling slightly, I open my packet to reveal a necklace with a round wooden token, painted purple. I slip the insignia over my head and remain where I'm standing, since I'm already on the correct mat. Meanwhile, some of the others shuffle in both directions. Green Hat and Mustache, as well as a few others, move to stand over on the blue mat, leaving me with Model Two and some I don't recognize.

Meanwhile, the older Black woman who was on the boat with me comes over to the purple mat. "I'm Rhonda," she says, smiling warmly. Her voice has a heavy Southern accent, and I'm guessing she's probably from Alabama or Mississippi or somewhere like that. "Nice to meet you, young man."

"Ryan," I reply, holding out my hand for her to shake. Her grin seems genuine, and she has an air of trustworthiness about her that comes through even in our brief interaction. Of course, that doesn't mean I can *actually* trust her, but I already feel like we could work well together.

Out of the corner of my eye, I see someone else stepping onto our mat. "Hi there," I say, turning to introduce myself again. "I'm Ry—"

The words die in my mouth as I get a good look at who I'm introducing myself to: a tall man with short blond hair and eyes the color of the ocean. He looks to be around my age—maybe a year or two younger than me, if I had to guess, and he's wearing a light blue T-shirt and khaki shorts. While his muscles aren't exactly bulging like Mustache's, they're perfectly defined, like he was sculpted out of marble by Michelangelo. I know, somewhere deep in my mind, that I shouldn't stare at him, but that's exactly what I'm doing.

To my great discomfort, he chooses that moment to give me a dazzling smile. "Nice to meet you, Ry," he says, his perfect white teeth glinting in the sun as he holds out his hand. "I'm Cole."

I take his hand and shake it. I don't know whether Cole means to be a charmer or not, but either way the absolute *last* thing I need right now is to be distracted from my goal. Even if—*especially* if—he happens to be one of the most handsome men I've ever met. "It's Ryan," I correct myself. I need to be polite, so I add, "But you can call me Ry if you like."

He shrugs, still grinning lightly. "If you say so, Ry." He looks like he's about to say more, but a young Asian woman who barely comes up to his shoulder walks up to him and introduces herself. He turns his attention away from me, giving me a chance to breathe again and greet the rest of my tribe.

Or maybe not, because the producers signal Alex again, even though it's been less than a minute. "I'm glad to see you're all excited to meet each other," our host says, the rest of us quieting down and turning to face him. "However, there are still a few more things to do before we can send you to your beaches."

He gestures to the blue tribe and throws a small burlap bag to Green Hat. "Your tribe name is Sika," Alex says. "In that bag is a map to your new home, and a flint to help you get started making fire. Be careful, because if you lose your flint, we won't replace it, and you'll be on your own."

Next, he turns and tosses a bag to Cole, who snatches it out of the air one-handed. "Purple tribe, your name is Meru. Same thing as I just said for Sika goes for you: lose your flint, and you're out of luck. Now, one last piece of advice for both tribes …"

He pauses, and when he speaks again, his expression is serious. "Remember, this is a zero-sum game. Only one of you will win, and the rest will lose. But in order to make it to the end, you'll have to work with your tribemates. As with life, there's no correct way to succeed, and how you play is up to you. Just know that if there are a hundred ways to win, there are a hundred thousand ways to lose. Always keep your focus on the game, and don't let anything distract you from your goal."

I've heard those words, or ones like them, coming out of my TV, phone, or laptop countless times over the last decade or so, ever since the very first episode aired when I was a kid. But now, hearing them in person, standing underneath the Samoan sky, they feel different—almost like they were meant for me, and me alone. Somehow, hearing them drives home the fact that I'm about to play this game that could change my life forever. The only thing standing in my way is the other contestants, and I'll do everything I can to make sure that none of them steal my prize.

If it wasn't already clear from all the cameras and producers and whatnot that this is a TV show first and foremost, what happens next would make it even more painfully obvious. The eighteen of us are told to get into two rowboats, one for each tribe, row about a hundred feet or so away from the pirate ship, then stop.

We, the newly-minted Meru tribe, paddle away in our purple-clad canoe, while the Sikas go in the opposite direction. Meanwhile, the hovering drone and the camera crew on the pirate ship film us majestically conquering the seas and navigating to our new homes.

Then, once we've reached the appointed distance and stopped paddling, one of the motorboats comes up alongside us, and we leave the rowboat behind. Once we're underway, Cole takes out the 'map' that we were given and silently shows it to the rest of us. As I expected, it's a cutesy little parchment with a vague outline of a coast and an X marking our tribe beach that I'm sure looks nice on TV but is essentially worthless for navigation purposes.

Thankfully, the captain seems to know where he's going, and the motorboat circles around the big island. It only takes a few minutes for us to come to a small cove on the western side of the island with a large purple flag on the shore, which I assume is our camp. The beach is beautiful, with white sand and palm trees waving lazily in the gentle breeze, but I have a feeling I'll think differently after a few days, if not a few hours.

The motorboat slows down as we approach the shore, pulling up beside a purple canoe that's an exact replica of the one we just got out of a few minutes ago. Waiting for us on the beach are several people holding large TV cameras, ready to make it look like we rowed the whole way here. The motorboat pilot tells us to get into the canoe, wait until he's out of sight, and then paddle the rest of the way in. It's nowhere near as majestic a landing as I imagined it would be from watching previous seasons, but as long as this ends with me winning a million-dollar check, I don't really care how authentic it feels.

Once the motorboat is gone and we've finally made our way to the beach, the nine of us take a few moments to admire our new home. The camera crew surrounds us, making sure to get all of our reactions while staying out of each other's shots.

"Should we all introduce ourselves?" asks one of my tribe-mates, a man with thick, curly hair and a full-Viking beard and mustache, who looks to be in his thirties. He's dressed like a lumberjack, with a flannel shirt and washed-blue jeans, which looks slightly out of place given that the only trees here are palms and mangroves. "My name is Becker," he continues as we gather around in a circle, "but you can call me Beck for short. I was born in Michigan, but for the last fifteen years I've lived in Oregon, where I run a small vineyard."

He turns to his right, where Model Two stands. "I'm Ashley," she says, idly playing with her hair. "I grew up in Wisconsin, and I'm a college student studying biology. I'm really excited to meet all of you."

I'm up next. "My name is Ryan," I say. My gaze jumps to Cole, who gives me a wink. "But you can call me Ry if you prefer," I continue, my face flushed, and not just from the heat. "I'm a lawyer, and I'm originally from North Carolina, but now I live in D.C."

Next up is Rhonda, whom I met earlier on the pirate ship, and who tells us she's a nurse from Georgia. Then there's a tall Black man with close-cropped graying hair named Joe who's dressed in a suit and is a doctor from New York. He makes it a point to shake each of our hands, his grip firm and dry even though we were just wading through the ocean. After Joe is a white woman named Katie, who has thick glasses and shoulder-length brown hair, and who is a graduate student in nuclear engineering at MIT. She also tells us that she transitioned about five years ago, which thankfully means I won't be the only queer person on this beach. Following Katie is Jing, a slender Asian woman with straight black hair tied up into a ponytail, who's a personal trainer in L.A., and Marina, a Hispanic woman with a wide smile, who works in a grocery store in southern Florida.

Last is Cole. "Nice to meet everyone," he says, grinning widely; I can't tell if it's genuine or not. "I'm Cole, and I'm a line chef at a French restaurant in Philadelphia. I'm really looking forward to working with you all."

"Same for me," Beck says. "Now that we all know each other, maybe we should take a look at our supplies next? Can't hurt to know what we're working with."

Nobody seems to disagree, so we all set off towards the large purple flag. My mind works furiously as I walk, trying to memorize all the names and locations and occupations I just heard. *So that's it, then—the people who will determine my fate in this game for the next two weeks.*

Even though we officially just met each other, I'm already starting to think about whom I might want to work with. I got a good feeling from Rhonda when we were on the ship, and that impression hasn't changed. Meanwhile, it sounds like Katie and I have a lot in common, so maybe I'll try to ally with her. Jing seems nice too, and if she's a personal trainer, she could really help us with challenges. It didn't escape me that Beck took the lead in getting us all to introduce ourselves to each other; it could be good for me to pair up with someone who's more self-assured. As for Marina, Joe, and Ashley, I didn't really get a great read on any of them, although I'm sure I'll have quite a few opportunities to do so over the next few days.

Cole, though … my first impression is that he's the sort of person who makes friends easily, and someone people generally like to be around. Even now, as we're walking up the beach, I can hear Katie laughing at something he just said. But I've met plenty of men who *seem* nice at first, only to reveal their true selves later on. Sometimes I even wonder if there's something in the water in D.C. that corrupts otherwise normal men and turns them into douches.

I shake my head at that last thought. We're barely five minutes into a game that lasts more than a month, and I can't let my preconceived notions get in the way of reality. Maybe Cole will turn out to be genuinely nice, or maybe he won't. All I can do for now is keep my eye on him and constantly remind myself not to let my guard down because out here, there are no second chances, and it will only take one mistake to send me home empty-handed.

CHAPTER 3

DAY 1

It turns out that we have very few supplies available, which is discouraging, but not really a surprise. The show is called *Marooned* for a reason, after all. In addition to the flint we got from Alex, there's a machete, a pot with a lid, a bag of rice, and another "map" that supposedly shows the way to a well. If I had to guess, I'd say the map is just as useful as the one that directed us to this beach, which is to say not at all.

Fortunately, one of the producers, an Indian woman with short gray hair and a weathered face, who introduces herself as Neema, gathers us together. "Welcome to *Marooned*," she says, her voice surprisingly deep. "I've been assigned to your tribe, which means I'll be here with you between eight and twelve hours each day. During that time, I may pull each of you aside to film individual confessionals, schedule permitting. Nothing you say in a confessional will be shared with your tribemates during the game, so please be as open and honest as you can. Otherwise, I will be available to answer any production-related questions you may have. If something comes up while I'm not on the beach, speak to one of the camera crew, and they'll make sure your concern gets to me. Having said that, be aware that we are *not* part of the game, and outside of confessionals, you should try your best to ignore us." She pauses for a moment, presumably to let all that sink in. "Now then, if you will all please follow me?"

We trail behind her as she walks down a path swept of underbrush and marked every so often with pieces of purple cloth tied to palm trees. Neema walks slowly and points out landmarks, making sure we all keep track so we can get there and back without her help. The path ends at our well, which Neema informs us is the only remotely safe source of drinking water. It's a short walk, perhaps five minutes, but I imagine it'll seem longer when we're lugging water back to camp.

Once we're all gathered at the well, she shows us how to uncover it and draw water from it. She also tells us that technically we don't *need* to boil the water before we drink it, since we all signed a waiver form before we came out here, but she strongly recommends that we do so if we want to avoid getting sick. I make a mental note to myself to do as she suggested unless I'm actually dying of thirst.

Back at the beach, she points out a container cleverly disguised as a log that holds any prescribed medications that the nine of us need to take, as well as sunscreen, toothbrushes, and toothpaste, the former so we don't sue them if we get skin cancer, and the latter to ensure that we have nice white teeth for the camera. Also in the cache is a small two-way radio, only to be used in actual emergencies. "And I mean *real* emergencies," she says, eying us each in turn. "Like, 'I accidentally chopped off my finger with the machete' kind of emergency. If you use it to tell me you can't find your socks or something like that, rest assured that I *will* ignore you."

Besides that, she tells us that we're on our own and reminds us that we are considered to be "on-camera" at all times while we're on our beach unless explicitly told otherwise. "Just do your best to pretend the cameras aren't there," she says. "As I'm sure you can understand, we want this to feel as authentic as possible."

Easier said than done, I think to myself, as one of the camera crew hefts a camera onto her shoulder and points it at me.

Neema sees me looking and gives a faint smile. "Don't worry, you'll get used to it much faster than you might expect," she adds. "Well, that's all I have to say, so you're free to go about your business." She pauses, giving us what might be a wink. "And remember, we're all rooting for you."

With the formalities taken care of, the nine of us convene and collectively decide that the first thing we need to do is build a shelter. It turns out Beck is an amateur carpenter, which I guess fits the lumberjack theme, so he takes the lead. "Cole, you and

Marina clear a space on the beach," he directs. "Preferably under the trees, so we can get some extra shelter from rain, but not too deep into the woods, or we won't have any place to put a fire. Joe, I'd like you, Ashley, and Rhonda to collect palm fronds that we can weave to make a roof. And then Ryan, Jing, Katie, and me will gather bamboo for the actual structure. Is that all right with everyone?" He claps his hands without waiting for an answer. "Wonderful. Let's get started, then!"

As instructed, I go off into the woods with Beck, Jing, and Katie, looking for logs to collect. Beck tells us to search for ones that are about ten feet long and not too dry, so they'll still be pliant. I'm not sure if he knows what he's talking about or is just pretending, but either way, I'm okay with following his lead for the moment. Stepping up and leading this early on can rub people the wrong way, and I'm happy to let him be the one to put a target on his back.

At first, the work isn't too strenuous, and the four of us have enough energy to talk while we work. I learn that Jing was born in China and moved to the US when she was three years old, that Katie transitioned in her freshman year of college at Stanford, and that Beck has dreams of expanding his vineyard and making a name for his wine. Eventually, though, the combined effect of the hot sun, the lack of water, and the fact that the bamboo logs are heavier than they look take their toll, and the conversation trails off. I wish I could find out more, maybe begin to build a little trust with them, but every little step counts.

It takes an hour or so to collect enough bamboo to satisfy Beck. By the time we've deposited the last log on the beach, the others are finishing up their tasks too. After a quick rest, Beck directs all of us to begin the process of actually building the shelter.

Ashley raises her hand. "Should all nine of us be working on the same thing?" she asks. "Maybe some of us should get started on something, you know, less exhausting."

Beck shakes his head. "It's better to get the structure done first. That way we'll at least have a base to work from. Plus, it's really important to get this done as quickly as we can. I don't know about you, but I'd like to increase my chances of getting a good night's sleep tonight."

He looks to Ashley as though he's inviting her to argue with him, but she just glares back at him. No one else objects, so we all begin working together to build a lean-to out of the bamboo logs we collected.

The shelter comes together faster than I expected. Fortunately, we all work together as a group. Or, at least, nobody starts an argument or goes off in a huff and refuses to work. A few times I see Ashley glaring at Beck as though she'd like to quit.

But in the end, she does her part, and after what feels like a good three hours, we've got an adequate-looking lean-to that wouldn't meet a single building code anywhere in the world, but also won't fall over the minute the wind starts blowing more than five miles per hour. At least, I hope it won't.

The nine of us stand there looking at it for a few moments, in various stages of being out of breath and/or dehydrated.

"Right," Beck finally says, breathing heavily. "I guess we should probably move on to other things, huh?"

Once again, nobody disagrees. Technically, we've reached the end of the part where he has more expertise than the rest of us, but it seems like no one else wants to step up. I can't speak for the others, but I certainly don't want to take charge, not this early.

Whatever the others are thinking, Beck apparently takes our silence as acquiescence. "Joe and Jing, you two see if you can get a fire started. Ashley and I will go to the well and fill up our canteens. Hopefully, we'll have a fire started by the time we get back. Everyone else, maybe start weaving palm fronds for the roof of the shelter."

With that settled, the five of us who were assigned to weaving palm fronds—namely, me, Rhonda, Katie, Cole, and Marina—take a seat on the beach and get to work. To my great relief, weaving fronds together is exactly as strenuous as it sounds, which is to be quite a bit less than collecting logs or constructing a shelter.

More importantly, we're able to talk as we work, which means I can begin to build the relationships I'm going to need if I want to have a chance at winning this game. The women, especially, are easy to talk to, each in their own way. Katie and I immediately discover that we're both nerds, so I already like her. We spend a good few minutes discussing our favorite Marvel movies—she prefers *Thor: Ragnarok*, but I think *Captain America: The Winter Soldier* is better. Meanwhile, Marina is bubbly and loves to talk about her three kids, her pets—a cat and a golden retriever named Leo, who sounds incredibly cute and who I want to meet as soon as possible—and her extended family that lives with her in Miami. Rhonda is quieter than the others, but she exudes a calmness that's welcome in this anxiety-inducing situation. When she does talk, her voice is light, but has a touch of gravitas to it, as though she's a Southern gentlewoman holding court with her friends and not sitting on a beach weaving palm fronds together.

Just as I expected, Cole is pretty pleasant too, jumping into the conversation occasionally with a joke or a polite comment in response to something one of the other four of us said. He and Marina bond over their shared love of cooking, even agreeing to share some recipes with each other once we're back home. More than once, I catch myself staring at his absurdly toned biceps and have to look away, but other than that I'm laughing and joking and telling stories with the rest of them. I'd say we're all enjoying each other's company, which is a good sign this early in the game. True, nobody brings up the possibility of an alliance, but it's still pretty early to be worrying about it.

Although I sincerely doubt that the topic hasn't crossed anyone else's mind. Alliances can get you far in the game, and all we have to do is mutually agree to vote the same way and not vote each other out. With nine people on the tribe, five is a majority, so we could take out the other four and get ourselves that much further in the game. Besides, everything else being equal, I'd rather be aligned with people I like than with people I don't.

My line of thinking is interrupted when Rhonda abruptly laughs out of nowhere. "I'm sorry," she says, "but I just realized that I'm actually lookin' forward to sleepin' in that shelter, even though it looks about ready to collapse." She shakes her head, still chuckling. "Y'know, my husband could barely believe it when

I told him I was applyin' to be on the show. 'You don't even like campin' in a tent, Rhonda,' he said. 'So how are you gonna sleep on the beach, with sand in your feet and no pillow or nothin'?' Well, I guess we'll find out tonight!"

Marina rolls her eyes. "*Men*," she says, with a heavy sigh. "No offense to you two guys, of course." She smiles at Cole and me. "My husband asked me if I was really going to live on rice and coconuts for a month. I told him, 'We've been married for nearly ten years now, mi amor. Don't you know that Cubans already eat rice every day?' That got him good!"

"Oh, that's nothing on my girlfriend," Katie adds, grinning. "She told me she'd faint if she saw a single bug, or heaven forbid, a rat. I said it's a good thing I'm out here and not her, because if that's how she'd react, she'd probably spend more time unconscious than awake!"

We laugh at the three significant others and their antics. "What about you, Ryan?" Marina asks. "Anyone special in your life?"

"Not really," I say, shrugging. *As though I'd have time for dating and taking care of Arielle.* But they don't need to know about any of that yet, so I just say, "Still waiting for Mr. Right to come along, I guess."

Marina nods. Fortunately, either they didn't catch me say *Mister* or they don't care. Not that I really *expected* anyone to care that I'm gay, but you never know. Before I came out here, I considered pretending to be straight, but I knew people would find out the truth eventually. Trust is key in this game, and I'd be shooting myself in the foot if I lied about something so irrelevant this early on.

Besides, everyone reacted pretty well to Katie coming out as trans. If I hadn't already decided to be open about my sexuality, that would have convinced me. And so far, it seems to have been the right decision.

In any event, the conversation continues without even a hiccup. "And you, Cole?" Marina continues. "Someone waiting for you back home?"

Cole shakes his head. "Nope," he says. "I dated one of my classmates from culinary school for a while, but we broke up a couple of years ago, and now I guess I'm just waiting for the right person." His eyes flick to me so briefly that I'm not sure whether it was just a trick of the light. "Like Ry."

The rest of the day passes uneventfully, or at least as uneventfully as it can on a desert island with nine strangers trying to build a campsite and twice as many camera crew running around filming every little thing we do. The only time I'm not on camera is when I go off into the woods alone to relieve myself, not because it's decent, but because there's no drama to film when I'm by myself. Just another reminder that this is entertainment first, last, and everywhere in between.

By the time we've finished weaving what feels like an adequate number of palm fronds, the others have gotten a fire started and boiled some water, which I drink down gratefully. It's not too hot out here, at least in the shade, but I've had nothing to eat or drink since I got on the motorboat hours ago. Joe also cooks us some rice; none of us is *that* hungry just yet, but we all agree it's better to eat something now rather than wait until we're truly starving.

We finish eating just in time to watch the sun go down over the ocean, lighting up the sky like a Monet painting. Then we rush to put the finishing touches on the shelter before it gets completely dark, lacing the weaved palm fronds through the roof and putting a few on the floor to make it more comfortable. We manage to finish the shelter just as the last rays of twilight begin to fade, and all of us take a step back to admire our handiwork in the light of the fire Joe and Jing built. It's no five-star hotel, or even a one-star hotel, but it'll do. Besides, we can keep working on it over the next few days. It's not like we'll have much else to do, honestly.

As soon as the sun is fully below the horizon, Neema and most of the camera crew pack up their equipment and leave, with only one, a tall, skinny man with dreadlocks who looks to be about my age, staying behind. He'll probably be enough until tomorrow morning, considering how worn out we all are from our hard day of work. It's not like we need a multitude of cameras just to watch us sleep—or, rather, try to sleep.

As the stars begin to shine, we sit around the fire for a little while, but it's obvious everyone is exhausted, so we all head off to bed fairly quickly. I try to struggle through, but eventually I can feel my eyes closing on their own, and so I make the short walk over to the shelter, ready to get what rest I can. With a sigh, I squeeze in between Rhonda and Joe, putting my pack underneath my head and pretending like it's a pillow, trying to find a comfortable position. *One day down,* I think to myself drowsily, my eyelids heavy as anchors. *Only thirty-two to go.*

CHAPTER 4

DAY 2

I wake up rather early the next day, not feeling anywhere near as rested as I might have hoped. The bamboo logs we spent so much effort collecting dug into my hips and back the whole night, and I shivered every time the wind picked up more than a gentle breeze. Plus, someone—I think it was Beck, but I can't be sure—started snoring ten minutes after I went to bed and kept it up the entire night. At least that means that *someone* got some shuteye, but I got two, or maybe three, hours of rest, and that's probably a generous estimate.

Even as tired as I am, I doubt I'll be able to fall asleep again, so I sit up and look around. Most everyone else is still in the shelter, even though the sun is up and the birds are chirping, so I might as well get a head start on chores. Maybe I can build up the fire and boil some water so everyone will have some ready to drink by the time they get up. *Can't hurt to get some brownie points.*

Yet as I slowly extricate myself from the shelter, taking care not to wake any of the others, I see that someone else has already beaten me to it. Cole sits by the fire, leaning against a log that we put there yesterday for that exact reason. He's got the fire going already, and it bathes him in a flickering golden light that contrasts with the shadows of palm fronds from the trees behind him. He's looking away from me, towards the open ocean, and he looks so peaceful that for a second I consider just turning around and going back to the shelter before he notices me. If I talk to him in my sleep-deprived state, I might slip up and let him know that I think he's a threat. That might not be a disaster, but it certainly wouldn't be good for my game.

Then I remember that we're stuck together on this desert island at least for the next few days, so I'm going to have to talk to him eventually. Plus, I need to start building relationships with my tribemates if I want to avoid being the first person voted out. Better to go hang out with him now, so he doesn't start to think I'm difficult to work with. *Besides, it can't hurt to get to know him a little, right?*

So, I sit next to the fire, close enough to him that we can talk without waking the others, but not so close that we're touching. Out of the corner of my eye, I see the overnight cameraman perk up and point his camera in our direction, but it barely registers. Maybe Neema was right, and I'm getting used to being filmed constantly. *Now* there's *a scary thought.*

Cole nods at me as I sit down. He's already starting to sport some stubble around his chin and cheeks, making him look even more annoyingly cute than he did yesterday. "Morning, Ry," he says, his voice scratchy. "You're up early. Couldn't sleep?"

"You could definitely say that," I reply, trying and failing to stop a yawn. "How about you?"

"I'm always up this early. Granted, usually I actually, you know, *sleep* during the night rather than just toss and turn for hours, but I guess it's just routine by now."

"Really? I would have guessed that chefs would be more on the nocturnal side. Staying up late to clean up after dinner, and everything."

"Yeah, you're not the first one to think that," he says, giving me a sardonic grin. "The restaurant I work for is known for breakfast and brunch. Usually I'm done before three in the afternoon."

"Oh. I guess that makes sense." I shift against the log, trying to find a more comfortable position. "Sounds pretty nice, if I'm being honest."

"I'm not complaining." He turns his head and looks at me, his gaze holding mine. "You should come visit once we're all back home. I'll make you the best eggs Benedict you've ever had in your life."

"I'd like that." I honestly don't know whether or not I mean it. Cole seems fine so far, and he's exactly the type of guy I usually go for, but my goal here is to win a million dollars for my sister and me, not to find a new boyfriend, even if I'd get some good food out of it. Still, I *am* trying to build a connection here, so I add, "I'm a sucker for a good brunch."

"Perfect." He grins at me, and it takes a conscious effort not to return it. "What about you? You must be used to getting up early to go to court every day, Mr. Fancy Lawyer."

I let out a laugh before I can stop myself. "I haven't been in a courtroom since the day I was sworn into the bar. My job is very much a 'nine-to-five, five days a week in the office' sort of thing. To be honest, I don't even wear a suit most days."

"Wait, really? I thought all lawyers were supposed to get dressed up and take their briefcases to court every single day."

"Not all of us," I say wryly. "If I'm in court, it means I've messed up pretty badly. That, or I've been arrested."

He chuckles at the last bit. "Okay, okay. I'll take your word for it."

We continue to sit together, chatting about the weather and our jobs, both of us apparently deciding that it's far too early—both in the day and in the game—to discuss important things like strategy or our fellow tribemates. Truth be told, I'm happy to avoid those subjects. We're less than a day in, and if I'm seen strategizing and laying out plans now, when we all barely know each other, people might start to think *I'm* a threat and send me home first. Far better to stick to small talk for now, and let someone else paint a target on their back.

Plus, if I'm being honest, this feels … nice, in a way I can't quite put into words. It's almost like we're just two friends who are catching up with each other after a long absence, rather than strangers who just met each other yesterday. Of course, that's part of the problem—if Cole can connect with everyone this easily, he'll be that much harder to vote out. And yet, there's a voice in the back of my head telling me nobody's getting voted out just yet. So, I continue my little chat with Cole, content to just enjoy the moment while I can. I just have to remind myself not to enjoy it *too* much.

We both keep our voices down so as not to wake the others, but it isn't long before Rhonda joins us, rubbing her eyes and yawning. That seems to open the floodgates, and soon we're all sitting around the fire in various stages of wakefulness. All of us, that is, except Ashley, who's apparently still sleeping.

We're all still hungry from last night, so we decide not to wait for Ashley to wake up before we make breakfast: plain white rice boiled in our single pot, just like we had for dinner last night. While we're eating, the cameraman who's been filming us for the past twelve hours radios in, and soon after, we're joined by more camera crew and Neema.

The latter makes a beeline for us, her shoulders squared. "Good morning, contestants," she says, her voice chipper, like she actually slept in a real bed last night. "Once you're done eating, we'll start filming confessionals one at a time. Meanwhile, the rest of you can go about your day and do your best to pretend like I'm not here. Understood?" She waits for us all to nod, then claps her hands together. "Anybody want to volunteer to go first? I promise I won't bite."

The eight of us share a look, and then Jing raises her hand. "I'll do it if nobody else wants to."

Neema smiles. "Perfect. In that case, come with me, please. We'll find a good spot for filming." Gesturing to one of the cameramen, she and Jing walk down the beach, leaving the remaining camera crew to film us.

Once Neema and Jing are gone, Beck turns to the rest of us. "I think there are a few things we need to do today." Apparently, he's decided to continue gracing us with his leadership. "One: collect coconuts so we have something to eat besides rice. Two: do whatever we can to make the shelter more comfortable. And three: gather some firewood so we don't have to worry about our fire going out. I figured we could split into groups and get everything done in parallel. Anyone have any objections?" He waits less than a second before nodding, as though we've all acquiesced. "All right! In that case, let's all get to it. The sooner we start, the sooner we'll finish."

Beck evidently didn't feel like assigning us to specific chores today, so after a quick discussion, the seven of us, minus Jing and Ashley, went about our tasks. Rhonda, Katie, and I all chose to collect coconuts, so we head off down the beach while Joe and Cole head to the forest to look for firewood, and Marina and Beck discuss what can be done about the shelter. At first, it's fun, almost like a game. We walk up and down the shore, searching the ground around the palm trees and looking for fallen nuts. None of us is quite hungry enough yet to try climbing one of the trees so we can harvest the fruits at its crown, but I imagine we might get there someday soon. Some of the coconuts we find are rotten, but a good number are suitable for eating.

As time passes, however, the sun grows higher in the sky, and it starts to get uncomfortably warm. We also make the mistake of starting with the trees closest to our camp, which means that we need to walk farther and farther away to find trees that we haven't already harvested.

Thankfully, just when my arms are starting to get tired from endlessly carrying coconuts back and forth, I get a reprieve. "Ryan, it's your turn to film a confessional," Neema says. She gestures to the coconuts I'm holding. "Once you get back to camp, put those down and follow me."

Breathing a sigh of relief, I follow her for about five minutes until we reach a spot out of earshot and eyeshot of the rest of the tribe. Of course, one of the ever-present camera crew comes with us. When we reach the appointed location, Neema has me sit against a large mangrove tree and positions the cameraman so the ocean is behind me. I imagine it's a pretty shot, and I'm sure it'll look very nice when and if it's edited into the show.

While the camera is being set up, Neema gives me a few instructions. "Since this is your first confessional, at the beginning, I'll ask you to introduce yourself. Then I'll proceed to ask you some open-ended questions. You can talk as much as you like, but keep in mind that we're on a schedule, and whatever you say will be edited down in post-production anyway. Also, please remember to restate the question in your answer so the viewers know what you're talking about. Other than that, feel free to say whatever's on your mind, although I remind you that any and all confessionals may be aired in the show, so you may want to avoid saying anything *too* mean about any of your tribemates. Oh, and look at me, rather than at the camera. Understood?" She waits for me to nod. "Good. In that case, just give me one more minute, and then we'll get started."

She goes over to the cameraman and checks his positioning, making sure it's just right. Then she checks to make sure I'm in frame, having me adjust my position slightly. Finally, she attaches a small mic to my shirt and tests the audio.

Once everything is set up to her satisfaction, she nods to the cameraman, and a red light turns on. Then she looks at me. "Okay, we're rolling. So, Ryan, tell me a little bit about yourself."

"My name's Ryan Levine, and I'm twenty-eight." I remind myself to look at Neema instead of the camera; it's a little counterintuitive, but at least I'm directing my answers to a person rather than to thin air. "I'm a corporate lawyer, and I live in Washington, D.C., although I grew up in North Carolina."

She gives me a thumbs up and mouths *good start.* "What do you think about your tribe so far?"

"I think my tribe is pretty good. I've only known them for a day, but I feel like I'm getting along with everyone just fine. I don't know how long that will last, but it's nice for now."

"Is there anyone you feel particularly close to?"

"I'd say I'm pretty close to Katie, and maybe Rhonda and Marina too. They're the ones I've spent the most time with, at least."

"What about Cole? It seemed like you and he had a good chat this morning before everyone else woke up."

"Cole seems nice, too," I say, trying not to sound as guarded as I feel. "We did get the chance to talk a bit this morning, and that was nice. And he seems pretty strong, so hopefully he'll be able to help us in challenges. But that could make him a threat, too."

"Anyone you *don't* particularly like, or that you don't really get along with?"

I allow myself a small smile. I knew it wouldn't take long for her to get to the point. *After all, who'd watch the show if there wasn't any drama*? "Well, if we did lose the next challenge, I suppose I won't be upset to see Ashley going home." I don't know if I'd be *happy* about it, but what I said is true—anyone would be acceptable at this point, as long as it's not me. "She hasn't really been much help around camp, and the rest of us have to pick up the slack. Or maybe Beck—he's been a good leader so far, but I don't really like being bossed around, and his whole act might get a little irritating if it goes on too much longer. Plus, like I said, Cole could be a threat down the line, so maybe it's better to get rid of him now, before it's too late."

She smiles and gives me another thumbs-up, so I guess that was enough of a soundbite. "Fair enough," she says. "Let's change topics a bit. Tell me why you want to win the million dollars. And I mean the *real* reason—why are you willing to starve for more than a month just for the chance to win some money?"

Now *this* one, at least, is easy. "I want to win for my sister, Arielle. Our parents died when I was sixteen, and she basically raised me after that. Then, a couple of years ago, she was diagnosed with Stage III breast cancer. She's cured now, but it hasn't been easy, and treatments are expensive." I'm tearing up just thinking about her. She's the strongest person I know, which is the only reason I agreed to come out here and be away from her for a month, even though she's still recovering. "If I win the million dollars, the first thing I'm going to do is pay off her medical bills. She's done so much for me, and now it's my turn to give back to her."

Neema nods. She and the rest of the production cast know all about my family situation since they were very thorough in the casting process, so I'm sure she was expecting this answer. "Great, thank you," Neema says. "You did a good job, Ryan. I think we've gotten all we need."

I get up and prepare to return to my tribe, my hands moving by rote while my mind is occupied with thoughts of my sister. I meant what I said about wanting to do something for her after all she's done for me, and if that means I have to outlast seventeen strangers to win a million dollars, then that's what I'll do. *This is for you, Arielle. The others may not know it yet, but I'm coming for them, and I don't intend to lose.*

CHAPTER 5

DAY 3

The next morning, a motorboat stops at our beach, and Neema tells us all to get on board. The rest of yesterday, our second day on the island, passed much like the first day did, with all of us trying to improve our living situation as much as we could. Well, all of us except for Ashley, who spent a good amount of time in the shelter while the rest of us worked, claiming that she was trying to conserve her energy for the upcoming challenge. It didn't really bother me—it's not like having nine people working makes a huge difference compared to eight people—but I could tell that a few of my tribemates were upset. Especially Rhonda, who frowned slightly every time she looked in Ashley's direction. "Conservin' her energy, my rear end," I heard Rhonda mutter at one point. "She better hope she's right, 'cause if not, she might be goin' home first."

Now, we're on our way to a different island, where our first immunity challenge awaits. As with the other times we've been off camera, we're not allowed to talk to each other, so I just sit back and try to relax a little bit. The thought of competing in a challenge makes me nervous—I'm not exactly the most athletic person, and I don't want us to lose because of me. I tell myself that all I can do is try my best, and whatever happens will happen. It doesn't really help, but it's better than nothing, I suppose.

After about fifteen minutes, we pull up to yet another perfect little island surrounded by turquoise water. Just like the last two days, there's no rain, and the sun shines down on the green trees and the yellow-white beach like we're in a magazine ad for a high-end resort. Honestly, add a real bed, a roof, and some good food, and you probably *could* market this place as a five-star luxury destination. I'd never be able to afford it, not until Arielle's bills are paid off and I can start saving some money, but I'm sure the rich and famous would absolutely love it.

As soon as the boat reaches shore, we get off, pausing for a moment so the producers can mic us up. Then, Neema has us get in a line, and hands Beck—he's at the front, because of course he is—a bamboo pole with a purple flag that says "MERU" on it, along with this season's logo.

Once everyone is in position, we march into the challenge area: a large, rectangular, cleared-up space on the beach that has some wooden boxes and poles scattered throughout. A large wooden fence running the entire length separates the area into two halves; in one, all the wood objects are painted purple, and in the other, they're painted blue. At the near end of each half is a large mat, again painted in the respective tribe's colors. As we walk in and stand on our mat, the other tribe comes in from the other side and stands on theirs. Of course, tons of cameras are positioned around the space, ready to catch the upcoming action, while a few people that I assume are producers stand off to the sides, out of view of the cameras.

Standing about ten feet past the mats is Alex, who waits for us with a TV-ready grin on his face. On either side of him is a small wooden platform, each with a burlap sack covering something; the one on the left is tall and cylindrical, while the one on the right is short and flat.

Once we're all set, one of the producers motions to Alex, and the latter's grin widens. "Meru, Sika, welcome to your first challenge," he says. "For this challenge, each tribe will be split into groups of three. The first group will work together to carry a heavy box containing three bags of puzzle pieces over and around several obstacles. They will then hand the box off to the second group, who will open it by untying a series of knots and make their way over a balance beam, each carrying one bag across. After all three members of the second group have gotten across the beam with their bags, they'll give the puzzle pieces to the third group, who will use them to complete a puzzle. The first tribe to correctly complete the puzzle wins the challenge."

He pauses to let it all sink in. "Now, today's challenge may seem complicated, but the prizes are not." He turns to the platform on his left and pulls off the burlap there, uncovering a two-foot-tall wooden carving of a bird with its wings spread wide. "Most importantly, the tribe that wins today's challenge will take home this immunity idol, meaning they will not attend tonight's tribal council, where someone will become the first person voted out of season nineteen of *Marooned.* The losing tribe, however, *will* attend and will vote out one of their own members tonight.

"In addition, you're also playing for reward." He turns to his right and reveals a large tarp. "It may not seem exciting," he continues, "but it will help keep you dry when the rain comes. And unlike the immunity idol, which you'll only retain until the next challenge, the tarp is yours for the rest of the game. Sound like something worth playing for?"

We all nod, and there are a few scattered cheers from the castaways.

Alex claps his hands together. "In that case, I'll give you a minute to strategize, and we'll get to it."

As soon as Alex finishes giving his spiel, the cameras surrounding all of us turn off, and Neema comes over to us. "Despite what Alex just said, you're not quite ready to begin yet," she says. "Before we run the challenge, Steve and I"—she gestures to the producer we met aboard the pirate ship on day one, who's currently talking to the Sika tribe—"are going to walk each tribe through it separately to make sure you all understand what you're expected to do. If you have any questions while we're doing the walkthrough, I encourage you to ask them, and I will do my best to answer. Afterwards, we'll give you a few minutes to decide which tribe members will take part in each phase of the challenge. Once both tribes are ready, we'll get started. Any questions so far?" Nobody says anything. "All right. Your tribe will do the walkthrough second, so just hold tight here for a few moments."

She goes over to join Steve, and the Sikas follow the two of them as they walk around the various obstacles. Then it's our turn, and Neema explains each portion of the challenge as we walk through it, answering our questions patiently before leading us back to the mat to strategize.

Once we get back, we huddle together to decide who will do each of the three portions. "I can do the first part, carrying the box," Beck says. "Cole and Jing, you're both pretty strong—do you want to join me?"

Ashley raises her hand before Cole and Jing can respond. "Actually, I'd like to do the first part," she says. "I think I'd be pretty good at it."

Rhonda looks at her, one eyebrow raised. "Are you sure, honey? That box looks pretty heavy to me."

"I'm sure," Ashley replies, her jaw set. "I may not look very strong, but I can pull my weight. Trust me."

Rhonda looks like she wants to argue more, but Jing steps in. "It's all right," the latter says. "I can do the second phase. I've got pretty good balance."

"I can do that part too," Marina adds. "I don't think you want me on the puzzle anyway."

Joe jumps in right after her. "I'll take the balance beam too, if that's all right."

"Excellent," Beck says. "So that leaves Ryan, Katie, and Rhonda for the puzzle. Does that work for everyone?"

Rhonda frowns and crosses her arms, but in the end, she just nods, and after a second so do I. Personally, I would have volunteered for the puzzle portion anyway, and if Ashley says she can carry the box, I'm not going to argue with her.

Hearing no dissension, Beck gives us all a winning grin. "Awesome. Then let's get out there and win!"

A few minutes later, we're all in position and ready to get started. Rhonda, Katie, and I are all at one end of the challenge, standing in front of a large wooden board on a platform about three feet off the ground, where we'll eventually make the puzzle.

Some distance away, in the middle of the course, Jing, Joe, and Marina wait, while the remaining three are at the far end, my view of them partially obstructed by the box they'll be maneuvering through the challenge. Across from us, the other tribe is set up similarly; Green Hat, Mustache, and a middle-aged blond woman stand ready to carry their box, while an athletic-looking Black woman, a short Asian man with wisps of gray hair coming off his head, and Model One stand across from Joe, Jing, and Marina. At the puzzle station for the Sikas are a middle-aged woman with frizzy light-brown hair and glasses, and two men, one tall and young and the other shorter and maybe my age, wearing a blue polo shirt and thick glasses.

Meanwhile, Alex stands in the very center, waiting for the all-clear from production. Once he apparently gets it, he raises his hand in the air. "Castaways: ready … set … GO!" he shouts, dropping his arm on the last word.

I can barely hear him all the way down here, but Beck, Cole, and Ashley shoot off like rockets towards the box, reaching it at about the same time the Sikas reach theirs. The three Merus work together to lift the box and begin walking towards the first obstacle; based on the strain in their expressions and the pace at which they're moving, it must be really heavy. Still, they reach the first obstacle—a triangular protrusion that pokes about five feet out of the sand like a shark's tooth—relatively quickly.

"Come on!" I shout. "You can do it!" Rhonda and Katie join me in cheering, while the Sika puzzle-makers do the same for their tribe.

The Meru trio gets the box up and over the first obstacle without stopping. But by the time they reach the second obstacle—a series of wooden poles that they have to weave the box around—they're slowing down, the effort clearly taking a toll on them. The Sikas are having trouble too, though, so we're still in good shape.

Then, halfway through the poles, Ashley lets go of the box and bends over, her hands on her knees, taking a break while Cole and Beck struggle on without her. With Ashley out, the two men move noticeably slower, and Sika quickly gains a lead, reaching the third obstacle—a raised set of tracks that the box has to be lifted onto and pushed for about fifteen feet—well before Cole and Beck. A cold spike of fear shoots through my body despite the warm sun; if we don't pick up the pace *now*, we might lose this challenge in a landslide. Ashley rejoins the men just as they finally get their box to the third obstacle, but by then the other tribe has already finished the first phase, untied their knots, and sent the first person across the balance beam.

Finally, after what feels like forever, Cole, Beck, and Ashley finally lug the box to Joe, Jing, and Marina, who take over while Ashley collapses to the ground next to them. By the time they finish with the knots, two Sikas have already made it over the balance beam, and the third, the young woman, is halfway done, a determined look in her eyes. She makes it to the end while Jing is just getting started on our beam, and the other tribe quickly gets to work on their puzzle.

Thankfully, Jing makes it across the beam without falling, as does Marina. "You got this!" I cheer as Marina crosses, despite a sinking feeling in my chest. Joe falls once, sending my heart rate spiking again. I studiously avoid looking at the other tribe, trying with all my soul to will my tribe to go faster.

It must be working, because Joe quickly makes his way back to the beginning of the beam and crosses again, this time successfully. Then he, Marina, and Jing run to us as fast as they can, and hand us the bags with the puzzle pieces in them.

As soon as I take my bag from Jing, I tune out everything but my job. The pieces are heavy and wooden, each of them maybe six inches in diameter, and we dump them all on the board before getting started on the puzzle. It takes me less than a minute to figure out what the final image will be—the logo of this season, the same one that's on our tribe flags—which means that all we have to do is find the right piece in the pile we've made, place it, and search for the next one.

Fortunately, Rhonda, Katie, and I work well together, and after a few false starts, we've got the edges of the puzzle complete. I have no idea how the other tribe is doing, but I think—I *know*—we're still in this. We place another piece, and another, and another, as the pile of unused pieces shrinks—ten pieces, now eight, now seven, as the three of us work to catch up to the other tribe.

But then, just as I grab another piece from the pile—*only five left, we can do this*—I hear cheering off to my left, and screams of "Alex!" from the other tribe. I glance up for what feels like the first time in hours to see Alex running over to the other tribe's board, and my heart sinks. *Maybe they missed a piece or something,* I tell myself, continuing to work frantically just in case. *It might not be over just yet.*

Placing one last piece, I look up just in time to see Alex raise his hands in the air. "Sika! Wins immunity!" he shouts. It takes a moment for his words to sink in, but once they do, I deflate like a popped balloon, bending over and resting my head on the unfinished puzzle as the Sikas begin to celebrate.

CHAPTER 6

DAY 3

We're a somber bunch when we get back to our beach an hour or so later without the tarp or the immunity idol. We all know that someone has to go home tonight, and nobody wants to be the first one to get voted out, least of all me. I have a feeling that the next few hours are going to be very frantic, with everyone scrambling to make sure that their name doesn't come up tonight. Besides, I don't doubt that some people already have an idea in their heads as to who should go home first. I've already decided that I don't want to be the first one to throw out a name—if previous seasons are anything to go by, trying to get your way this early in the game is just as likely to backfire on you—so I'll wait a bit and see if anyone comes to me.

I don't have to wait very long, because I've barely taken five steps towards the shelter when Rhonda sidles up to me. "Ryan, would you mind walkin' to the well with me?" she asks. "I don't know about y'all, but I could use a drink after that challenge."

I'm thirsty too, so I agree, although I have a strong feeling this is more of an excuse to talk strategy more than anything else. We collect everyone's canteens, then set off down the trail towards the well, a cameraman walking slightly in front of us.

Rhonda waits until we're out of earshot of the rest of the tribe before turning to look at me. "I know we don't have a ton of time before we have to go to tribal, so I'll be blunt," she says. "I've been around long enough to know that there are some people in this world that I get along with, like you, and some that I don't. All else bein' equal, I'd like to play this game with the former. It's gonna be hard enough dealin' with the starvation and the lack of sleep and whatnot, and I don't want to add to that stress if I can avoid it."

"That makes sense," I reply. "Just for the record, I like you too. I certainly wouldn't mind working with you."

She accepts this with a nod and a smile. "Thank you, Ryan. I was hopin' you'd say somethin' like that. In fact, I think you and I—and perhaps a few of the others—could work well together, if'n we put our minds to it. In an alliance, I mean."

Ah, there it is. "I could see that happening," I say, choosing my words carefully. I'm not opposed to allying with Rhonda, but I'm not ready to commit to anything just yet. "Who were you thinking of voting for tonight?"

"Ain't it obvious?" Her brows pinch together in an expression of distaste. "The way I see it, on this tribe, there's eight of us, you and me included, that work as hard as we can around the camp. And on the other hand, there's Ashley. Don't get me wrong—she seems like a nice enough young lady, and maybe the dehydration really is gettin' to her more than the rest of us." The corners of Rhonda's mouth turn up in a sneer. "But you saw what happened at the challenge today. She insisted on carryin' that heavy box and then gave up halfway through! Now, if nobody else had wanted to do that job, and she'd gotten stuck with it, I'd cut her some slack. *I* sure as heck couldn't have carried that box around like them boys did. But she *volunteered.* She told us to trust her, and then she showed us we can't. And you know as well as I do that trust is the single most important thing in this game."

We reach the well just as Rhonda finishes, giving me a chance to think about how I want to respond. I don't disagree with Rhonda's reasoning. I said something similar to Neema in my confessional yesterday, and that was before the challenge debacle. Plus, I haven't really bonded with Ashley, so I wouldn't be betraying her if I were to write her name down.

But I'm not fully on board just yet. "I certainly wouldn't mind it if Ashley went home tonight," I finally say, ladling water into a canteen. "You said you think a few of the others might work with us, too. Did you have any names in mind?"

"I think we can convince Marina and Katie without too much trouble. I like those two ladies a lot—they ain't afraid to get their hands dirty if they need to. And I bet we could bring in Cole, too. He's another one I wouldn't mind workin' with. Plus, you and he seem to get along pretty well."

I do my best not to wince at the last part. Rhonda may think that Cole and I get along, but that's only because I've been doing my best not to slip up around him. If he knows that I think he's a threat, he might turn on me. Besides, if I'm not careful, I might start to get distracted by his washboard abs or his perfect arms. But at the same time, at least I have *some* connection with him, so maybe she's not completely wrong.

"Anyway," Rhonda continues, "if we manage to bring all of them in, that'd make five, and then we'd have the majority." She looks up at me, her eyebrows raised. "Of course, that only works if you're in too, chile."

Again, I take a moment to consider my response before I say anything. "I could definitely see myself voting for her," I eventually reply. Truthfully, I'm not convinced yet. I want to hear what some of the others think before I make up my mind. But it's not a bad plan, and if I seem *too* noncommittal, Rhonda might get spooked and target me instead of Ashley, which would be a disaster. "I'm glad you came to me, by the way. It's nice to know that someone wants to work with me."

"Of course, Ryan. Like I said, I like you quite a bit." She lightly touches my hand, giving me what looks like a genuine smile. "In fact, I think that you and I are going to go very far in this game."

We finish filling up the canteens and return to camp shortly after that. However, I've barely had time to empty the now-full canteens into the pot for boiling before Beck comes up to me and asks if he can talk to me for a few minutes.

As with Rhonda, I agree to talk to him, and he leads me down the beach. As usual, we're trailed by one of the ubiquitous camera crew, who are ready to record every last detail of our conversation.

Once we've gotten a good distance away from the camp, Beck suggests that we sit on the beach before launching into his spiel. "I'm guessing Rhonda just asked you to vote for Ashley," he says, idly running one of his hands through the sand. "It's clear that she doesn't like Ashley, especially after what happened at the challenge today. And look, I get where she's coming from—really, I do. But I think it would be a mistake to get rid of Ashley. After all, it was just one challenge, and who knows what the next one will be?" He shrugs, as if to emphasize his lack of foreknowledge. "Besides, this game isn't about who can lift the most weight or who does the most work around camp. No, it's about finding people you can work with, who you can *trust.* I trust Ashley, plus a couple others, and I don't trust Rhonda. It's as simple as that."

It isn't lost on me that he and Rhonda both emphasized trust above all else. "I see," I reply, just as careful as I was with Rhonda. "And who are the other people you trust besides Ashley?"

"Honestly? Jing and Joe." He stops playing with the sand and looks me in the eye. "I know what you're thinking, and the answer is no, you're not on that list, not yet. But I get a good feeling from you, and I'd like to think that we could develop that trust pretty quickly."

I stop myself from rolling my eyes with some difficulty. Given that our conversations so far have mostly been limited to him telling me what to do, it's more likely that he just sees me as a number rather than a true partner in his alliance. "That could happen," I say. To be fair, it's only been three days, so maybe I'm not giving him enough credit. "I'm guessing you want to vote out Rhonda?"

"Actually, I was thinking something different." He gives me a conspiratorial grin. "How would you feel about voting out Cole?"

Wait, what? I don't know why I'm so surprised to hear Cole's name being thrown out there. I pegged him as a possible risk on day one, and it's silly to think that I'm the only one who saw the obvious. "I … suppose I might be interested," I eventually reply. What's even more confusing is the flicker of revulsion that the thought of voting out Cole brings to my mind. *Isn't this what I wanted?* "Let me guess, you think he's a threat?"

"Exactly." Beck leans forward, his eyes burning with an inner light. "You saw him at the challenge today. Despite what it might have looked like, *he* was the one putting in most of the effort carrying that box. If he makes it to the merge, he could win every single individual immunity challenge and just coast to the end. Who *wouldn't* vote for him to win if that happens?"

"But … don't we need him to win challenges now?" I can't believe I'm arguing that we should keep *Cole*, of all people, around. I tell myself that I'm just playing devil's advocate, just making sure Beck has seriously thought this through before I commit either way. "It doesn't really matter what happens after the merge if we lose all the challenges before then."

"Who's to say that the tribe challenges will all turn on physical strength? You and the other two did a good job with that puzzle. You could probably have won the whole challenge for us if Joe hadn't fallen off the balance beam!" He sighs and leans back. "Look, you obviously don't have to decide right this second. But this is an opportunity to make a really strong alliance, and at the same time get rid of one of the biggest threats in the game. Just think about it for a little while, and I'm sure you'll come around."

I spend the entire rest of the time before tribal council doing as Beck suggested and thinking about who I want to side with—and, more importantly, who I want to send home. Jing and Katie both approach me at different points, but their pitches are pretty much the same as Beck's and Rhonda's. Just like before, I do my best to make them think I'm on their side without actually committing one way or the other.

In a perfect world, I'd be decisive and make up my mind quickly, because the longer I wait before I pick one side or the other, the more chance there is that both sides just decide to take *me* out instead of waiting to see which way I jump. But I have a feeling that what I do tonight could define the rest of my game, for better or worse, and every time I think I've settled on a name, I start to wonder whether I'm doing the right thing and just spiral back into overthinking the whole thing again. There's just so much riding on the outcome of this vote, for me and for my sister, and so many factors to consider.

On a personal level, I'm closer to Rhonda and her alliance than I am to Beck's. I mean, Beck and Jing seem nice enough, but I've barely talked to Joe or Ashley, and that's not a good sign for working with them long-term. Plus, I appreciate Beck's honesty in telling me that he doesn't trust me just yet, but if I join his alliance, I'll definitely be on the bottom, and I could easily see them cutting me loose later on without shedding a tear.

Rhonda, on the other hand, seems like she genuinely wants to work with me, and I get along well with her, Marina, and Katie. I could easily see the four of us and Cole getting to the merge, and maybe even further, if I'm lucky.

But I don't just want to get to the merge, I want to *win.* If I get to the final tribal council and I'm sitting next to the wrong person, it would be just as bad as if I were to be voted out tonight. In fact, it would be worse, because it would mean starving and freezing and getting no sleep for the next month, only to come up just short. And *Cole is* a threat, both to get to the end and win. If I'm sitting next to him at the final tribal council, I might not get a single vote.

Then again, I won't need to worry about getting to the end if my tribe loses the remaining immunity challenges. At least if I get to the final tribal, I have a chance to convince the jury, but if I get voted out before that, I'm guaranteed to leave with nothing. That absolutely cannot happen. Also, Cole being such an obvious threat could actually help me—once he's gone, people might start to see *me* as a threat. As long as he's in the game, he'll draw everyone's eyes, and that might give me the freedom I need to make some big moves down the line. But then, if I know how big a threat he is and don't get rid of him, will the jury hold that against me, assuming I can even get to the end?

I sprawl back onto the sand, pressing my hands against my temples, as though I can quiet the incessant thoughts. *This is why people hate lawyers*, I think to myself. *We can argue both sides until we're blue in the face, even if the people we're arguing against are ourselves.*

By the time the sun begins to sink below the horizon and the producers tell us to get ready for tribal council, I'm still undecided between voting for Cole or Ashley. There are strong arguments on either side, and making the wrong decision could mess up my entire game before I really have a chance to start playing. I won't let that happen, not if I can avoid it.

The motorboat ride from our beach to the tribal council set is blessedly short, and it seems like no time at all before we're lined up, mic'ed, and ready to go. At a signal from Neema, Joe—the first in line—walks forward, and soon enough we're all walking up a wooden ramp with rope handrails towards a well-lit area.

My first impression of the set is that it's bigger than it looks on TV. The ramp leads up to an open space with a fire pit in the middle; on the near side of the pit are nine stools, and on the other is a single stool and a podium, with another walkway stretching off into the distance next to the podium. In the background stands a thatched hut; I'm guessing that's where we'll go to cast our votes. The producers appear to have decided on a pirate theme for this season, since there's a skull-and-crossbones motif to the decorations, with a pair of cutlasses hanging over the entrance to the voting hut and the podium being carved to look like a treasure chest. The only things that spoil the effect are the cameras set up around the perimeter and the LED floodlights, making sure everything is visible on the average TV screen.

Alex waits for us standing in front of the single stool, wearing his typical tribal council outfit: a button-down shirt with the sleeves rolled up, this time in seafoam green, and full-length khaki pants. Once we're all seated, he sits down as well.

"Welcome to tribal council," he intones. "Even though nine of you walked in, only eight will walk out with a chance to win this game, because somebody will be voted out tonight. But first, I'm going to ask you a few questions." He points to Beck. "Beck, I'll start with you. What are you feeling being here at tribal?"

"Well, to be honest, part of me is super excited," Beck says, a gleam in his eyes. "I mean, I've been watching *Marooned* for nearly two decades, and I always dreamed about being here with you. But on the other hand, I think I speak for all of us when I say I'd much rather be spending tonight on our beach, not worrying about voting someone out. And there's some disappointment, too—if we'd just done a little bit better in the challenge, the other tribe would be here instead of us."

"Let's talk about that immunity challenge," Alex says. "Ashley, it seemed like you had a bit of trouble carrying that box. Are you afraid that the tribe might see you as a liability because of that?"

To her credit, Ashley doesn't wilt under the pressure; if anything, she sits up straighter. "I can't speak for the rest of the tribe, but I don't think I'm a liability. I admit that I struggled in the challenge, and it doesn't take a rocket scientist to see that I'm not ripped like Cole is. But that doesn't mean I don't have a lot to offer."

Alex turns to Rhonda next; I wouldn't be surprised if the producers filled him in on all the drama from our beach, so he knows where the fault lines in our tribe are. "Rhonda, do you agree with what Ashley said?"

"Oh, of course," Rhonda says smoothly. "I'm sure Ashley brings quite a bit to this tribe. The problem is that everyone else does too. And that's why tonight's vote—and probably *every* vote from here on out—is going to be difficult, because there ain't no benchwarmers on the Meru tribe."

Alex nods. "What about you, Marina?" he asks. "What were your first impressions of your fellow tribemates?"

I tune out Marina as she begins to answer Alex's question. I know I really should pay attention, but I also need to decide who I'm going to vote for tonight. Normally, in a situation like this, I'd just listen to what my brain is trying to tell me. But tonight my mind is truly split—there are arguments for and against both Ashley and Cole, and so many unknowns. *If only my gut would chime in, then it would be a real party.*

My reverie is interrupted when Alex points at me. "Ryan, what are you basing your vote on tonight?"

I grin internally at his question. *As though I haven't been debating that with myself for the last six hours.* "Well, there are a lot of factors," I say, getting ready to give him my best lawyer answer. "Who I get along with, who I trust, who I think can help win us challenges. But really, they all boil down to the same thing: who can best help me get to the end and win? That's all that matters, and the person I'm voting for tonight will be the one that I think benefits my chances of winning the least."

Alex nods sagely. "I think you've summed it up better than I can," he says. "And with that, it is time to vote. Jing, you're up."

Jing gets up and walks over to the hut while the rest of us sit in silence, coming back a minute later with an inscrutable expression on her face. Alex works his way down the line from left to right, sending Cole to vote next, then Marina, and so on. I'm sixth to vote, and as I get up, my mind is racing even faster than before. *Cole or Ashley?*

I take a deep breath as I walk into the hut, getting my first look at the voting setup. Opposite me is a table with several pieces of parchment and a marker, as well as a large urn that holds the votes that have already been cast. Behind the table is a camera. Earlier, Neema told us that after we write down the name of the person we're voting out, we should show the vote to the camera, say the name out loud, and briefly explain why we're voting for that person.

I walk over to the table, looking down at the parchment, and slowly open the marker. *It's now or never, Ryan. Who can help you win this game?*

And just like that, I finally, *finally* decide who I'm going to vote for—and, more importantly, who I'm going to keep. My heart thuds in my ears, but my hand is steady as I put the marker to the parchment and write down a single name.

Once we've all voted, Alex goes and confers with Neema and Steve in the hut where we voted. Presumably, they're rearranging the votes in the urn to ensure maximum drama when they reveal them to us, and by extension, the viewing audience. Now that I've made my choice, my heart has returned to its normal pace. I'm sure I'll find out whether I made the right decision sooner or later, but for right now, there's not much I can do other than try to relax.

After a few minutes, Alex comes over to the podium and places the urn on it, waiting until he has our full attention before speaking. "Once the votes are read, the decision is final, and the person voted out will be asked to leave immediately," he says gravely, the same way I've heard a thousand times before on TV. "I'll read the votes."

He opens the urn and takes out a parchment, revealing it to us. "First vote, Ashley." She nods, clearly expecting this.

"Next vote, Cole." Unlike Ashley, Cole frowns and shakes his head, as though he's surprised to see his name written down.

"Ashley.

"Cole.

"Ashley.

"Cole.

"Cole.

"Ashley. We're tied: four votes Ashley, four votes Cole, one vote left."

Alex pauses for a moment to heighten the drama, then takes the final vote out of the urn. "The first person voted out of season nineteen of *Marooned* is …"

Seeming to move as slowly as he can, he turns the parchment to reveal a name written in my handwriting: "Ashley." He gestures to her, and out of the corner of my eye, I see Cole breathe a huge sigh of relief. "Please hand me your insignia."

She stands up immediately and walks over to Alex, taking off her necklace as she does. Once she gets there, she hands the insignia to Alex, her expression resolute.

"Ashley," he says. "Your time in this game has come to an end."

As he speaks, he snaps the token on her necklace in half, symbolizing her exit from this game—the first person voted out, but far from the last.

CHAPTER 7
DAY 3

The vibe at the tribe beach later that night is tense, to say the least. The eight of us who remain sit around the fire, chatting quietly with each other, our voices a low murmur over the crackle of the fire. Beck, Joe, and Jing are all downcast—which is to be expected, I suppose—and none of them really says much, although they do occasionally glare at the rest of us. To be honest, their scowls don't really bother me. Nothing against Ashley, but nobody wants to be the first person voted out, and I'm just glad I'm still here.

The rest of my alliance seems equally satisfied, if not necessarily overconfident. Well, all of us except Cole, who alternates between being relieved that he's still around and shaken that it was so close in the first place. I guess he really didn't know he was being targeted. Or maybe he just didn't trust me not to vote him out. Not that he really should have trusted me, given how close I came to writing his name down.

And yet, even though I've had a chance to mull it over, I don't regret my choice to keep him around. In the end, I just felt more comfortable working with Rhonda and her alliance. Beck, Joe, Jing, and Ashley seemed like a tight foursome, and I knew that if I went with them, they'd cut me loose sooner or later. I couldn't take the chance of that, not with my and Arielle's future at stake. At least with Rhonda, Marina, and Katie, I feel like I'm on relatively equal footing, even if I *was* the last one to join the alliance.

As for Cole… There's no denying that he's a threat, in more ways than one. But it's still early, and it's not like he's some unstoppable juggernaut. As long as I'm careful and do my best to keep my focus on winning the game, I think I can work with him.

I'm sure I'll have multiple chances to get rid of him in the future if I need to.

Going to tribal council must have really messed with my head, because right now the thought of getting rid of Cole just feels … I don't know, *wrong*, somehow. And I could swear there's a little voice in the back of my head that's telling me to go talk to him, to assure him that I would *never* vote him out, if only to see him smile at me. *I must really be exhausted.*

That must be it, because as the adrenaline from going to tribal wears off, I can barely keep my eyes open. I feel like I haven't slept in years, and the makeshift bed calls to me, its siren song growing with every passing minute. I'm not the only one who hears it, because people are starting to drift off to the shelter, and we've only been back for fifteen minutes. I can't really say I blame them. It's been a long day, and if we're lucky, we've got a whole month of long days ahead of us.

But just as I'm about to join the exodus and go to bed, Rhonda comes up to me and lays her hand on my arm. "Can I talk to you privately?" she asks, her voice low. "Just for a moment, I promise."

I'd much rather sleep, but this could be important, so I nod, letting her lead me down the beach away from the camp. The one overnight cameraman looks torn as to whether to follow us or stay with the rest of the tribe, but after a moment of indecision, he settles on the former.

Once we've gotten some distance from the shelter, Rhonda stops walking and turns to look at me. "I just wanted to say thank you," she says, her face flickering in the light of the fire. "I know you could have voted with the other group tonight, but you made the right move in the end."

I shake my head. "You don't have to thank me," I say quietly. "I'm sorry I took so long to decide."

"Oh, don't you worry about that, chile," she replies, patting my arm. "Like I said at tribal, there ain't any easy votes out here. As much as I might have wanted it to be Ashley, it's God's honest truth that I still had a tough time writin' down her name on that parchment. Besides, I knew you'd make the right decision in the end." She sighs. "You know, you remind me of my son. He may not be the strongest or the fastest one out there, but he's got a good heart, and I can already tell that you do too." She taps me lightly on the chest. "I guess what I'm tryin' to say is that I already knew I liked you, but tonight proved that I can trust you. And that means you're someone I want to work with."

My vision goes blurry, and it takes a moment to realize it's because I'm tearing up a bit. She could be lying to me to gain my trust, but she really does sound like she means it. "I trust you too," I say. And I guess I really do, about as much as I can trust anyone I've only known for three days. "So it's you, me, Katie, Marina, and Cole to the final five, then?"

"That's the idea," she agrees. "But final two sounds a lot better than final five in my book." She holds out her hand. "What do you say, Ryan? You and me to the end?"

I only need a second to think before I take her hand and shake it. "You've got yourself a deal," I tell her. Even if she's not telling the truth, I'd be a fool to turn her down. "You and me to the end."

DAY 4

I wake up a few hours later, well before dawn, to find that it's raining. It isn't particularly heavy, but it's enough to soak through our shelter's palm-frond roof. I quickly leave the shelter and grab my bag, taking out a hoodie—one of the few pieces of clothing I was allowed to bring with me that I'm not already wearing—and putting it on. But soon it's soaked through, leaving me even wetter and colder than before.

Trying to sleep in these conditions is miserable, to the point that I almost feel jealous of Ashley. At least she has a roof over her head and a real bed to sleep on. Every time I manage to drift off, a raindrop plonks down on my head, or the wind picks up, and I'm awake again.

Finally, maybe a couple of hours after I first woke up, I give up and open my eyes. I don't think there's going to be a challenge today, so hopefully at some point the rain will end and I can nap.

But even though the sky grows marginally brighter as dawn turns to morning, the sun remains hidden by thick, gray clouds, and the rain stubbornly refuses to let up. In fact, if anything, it just gets heavier as the hours pass. As leaky as the shelter is, it at least provides *some* protection from the downpour, so the eight of us huddle together under the palm fronds, shivering and waiting for the weather to improve.

At one point, the rain lessens slightly, and Jing and Marina decide to see if they can get a fire started—assuming there's any dry kindling left—and cook some rice. Marina had been sitting between Cole and me, and when she gets up, he notices me shivering in my hoodie and holds his arm out with a tired smile.

"I don't have much body heat to give right now, but you look like you need it," he says, giving me a tired grin.

I internally debate whether to take him up on his offer, but only for a second. It feels awkward to cuddle up against a hot guy that I barely know, but right now I'll take *any* excuse to get even a tiny bit of warmth.

So I scootch up next to him, laying my head on his shoulder. It's not the most comfortable position, and he was right about not having much warmth to give. Plus, I'm not really sure I want to get any closer to him, at least in the metaphorical sense.

But it's better than nothing, and my hood works as a cushion to protect me from his rock-hard shoulder. In fact, if I wasn't currently soaking wet and colder than ice, I'd say this feels pretty damn good.

"Are you sure this is okay?" I ask, already dreading the answer. "I don't want you to freeze to death."

In response, he wraps his muscular arm around me, squeezing me and pulling me even closer. "Don't worry, Ry," he says, so softly I wouldn't be able to hear him if his mouth wasn't right next to my ear. "I've got you."

DAY 5

The rain continues throughout that day and into the next night, making all of us miserable. Once again, I get next to no sleep. I knew this game wasn't for the faint of heart, but it's one thing to know it and another to *experience* it. I just keep reminding myself that it's only a few days, and that Arielle had to deal with much worse when she was going through chemo. At least I know that I only have to do this for twenty-eight more days, max, and then I can go home and get back to normal.

The only other silver lining is that the other tribe has to be going through the same thing we are. They do have a tarp, but I don't think that would make a huge difference. At least, I hope it doesn't—not because I wish ill on them, but because it would mean they're more rested than us, and could have an advantage in the next challenge.

Speaking of which, once we're all awake, Neema lets us know that the motorboat will be in a few hours to take us to the challenge area. Soon thereafter, the rain begins to lessen, and when we all climb onto the boat, it's stopped completely. In fact, during our short jaunt, the sun starts to poke through the clouds, giving me hope that I'll least be able to get two or three hours of sleep tonight.

Of course, that's assuming that we don't lose the challenge. I don't think I'm on the chopping block, but you never know. Anything is possible in this game.

The challenge area has been completely redone since we were last here a couple of days ago, to the point that I almost wonder if the motorboat took us to a different island. Gone are all the obstacles from the last challenge; in their place are two contraptions, one painted blue and one purple. Each setup has a net suspended from four poles, one at each corner. Just beyond those are sixteen more poles, again half blue and half purple and about ten feet high with flat tops, in a single horizontal line. The entire thing takes up maybe a quarter of the space that the previous challenge did. I almost—*almost*—feel bad for the production crew, who must have worked all day in the rain to get everything done. *At least they could go to their base camp, eat some hot food, and sleep indoors.*

As with the previous challenge, Neema and Steve have us march into the area single file, with Katie leading and holding our tribe flag. This time, however, the other tribe goes in before us, and we wait until they're settled before entering. "Sika, getting your first look at the new Meru," Alex says as we reach our mat and plant our flag. "Ashley voted out at the last tribal council."

There are some muted gasps and exclamations from the other tribe at Alex's proclamation. I assume their shock is for the cameras, because it's not like they have any idea what our dynamics are like or why we'd vote out any one person over the others.

"Let's get to today's challenge," Alex continues. "Once again, you are playing for immunity. Sika, I'll take back the idol." Mustache hands the idol back to him, and he places it on a podium to his left. "You're also playing for reward. I'm sure you all remember the ship from the very first day, when you were divided into tribes. The winner of today's challenge will send two members of their tribe to 'plunder' that ship. We've stocked the hold with some items that you might have found in a real merchant vessel that plied these waters; your choices range from food to tools to luxury items, like blankets and pillows. Each person will be able to take either two small items or one large item. Some will be more tempting than others, but I promise you they're all useful. Sound like something worth playing for?" He pauses while we clap and cheer. "All right, then I'll explain today's challenge.

"First, two members of each tribe will work together to untie a series of knots, which will cause sandbags to release from the net. Then, each member of your tribe must throw a sandbag and land it on top of one of the eight poles behind me, in whatever order you like. However, if you accidentally knock another tribe member's bag off their pole, that person must go again until they've landed their bag a second time. The first team to have all eight members land their bags wins." He points to the other tribe. "Sika, you have one extra member, so someone will sit out. Who's it going to be?"

The other tribe confers for a moment, and the frizzy-haired woman raises her hand. "Alina, sitting out of the challenge," Alex continues, gesturing for her to sit on a small bench off to the side. "The rest of you, get in position, and we'll get started."

As with the previous challenge, Neema and Steve walk both tribes through everything before it actually starts. This one is fairly simple, at least compared to the last one, so it goes rather quickly. After answering our questions, they give us a moment to choose who will untie the knots in the first part of the challenge. Since they did a good job with that in the last challenge, we decide on Joe and Marina this time with a minimum of fuss.

Shortly, we're all ready to start, and Alex waits for the all-clear from Neema. Once he gets it, he raises his hand and says, "Cast-aways: ready … set … GO!"

As soon as he says the last word, Joe and Marina sprint to the net weighed down with sandbags and begin untying knots, as do two of the Sikas. Both groups work quickly, but it looks like they're evenly matched. Alex narrates and exhorts the four knot workers, but it's more irritating than helpful, and I tune him out so I can focus on watching the challenge.

After what feels like forever, but is probably only a minute or two, Marina and Joe finish the knots, and the purple sandbags fall from the net into a wooden crate. The two of them sprint back to the mat, and Beck runs forward, picking up a sandbag as he goes. The other tribe follows close behind, and Green Hat goes to throw his own bag.

It only takes Beck four or five throws to land his bag on the left-most purple pole, but unfortunately, Green Hat lands his a few seconds behind. Marina runs up to take Beck's place, then Rhonda, then Jing. Each of them takes a few tries to get it, with Rhonda in particular struggling a bit, but they get it done. The other tribe matches us, bag for bag; sometimes they land it first and sometimes we do, but the lead is never more than one at any given time. The closest we come to pulling away is when Joe lands his bag on the second try, but Katie, who follows him, has a few close misses, allowing Sika a chance to catch up. Meanwhile, my heart beats even faster. Everyone else has done pretty well, meaning that if I mess up, it might cost us the challenge.

Finally, Katie lands her bag, giving us a six-to-five lead, and I run out there, my heart pounding. As I approach the line, Mustache lands his bag, tying us once again.

Taking a deep breath, I toss my sandbag in the air; it comes close to the top of the pole but doesn't quite reach it. For my second throw, I overcompensate, sending it sailing over the top of the pole and coming down the other side, costing precious seconds as I have to run around the pole to pick up the bag and come back across the line. My third and fourth throws are closer, but not on target, and anxiety begins to close in on me. *Come on, you can do this!* The fifth attempt grazes the top of the pole but falls off again almost immediately. My teammates scream encouragement, but I tune them out. My hands sweating, I fight down a rising feeling of panic as I pick up the sandbag and run back to the start. *We can't lose because of me*!

But then, just as I'm about to make my next attempt, there are groans from the other tribe, and I quickly steal a glance over to my left. It takes a moment to realize what I'm seeing, but when I do, it's all I can do not to laugh out loud. The Sikas are down to five bags again, and there are two on the ground, about five feet apart. Their seventh thrower, the young Black woman I noticed in the previous challenge, must have hit another pole with one of her throws, knocking her teammate's bag off. I'd feel bad for her if I didn't want to win so badly.

With a start, I realize that I'm wasting precious time, and that I still need to land my own bag if I want to win. A sense of calm descends over me, and I turn back to my task. *Focus, Ryan.* I take another deep breath, then throw the sandbag again. It arcs through the air, almost seeming to move in slow motion, and lands directly on the top of the pole, right where I was aiming.

For a bare second, I almost can't believe I did it, and I just stare at the pole, unmoving. Then I remember that we're not quite done yet, and I turn and run back to the mat and my cheering tribemates. *I did it!*

As soon as my foot touches the purple, Cole sprints past me in the other direction, grabbing his sandbag and stepping up to the line. As he does, a feeling of weightlessness starts deep within my chest, spreading out to the rest of my body, like I'm walking on the moon. Meanwhile, Cole squares his wide shoulders, determination written like poetry in the way he stands, as though he's a sculptor's masterpiece come to life.

"You can do it, Cole!" I scream. "I believe in you!"

He doesn't turn around—I don't want him to, I'd rather he focus on winning the challenge for us—but I think he perks up just a little, stands a little straighter than before. Then he throws the sandbag underhand, and it rises in a perfect arc and lands on the very center of the pole.

CHAPTER 8

DAY 5

I'm still riding high when Alex hands Katie the immunity idol a little while later, as though my body is somewhere up in the clouds. Just knowing that none of us is going home tonight, that I can spend the rest of the day not having to strategize, is an excellent feeling.

Actually, I quickly correct myself, *that's not* exactly *right*. I don't think it's ever possible to completely stop strategizing, not in this game. But at least it won't be nearly as bad as if we had lost, and more importantly, I'm safe for another few days.

Alex lets us cheer for a moment longer, then gives us a grin. "Congratulations, Meru," he says. "Nobody's going home from your tribe tonight." He pauses as we clap at the reminder. "However, you still have to choose two people to go to the ship for your reward. Take a moment to confer amongst yourselves."

The eight of us huddle together. I'm expecting Beck to nominate himself, and assuming he gets his way, that leaves one spot. I wouldn't mind going with him, if only to get away from our camp for an hour or two, but I'm not so enthused that I'll argue if someone else really wants to go. In fact, it might be best if Joe or Jing goes with him—I don't want to give him the chance to convince one of my alliance to flip on us.

But to my surprise, Jing speaks up before Beck. "I think Cole should go," she says, nodding in Cole's direction. "Alex said there will be large items, and he can probably carry the most weight. That gives us the biggest range of options, and we won't have to worry about leaving something really useful behind because it's too heavy."

"Sounds like a smart move to me," Rhonda agrees. "Cole, is

that all right with you?"

"That's fine," he says. He turns to me, his ocean-blue eyes glinting in the noonday sun. "You should come with me, Ry."

I certainly wasn't expecting that. "Me?" I ask, swallowing. "Are you sure?"

He nods and gives me an encouraging smile. "Of course I am! You're pretty smart, right? I could use someone to tell me what would be most helpful around camp."

I'm not sure how I feel about this. If the rest of the tribe doesn't like what we bring back for whatever reason, I might get blamed for it.

But before I get a chance to respond, Beck cuts in. "All right, so Cole and Ryan will go," he says. "Choose wisely, guys. We're all counting on you."

A half-hour or so later, Cole and I are sitting in a motorboat, speeding away from the challenge area over the open ocean. Unlike before, it's just us and the captain, but the no-talking-off-camera rule is still in effect. Maybe that's a good thing, because I really have no idea what I would say.

I glance over at Cole, wondering what he's thinking. He certainly doesn't look pensive. His eyes are wide as he watches the waves pass by, his hair whipping back and forth in the wind, and a tiny smile rests on his face like he doesn't have a care in the world. Spray from the ocean coats his shirtless, well-defined chest, making him gleam like a Greek god. I turn away so he doesn't catch me staring, but it takes more willpower than I care to admit not to peek. Not for the first time, I silently curse the producers for putting Cole and me on the same tribe. *How am I supposed to think when he's around?*

Thankfully, our destination chooses that moment to come into view, and it doesn't take long before the motorboat draws up to the larger ship. Cole and I climb a rope ladder, stepping carefully as we pull ourselves up the rungs.

Waiting for us at the top of the rope ladder are two cameramen and Neema, who attaches small microphones to our clothing. "Remember, you can each take two small items or one large item," she says, fiddling with my shirt to ensure the mic is hidden from the camera. "You don't both have to do the same thing—one of you can take a large reward, and the other can take two small ones. Large items are to your right and small items are to your left." She finishes with my mic and moves over to Cole, who has unfortunately put his own shirt on in the interim. "You can, of course, confer with each other. Just pretend like I'm not here, and ignore the cameras. Once you've made your selections, however, you will have to show them to me so I can make sure you aren't taking more items than allowed. Got it?" She waits for us to nod. "Awesome. In that case, go ahead. Take as much time as you need."

With that, Cole and I start walking towards the supplies. Some of the slats on the deck above have been removed over the last five days to let in some light, so it's easy enough to see what we're working with.

Cole glances at me, his eyebrows raised and his nose wrinkled. "You take the left, I'll take the right?" he asks.

I nod, not quite trusting myself to say anything, and we go off in our appointed directions. As Neema promised, the whole right side of the hold is lined with wooden barrels and crates, each topped by one or two potential choices. Immediately, I see things that could be useful: a handsaw that we could use to cut down bamboo for the shelter or chop firewood, a pack of matches wrapped in oilcloth, a burlap sack full of fresh fruit, a set of herbs and spices in glass vials, and a thick waterproof blanket. The matches are tempting—they would make starting our fire so much easier, as long as it's not raining—but I only count twenty of them, and I imagine we'd blow through them fairly quickly, so I continue on down the line.

"Anything good over there?" Cole calls over as I'm examining a toolbox, complete with needles and thread, as well as a small pair of scissors, a hammer, and a few other tools that could be useful around camp. "I've got some good options."

"I do too," I reply, pausing my examination long enough to glance up at him. "Matches, a blanket, some seasonings—"

Cole perks up at the last. "Seasonings?" he repeats, tilting his head slightly. "You mean, like, salt and pepper?"

I stifle a laugh with some difficulty. "Uh, yeah," I reply, walking back to where I saw the set and reading the labels on the bottles. *I can't believe I forgot he's a chef.* "Looks like there's salt, pepper, thyme, rosemary, paprika, a couple other things."

He comes over to see for himself, handling the glass with extreme care. "Oh yeah, we are definitely taking these. No more bland rice for us, you can count on that." He looks up and gives me an abashed grin. "You know, this is going to sound incredibly nerdy, but when I graduated from culinary school, my mom got me this super fancy hand-carved spice rack with real glass bottles, just like these ones. I can't wait for her to see this when it airs. I know she'll get a kick out of it."

I smile back at him, even though there's a twinge of pain somewhere in the back of my head. "I'm sure she will."

He grins at me for a moment longer before the moment breaks and we get back to looking through the items. "What about you?" Cole asks as I move on to the next one, a jar of pickled lemons. "Are you going to watch the show with your parents?"

This time the pain is much more than a tinge, and my eyes burn as they tear up. "Actually, no," I reply, trying to keep my voice even. "My parents died in a car accident when I was sixteen."

I look up just in time to see Cole's face fall, a stricken expression crossing his face. "I'm so sorry, Ry," he says. "I had no idea."

I wave a hand and force a smile. "Of course you didn't," I reply. "Don't worry about it. I'll watch it with my sister."

He opens his mouth, but closes it again without saying anything, which is probably for the best. Even though it's been more than a decade since my parents died, I still find it hard to talk about them. I know I'm hardly the only person who's lost loved ones before their time, but sometimes I feel like nobody understands how hard it is to have your whole life shattered in a single moment like so many pieces of glass, and then to have to rebuild it without getting sliced to ribbons by the shards. I could never have done it without Arielle, and I'm sure she'd say the same about me. She's the only person I can truly rely on, my rock in the raging sea that is life.

And if there's a small part of me that insists that it doesn't have to be this way, that I can afford to let other people in … well, I can worry about that when the game is over, because right now the only thing that matters is winning, no matter how hard it gets.

Cole and I continue cataloguing our respective halves of the hold in silence, which is probably for the best. I don't pay as much attention as I should to the remaining items, distracted as I am by thoughts of my parents and Arielle.

Eventually, though, I reach the end of the line, and with a not-insignificant amount of effort, I mentally wrench myself out of my funk and back into game mode. *I need to stay focused if I want to have any chance of winning at all.*

Putting on my best face, I join Cole in the middle of the hold, where we discuss which items we should take. Cole is set on taking the spices, and I think the toolbox will be useful, so we agree to take those as my small items without much debate. For Cole's pick, we eventually settle on a large bag of dried black beans. It's not the most exciting choice, but it'll help keep us fed for a few days, and hopefully that will give us an advantage in the next few challenges. Plus, it'll be a change from rice.

After we make our selections, we take them over to Neema, who gives us her approval after a cursory inspection, before loading us back onto the motorboat with our plundered riches. The captain drops us off on the beach about half a mile up from our tribe camp; Steve waits there with a couple more camera crew, and as we get off the motorboat, careful not to get the bag of beans wet, he tells us that production wants to film us walking back to the tribe. "It'll look more authentic," he says, shrugging.

I don't really want to waste the calories, and I doubt anyone watching will be fooled, but I also don't think arguing the point would change his mind. So, Cole and I get started down the beach, one of the cameramen in front of us and the other to one side as we carry our rewards back home.

After we've been walking for a couple of minutes, Cole turns to me. "By the way, I never did get a chance to say thanks," he says, rubbing the back of his neck. "So … thank you, Ry."

"No problem," I reply, frowning slightly. "But, what exactly are you thanking me for?"

"For not voting me out the other night. I know that you were thinking about siding with Beck and them up until the last minute, and I'm glad you decided not to."

Whatever I thought he was going to say, it wasn't that. "You're … welcome, I guess? I didn't realize it was so obvious that I was torn."

He winks at me. "Come on, Ry. You didn't think I didn't notice you were avoiding me for the first three days? At first, I thought you just didn't like me, but then I realized you were leaning towards voting with them and didn't want Beck to get suspicious. I thought about talking to you myself, but Rhonda swore you'd see the light before we voted, and she was right." He laughs. "Granted, I only listened to her because I thought she was the one on the chopping block. If I knew they were targeting *me*, I would have tried a little bit harder to get you on our side. But then, it all worked out in the end, so I'm not upset."

I stare at him silently, not entirely sure how to respond. *Had I been avoiding him*? I didn't think so, but if he felt that way, then clearly I was doing something wrong. "I'm sorry," I eventually say. Even if he's wrong, I need to stay on his good side. "I certainly didn't mean to come off as if I was avoiding you. Please don't take it personally."

"Don't worry about it." He gives me an easy grin; either it's real, or he's the best liar I've ever met. "I'm just happy we're on the same side now. I really like you, and I think we're going to do well together."

My heart does a little flip, and I take a second to remind myself that now is *not* the time to be distracted by an attractive man, even one as gorgeous as Cole. "I'm glad to hear that," I say, hoping beyond hope that the sudden heat I feel on my face is not a blush. "And, speaking of which, I really should thank you too."

"Oh?" He arches an eyebrow at me. "For what?"

"For warming me up in the shelter yesterday." I shudder just *thinking* about the rain. "Or, for trying to, at least. You didn't have to, but you did. I really appreciate that."

"Of course, Ry. It was nothing, really." His eyes shine, and he lowers the bag of beans slightly, as though he's going to put it down, before thinking better of it. "We're allies now, and I meant it when I said I've got you."

CHAPTER 9

DAYS 5-6

We get back to the tribe beach pretty soon after that. Once they see us coming, our tribemates stop what they're doing and run out to meet us, excited to see what we've brought them. Most everyone seems pretty pleased by our haul, although Joe mutters that he would have preferred something to keep us dry. I don't really mind. You can't please everyone, and I'm confident we made the best choices we could have.

If anything, I'm even more convinced when dinnertime comes and Cole, true to his word, somehow makes rice and beans taste like a world-class meal using the spices. Honestly, I don't know if it's *actually* that good or if I'm just starving, but at this point I couldn't care less. From my tribemates' expressions, they're not questioning it either. Marina even pronounces it to be almost as good as her abuela's Moros y Cristianos, which makes Cole flush with pride.

Besides that, we spend some time over the next two days using the tools from the toolbox to improve the camp. The scissors are very useful for cutting palm fronds to size so we can weave them into bowls, and Beck uses the hammer and some wooden nails he carved to make the shelter more structurally sound. Meanwhile, Rhonda grabs the needle and thread as soon as Cole and I get back, and within a few hours, has repaired all the holes in our clothing. "I just wish I had more fabric so I could make a blanket to keep us warm at night," she says as she hands me back my socks. "But somethin' is better than nothin', I suppose."

Of course, we can never truly forget that we're in a game, so there's always strategy talk that goes on while we work. Even though we come together to eat and sleep every day, there's still a clear division in the tribe between the two alliances. The five members of my group discuss who should go home next without coming to a consensus. Meanwhile, I assume Beck, Jing, and Joe are trying to figure out how they can get back on top. Barring a twist or someone flipping, they don't seem to have much of a chance, but I've seen enough episodes to know that's not always a given, so I keep my ears and eyes open.

If we needed any further reminders, Neema and her confessionals would do the trick. It's a little bit annoying when she interrupts me having a chat with someone to pull them aside, but ultimately, we're at the mercy of production. At least we all have to go through the same thing, so we can all joke about it.

My turn comes just after we finish eating breakfast on day six, when Neema grabs me and takes me to a spot on the beach, where she has me lean against a boulder.

"So, Ryan," she says, once everything's set up. "You were in the majority in the last vote. How are you feeling about your position in the game?"

I smile inwardly, even as I keep my expression blank. She's obviously giving me a chance to brag about how powerful I am right now, but I've seen too many contestants be overconfident and then immediately get voted out to fall for *that* trap. "I'd say I'm feeling pretty happy about where I am," I reply. "I mean, I'm in the majority alliance, so that's good. But anything could happen between now and our next tribal council, and I'm not counting my chickens before they hatch."

"Fair enough. In that case, who would you vote for if you do go to tribal tonight?"

"If we go to tribal, I'd definitely vote for either Beck, Joe, or Jing. But as for which one of them specifically, I don't know. I'd have to come to a consensus with my allies first."

Neema's wearing sunglasses, but I swear I can see her roll her eyes anyway, and I can guess what she's thinking right now: *Stupid lawyers and their lawyer answers*. "So, you trust your alliance, then?"

"I'd say I trust my alliance about as much as I can, under the circumstances. I'd be happy to go to the final five with them, and Rhonda and I have a deal to go to the final two together."

"And do you intend to keep up your end of that deal?"

"I wouldn't have made it if I didn't intend to keep it," I answer, with a shrug. "But in the end, only one of us can win the game, and I want that to be me. I'm trying to keep my options open as best I can to make that a reality."

"What about Rhonda? Do you think she's telling the truth about wanting to go to the end with you?"

That brings me up short. "I … guess I'm not really sure," I finally say. "I mean, I hope she is, and she *sounded* sincere, but she could be trying to fool me."

Neema nods. "You've gotten pretty close to Cole recently, haven't you? Do you think you might want to go to the end with him instead of Rhonda?"

I frown at that. *Have I really gotten close to him?* "I could see going to the end with Cole," I reply. I did go to the pirate ship with him for the last reward, but I wouldn't really say we're close. *Maybe she's just trying to make it seem like we're buddies or something for TV purposes.* "But then, I can see myself at the end with Katie, or Marina, or whoever. A lot can happen between now and then, and as long as I'm the one who gets that million-dollar check, I don't care how I get there."

"Wise words," Neema says. She signals the cameraman, and the red light turns off. "Thanks, Ryan. That's all for now."

At her signal, I get up and take off my mic, returning it to her before heading back to my tribe. As I walk, I mull over the last thing I said in my confessional: that I don't care how I win, as long as I do. Before I left the States, I told myself that I would do anything to win—lie, cheat, steal, whatever. I'm sure Arielle wouldn't be happy if I told her that, but I'm the one out here, not her. I don't *want* to hurt anyone, and it's harder to imagine myself backstabbing my allies now that they're real people instead of imaginary strawmen.

Unbidden, an image of Cole comes to my mind, his eyes shining as we walked down the beach yesterday, returning to our tribe with our rewards from the pirate ship. Could I really betray him—or Marina, or Katie, or Rhonda? They've all been nothing but good to me, and I'm sure they have their own families, their own reasons to want the million dollars.

But I shake my head, dispelling those thoughts before they can take hold. I may not want to hurt my allies, but only one of us can win. If there comes a time when I need to backstab someone in my alliance to get further in the game, I'll do it, no matter how much it would pain me to see Alex snap their insignia in half. I'm here to make Arielle's life better, and I won't let anything get in the way of that goal.

DAY 7

We have our third immunity challenge the following day. This time, we walk into the arena first. When the Sikas arrive, Alex announces that Model One, whose name was apparently Lauren, was voted out two nights ago. We all do our best to pretend to be shocked.

Next, Alex explains the challenge to us. "This one is simple," he says. He gestures away from us, where sixteen raised platforms, like miniature balance beams, sit, half blue and half purple. Each platform has a six-foot-long bamboo pole on top. "Each of you will stand on a narrow wooden beam, carrying a heavy pole. Every five minutes, we'll add twenty pounds to the poles of everyone remaining in the challenge. If at any point you fall off your beam or you drop your pole, you're out of the challenge, and your weight will be distributed among the remaining players. As you can imagine, those poles will get heavy *very* quickly. The last one standing will win immunity for their tribe, as well as a reward in the form of fishing gear." He pauses, a glint in his eye. "It sounds simple, but there is a twist to this challenge."

I turn and share a look with Katie; she looks as I imagine I do, cautiously excited. We all knew there would be twists—anyone who's seen an episode of this show would know that—but what exactly those twists are, as well as their timing, is, of course, a mystery to us.

Alex waits for the news to sink in, then reaches behind the podium where the immunity idol sits and pulls out a covered tray, the kind you'd see a waiter carrying at a fancy restaurant. "I'm sure you've all gotten very hungry over the past week." He pulls the cover off the tray, revealing the most appetizing thing I've ever seen: a hamburger and fries, the latter still glistening with oil. "Any contestant can choose to sit out of this challenge," Alex continues. "If you do, you'll eat a full meal while the others compete. However, there is a downside, because the rest of your tribe will still have to bear your weight. Oh, and if your whole tribe sits out, nobody eats, and you lose by default." He gives us an almost predatory grin. "I'll give you all a moment to think about what you want to do, and then we'll see who's competing and who's sitting out. Make sure you choose carefully."

His last word is met with dead silence as we all consider our strategy. It's not an easy choice, at least not to me. Sitting out would be a bad look, and the tribe members who compete might resent those who don't. But at the same time, I've barely eaten since we landed on the beach, and I don't know if I'll have another chance like this. Besides, it's not like I'll be of much help in this challenge. It might be better for us if I fuel up while the Sikas tire themselves out, even if it means we lose this one challenge.

But then I look up to see Cole, his shoulders square and his expression etched with determination, and all thoughts of sitting out evaporate immediately. *Do I really want him to think of me as a quitter, as someone who puts their own needs above everything*? I don't even think he'd be angry with me, just disappointed, but somehow that seems even worse.

Alex clears his throat, snapping me out of my reverie. "On the count of three, I want those of you who have decided to sit out of the challenge to raise your hand," he says. "One … two … three."

Steeled with newfound resolve, I keep my hand down. The rest of my tribe follows suit, although Beck's hand twitches briefly. I'm a little surprised nobody took the bait, especially the three who are in the minority, since they have less to lose.

Meanwhile, two of the Sikas have raised their hands: the tall one who looks like he's barely over eighteen, and the older man with thin hair. "Elijah and Minh, sitting out of the challenge," Alex says. "I'll give the rest of you a moment to prepare, and we'll get started."

The cameras turn off, and the two Sika sit-outs, Elijah and Minh, stand off to the side while Neema and Steve give us a walk-through of the challenge. This time, the walkthrough lasts barely five minutes, less time than it takes for the fourteen of us who are competing to get situated on our platforms. I hoist my pole up onto my shoulders, trying to get comfortable with the weight. Meanwhile, Minh and Elijah sit on a bench that Steve brings out, eating their food. I do my best to ignore them.

As soon as we're all ready, the cameras turn on again, and Neema signals to Alex. "This challenge is on," the latter says.

Once again, he's met with silence, although this time it's punctuated by the sounds of delighted munching. I close my eyes, trying to tune them out. *I sure hope I made the right choice.*

The first few minutes pass fairly quickly, but soon after that, my shoulders begin to burn and my legs start to go numb. Every five minutes, a producer comes around and hangs sandbags off our poles—one on each side, to maintain balance—making it that much harder to carry. The pain grows higher, but I grit my teeth and push through, ignoring the sweat dripping down into my eyes. Finally, after twenty-five minutes of torture, I can take no more, leaving Cole, Beck, and Jing from our tribe, and Mustache and Green Hat from the Sikas. I'm impressed with them—each Meru is carrying a hundred and forty pounds, and the Sikas have even more, since they had two people sit out.

Less than a minute later, Beck drops out. He's followed almost immediately by Jing, leaving Cole up there alone, carrying the hopes of the Meru tribe on his shoulders. Thankfully, Green Hat steps down bare seconds after Jing does, setting up a showdown between Cole and Mustache. *Come on, Cole,* I silently urge him, not wanting to break his concentration. He barely moves, even when the producers add more weight onto his pole, but I can see cords standing out on his neck, and his hands shake. *I know you can do it.*

And then, seemingly out of nowhere, Mustache drops his pole. It takes a moment for us Merus to realize what happened, but when we do, we start cheering. "I knew you could do it, Cole!" Marina shouts, clapping her hands together. "Never a doubt in my mind."

Meanwhile, Cole waits for Alex to announce that we've won before dropping his pole, then steps off the platform and immediately collapses in relief. "I'm okay," he announces, laying spread-eagle on the muddy ground. "Celebrate without me."

DAYS 8-9

The next few days fall into a bit of a routine, or as much of one as is possible with cameras watching our every move. Most of the daylight hours are spent doing chores around camp or resting, except for when we have an immunity challenge. Then, at night, if we're not at tribal council, we sit around the fire talking to each other or just looking at the stars until bedtime. Our continued work on the shelter gets it to a point where sleep is bearable, rather than almost impossible. Even better, the weather holds up, although we do get some more rain on day nine. It still gets chilly at night, but our improved shelter does an okay job of breaking the wind, and we're all long past the point of feeling embarrassment at huddling together to conserve body heat.

Between the fishing gear and the extra beans, we're eating better than we were before. None of us has used a Hawaiian sling before, but Katie has some snorkeling experience— "My girlfriend is from Key West, and I swear it's like a religion down there, so we go whenever I visit," as she puts it—so she becomes our primary fisher, bringing in a few small fish each day. Meanwhile, on day eight, Marina discovers a papaya tree with several ripe fruits, which gives us a nice change of pace for a couple of meals. It's not enough to sustain us long term—I wouldn't be surprised if we've all lost ten pounds by now—but it's an improvement, no question. We may be hungry pretty much all the time, but at least we're not *starving.*

To be honest, it could be worse, because no matter how much I might think Cole is a threat, I can't deny that he makes what little food we do have downright delicious. Somehow, with the spices and the beans from the pirate ship reward, the rice we were given on day one, and whatever fish and fruit we're able to scavenge from the island, he's able to make meals that I never would have expected to find on a desert island. If we had actual plates and silverware, I could almost believe we're eating at a fancy restaurant back home.

"How do you do it?" I ask him while he cooks breakfast on day nine, trying and failing to keep a note of envy out of my voice. The others are doing their daily chores or recording confessionals; I should be with them, but Cole asked me to help him, so here I am, sitting uncomfortably close to him, chopping coconut meat with the machete while he stirs rice over the fire. "I mean it. How can you make this stuff taste like real food?"

"I've had a lot of practice." He looks up and gives me a quick grin before concentrating on the rice again. "Honestly, though, the ingredients are about as good quality as you'd get back home. Maybe even a little better, since they're fresh." He reaches for the glass vial of paprika and shakes a precise amount into the rice pot before returning it to its place. "The real trick is knowing how to treat them so that each element speaks for itself. It's pretty easy once you get the hang of it."

"Easy, huh? I think I'll have to take your word for it."

He chuckles. "Let me guess, you're one of those people who can't even boil water for pasta?"

"I'm not quite *that* bad, thank you very much. I've been known to make a mean grilled cheese from time to time."

This time, he outright laughs, and for a second, there's a warm feeling deep in my chest that has nothing to do with the fire. "My apologies for underestimating you," he says. "Seriously though, I'm sure you'd be a great chef if you had the time for it. You're really smart, Ry. I'm sure you could do anything you put your mind to."

The warm sensation returns with interest. "Thanks, but I really think you're puffing me up. I'll never be as good as you."

"Maybe not," he replies with a shrug. "But don't be so hard on yourself. You've been through a lot, and you still managed to get through law school and be a successful lawyer. There's no way in a million years I'd ever be able to do that."

His words hit me with unexpected force, and I barely avoid flinching. *He doesn't know about Arielle, does he?* I don't see how he could have found out, but that doesn't stop me from feeling irrationally anxious. "How did you become a chef?" I ask, desperate to change the subject. "You must have started early on if you're this good now."

"I played baseball in high school. Shocking, right?" He looks away, splotches of red on his cheeks. "The coach was a real hardass, and he insisted that we all go on a high-protein diet so we could build some muscle. I hated every second of it. I just wanted to eat what I wanted to eat, you know? So I started doing research into different types of diets, nutrition, that sort of thing. I guess I had this idea that I could convince him he was wrong, and I could go back to eating burgers and fries all the time."

"I'm guessing he didn't agree with you?"

He shrugs. "To be honest, I never got the nerve to bring it up. But I did find some cool recipes that met his conditions and didn't sound terrible, so I asked my mom if I could try to make a few of them, and she was all for it. The first few weren't great, but I learned quickly, and…" He gestures at the pot. "Well, here we are."

"That's awesome." Without even thinking about it, I gently pat his shoulder. "I'm glad it worked out for you."

Now he looks up at me, giving me a slow grin that makes my heart begin to race. "Thanks, Ry," he says. His eyes are locked onto mine, and I have this crazy feeling that he's going to reach out and touch my shoulder too, or maybe even wrap his arm around me and pull me close, or—

But then the moment passes, and he clears his throat and

looks back down at the rice. "How about you? Why did you become a lawyer?"

"Nothing quite as interesting as all that," I reply, a feeling of tightness growing in my chest. *What in the world just happened?* "People think being a lawyer is super intense, going to court and shouting all the time, but it's really not. It's more like solving puzzles—how do you get the best deal for your client while making sure everything meets all the rules and regulations? I know it sounds nerdy, but I guess I just liked the sound of that."

"I don't think it's nerdy. I think it's smart." He pauses, and when he speaks again, his voice is lower, more contemplative. "I know what you mean about solving puzzles. Cooking's the same way. I have these ingredients and this equipment; how can I use them to make a perfect dish? The difference is that in my job, there's no one right answer. Two chefs could start with the exact same stuff and come up with completely different dishes, and they could both be amazing."

"Huh." I lean back, pausing my chopping for a moment. "I never really thought of it that way."

"See? I'm opening your mind to new horizons." He gives me another smile that makes my stomach flutter. "I guess what it boils down to is that I love to create new things, especially ones that make people happy. I'm sure you do that in your own way too, but there's something really satisfying about watching people eat something you made, and knowing that they're actually enjoying it too."

He falls silent after that, and for a moment I just sit there quietly, letting the sound of the ocean wash over me. "You know," I eventually say, "my sister Arielle always tells me that I should have something to do besides work. Maybe I should take up cooking."

He laughs once more. "You definitely should." He looks up again, his gaze meeting mine, and for a moment, I could almost wish that this isn't a game, that I could win the million without having to vote Cole out somewhere down the line. "I know you'd be great at it."

When we enter the challenge area later that day, I'm hopeful that the extra food will give us an advantage over the Sikas. Since we won last time, we go in first, this time with Rhonda carrying our tribe flag as we march single-file up to our mat. A short time later, the other tribe joins us, with Minh, the elderly Asian man who sat out the last challenge, no longer among their ranks. I wonder if he was sent home because he didn't compete, or if he was already on the outs and figured it was better to get some food in his belly. If it were the latter, I can't really say I blame him. I'm still a little surprised Joe and Beck didn't take Alex up on his offer.

Once we're all present and accounted for, our charming host explains the challenge to us: a stereotypical *Marooned* challenge, with swimming and digging portions followed by a complex puzzle. "The first tribe to finish wins immunity and a reward," Alex says, pulling a cover off the podium next to him with a flourish to reveal a set of pillows and blankets. "Just a little something to make your time out here a bit more comfortable."

As usual, Neema and Steve give us the walkthrough, and then we get a few moments to decide who will do which portion of the challenge. Katie volunteers to sit out, leaving the rest of us to choose our roles. I quickly volunteer to do the puzzle, and Beck insists on joining me. Meanwhile, Cole, Rhonda, and Joe offer to swim, leaving Marina and Jing to do the digging. Even though I volunteered, part of me is nervous about doing the puzzle. If this challenge ends up being as close as the first challenge was, seconds could matter, and I don't want to be blamed if we lose.

But all my worrying is for naught, because the younger Black woman on Sika is like a dart in the water, retrieving all three of their keys while we still only have one. Their lead only grows from there, to the point where they finish their puzzle before we can even get a chance to begin ours. I wish we hadn't lost, since I could have really used one of those blankets, not to mention all the pillows that now belong to the Sikas. But at least it wasn't my fault that we did.

Of course, the bigger problem is that we have to vote someone out. The good thing is that now that the alliances are crystallized, there's less horse trading than there was on day three, before our first tribal. Instead, my alliance spends a good amount of time debating who we want to send home next. We quickly decide to keep Jing, since she's clearly an asset in challenges and nobody has anything against her personally, which means it's down to Beck or Joe.

Rhonda, Cole, and I want to vote for the latter, since he's by far the most aloof on the tribe. "I don't think he's said two words to me the entire time we've been here," Rhonda says at one point. I'm sure that's an exaggeration, but she isn't far off, and the fact that he hasn't even tried to get to know us means that we don't trust him very much.

Meanwhile, Katie and Marina are tired of Beck's continued attempts at leadership. I understand why they're upset—he does tend to railroad anyone who disagrees with him—but at least I know where Beck stands, and I can't say the same for Joe.

Fortunately, even though we all have our own opinions, we also recognize the value of voting together and presenting a united front, at least at this stage in the game, and we come to a joint decision well before tribal.

But just because we're united doesn't mean the other alliance is going to go down without a fight. A few hours before sunset, Beck and Jing pull me aside and try valiantly to convince me to vote for Marina. "I just think she's the least helpful in challenges," Jing says while Beck nods along. "Nothing against her personally, but someone has to go, and it might as well be someone who benefits the tribe the least."

Unlike last time, however, my mind is already made up, so I politely hear them out without agreeing to anything, doing my best impression of a brick wall, and after a while, they leave me alone. I don't want to rock the boat this early in the game, and I doubt my alliance mates do either, despite the best efforts of the three in the minority.

Even though I trust my alliance, there's always the possibility that something can go wrong. You never know in this game—someone might decide to flip, or there could be some twist at tribal council. Nothing is ever guaranteed.

But in what can only be considered a win for my blood pressure, everything goes smoothly at tribal that night, and Joe is voted out with five votes to Marina's three. I wouldn't say I'm *happy* to see him go home—the silver lining of our complete lack of interaction is that he didn't really have a chance to get on my bad side—but far better him than me.

Cole glances over at me as Alex reads the final vote, giving me a wink, and I amend that last bit. *Better him than any of my alliance.*

DAYS 10-13

In the coming days, we try our best to bounce back from our immunity loss, hoping that the loss of another tribe member will keep us focused. But on day eleven, we lose the next challenge, and the reward of PB&J sandwiches that comes with it. The mood around camp is gloomy that afternoon, despite the fact that the sun is shining high and there are no clouds in the sky. As well as losing another member of our tribe, this puts us one down on Sika. We don't know when the tribes will merge, but we *do* know that it's better to go into it with numbers. If they outnumber us, they could just pick the remaining Merus off one by one, until we're all gone.

At least we don't have to spend too much time worrying about who's going home this time. Now that Joe is gone, Beck is next on our list. He and Jing try once again to convince me and the others to flip on our alliance, but their attempts are desultory this time, presumably because they know it's even more of an uphill battle with a five-to-two disadvantage.

In fact, when we get to tribal council and the votes are tallied, the final vote is six to one against Beck, with the remaining vote—namely, Beck's—against Marina. I guess Jing saw the writing on the wall and voted against her alliance. Maybe she doesn't want to burn bridges in case we merge before we go to tribal council again. Personally, I wouldn't be opposed to working with her, but I trust her less than I do the others.

For our sixth immunity challenge, on day thirteen, we redouble our efforts to win, eating a substantial portion of the remaining beans to give our bodies some fuel. Perhaps because she knows she's going home next if we lose, Jing is invaluable in psyching us up. "Katie, you and Ryan are awesome at puzzles," she says as we wait for the motorboat to take us to the challenge. "Marina, you have great balance, and you're quick with knots. And Cole, you were an absolute beast carrying the pole with all the weight on it. I know we can pull it off, no matter what the next one is."

Rhonda glares at Jing, but the effect is lessened by her familiar smile. "And what about me?" she asks. "Am I just chopped liver?"

To her credit, Jing doesn't miss a beat. "I didn't think I needed to mention you," she says, matching Rhonda's smile. "We all know you're the heart and soul of this tribe."

Rhonda gives a stately nod while the rest of us laugh good-naturedly. "And don't y'all forget it," she says gravely. We all hasten to assure her that we won't.

To my immense relief, we win immunity that day, along with a reward of tins of coffee and tea and a couple of ceramic mugs. I'm excited for the tea, but everyone else seems to prefer coffee, especially Rhonda and Cole. *More for me, I guess.*

Even more than just the material rewards, the fact that we won again brings our spirits back quite a bit. While this win only means that we're tied with Sika again, rather than having an advantage over them, it still feels good to know that nobody from our tribe will be going home tonight. Jing seems especially relieved, but all of us are walking a little bit lighter that afternoon as we go about our daily chores. It's a good feeling, to say the least, and I savor it while I can. Something tells me that feelings like this one are going to become few and far between as we get closer to the merge.

That night finds us sitting around the fire, celebrating the fact that we don't have to attend tribal council for what feels like the first time in forever. Well, all of us except for Rhonda, who went to bed just after sunset. Now that Beck is gone, she claims that she actually has a chance to get some decent sleep since she doesn't have to put up with his snoring. "I swear, that man could knock the shingles off a house," was the way she put it.

Jing follows her a short time later, leaving me, Marina, Cole, and Katie to our own devices. As the sky darkens and the stars come out, the conversation trails off, and we sit in silence for a little while, enjoying the view. The moon is a barely-visible crescent just above the western horizon, so the only light is from the fire and the stars. If I didn't know better, I'd swear the stars are brighter out here. More likely, they just look that way because there are no streetlights and buildings to hide them and dim their light. Whatever the reason is, the effect is spellbinding.

My train of thought is interrupted when Katie abruptly clears her throat. "I want us all to be friends when this is all over," she says, her knee bouncing. "No matter what happens in this game, I mean."

Marina scoffs lightly and nudges Katie's foot with her toe. "Of course we will be," she says. "I, for one, am going to blow up all of your phones. Especially you, Cole—now that I've seen what you can do with a few coconuts and some white rice, I'm coming straight to your restaurant as soon as we get back home."

"Sounds like a great plan to me," Cole says, flashing that easy smile that I'm finding more and more difficult to ignore. "You're all invited to brunch as many times as you like. I'll make sure there's a table for you, even if we're all booked up."

"And you're all welcome to visit me in D.C. any time," I add. "I'll show you all the tourist sights. You'll love it."

"Thanks, guys," Katie says, laughing. "I appreciate it." Her laughter turns into sniffling, and she puts her head down.

"Oh, hey now, what's wrong?" Marina moves closer to Katie, wrapping an arm around her and gently massaging her shoulder. "Is it something we said?"

Katie looks up again, tears in her eyes, and gives Marina a

watery smile. "No, of course not," she says. "I'm just happy to have people like you around. It … hasn't always been easy for me, especially right after I transitioned. My parents were supportive, but my extended family—and a few people I *thought* were good friends—didn't really react well. And it's not like I had a ton of friends at the time to begin with. I was a stereotypical engineering nerd. More comfortable with books than people and all that." She shakes her head. "I don't know what I would have done if I hadn't met Rachael. And … I guess things haven't been as bad as they could have been, not really. But sometimes it feels like … like people just don't want to be me because of who I am, you know?"

"Well, *I* think you're wonderful," Marina says, giving Katie a one-armed hug while Cole and I chime in to agree. "And I'm glad you have someone you can count on, *tata*. When I met my husband, it was love at first sight. I didn't tell him right away, but I knew we were meant to be together after five minutes. But when my parents found out that I was dating a Black man…" She frowns at the memory. "Well, let's just say they weren't happy about it, if you know what I mean. They treated him like he was something they scraped off the bottom of their shoe, right up until our son was born. He put up with all of it because he loves me as much as I love him, but if he'd been a lesser man …" She pats Katie on the shoulder, her expression distant. "What I'm trying to say is, I'm glad you found your girlfriend. We all need someone in our lives who will back us, no matter what."

"For me, it's my mom," Cole adds quietly. "When my dad left, she could have given up and left me to my own devices, but instead she did everything she could to make sure I'd have a normal life. I may not have realized it at the time, but she really sacrificed a lot to raise me. And when I graduated from culinary school, she was there in the first row of the audience, with the biggest smile I've ever seen in my life. Everything I have, I owe to her."

"She sounds amazing," Katie says. Cole nods his thanks to her, and she turns to me. "What about you, Ryan? Do you have someone who's always there for you?"

I nod. "My sister, Arielle. Our parents died when I was sixteen, and she was twenty." I push down the pain that the thought of them always brings. Now is not the time to mourn. "We don't have any aunts or uncles, and our grandparents were all long gone, so she really was the only family I had left. There's no way I would have been able to go to college, let alone law school, if she hadn't pushed me. And then when she—"

I abruptly stop talking, catching myself just in time. I can't tell them about Arielle's cancer, about how terrified I was when she was diagnosed, how helpless I felt as she went through treatment, how we've barely made a dent in the bills even though we've pooled both our salaries for the last year. I can't tell them all of that, even though I trust them, because if I do, then they'll know just how badly I need the money, and then *they* might not trust *me*.

So instead, I just finish by saying, "When she wanted to go back to grad school and become a teacher, she had to scrimp and save for years to pay for it. But she took it in stride."

Thankfully, even if anyone noticed my slip, they don't question me further. "I'm sorry, guys," Katie says, rubbing at the back of her neck. "I didn't mean to kill the vibe."

"No worries, *tata*," Marina says. She starts to say more, but interrupts herself with a wide yawn. "I don't know about the rest of you, but I'm beat. I think it's time for bed."

"Me too," Katie adds. "Good night, everyone." She pauses, then looks at the three of us, her eyes glowing softly in the light of the fire. "And … thanks to all of you. I really appreciate it."

"Of course," Marina says, favoring Katie with a smile before turning to Cole and me. "How about you boys? You gonna stay out here, or come to bed?"

I shake my head. "I'm not too tired yet," I reply. "I'll be there soon, though."

"Same for me," Cole says. His eyes flick to me, then back to Marina. "You ladies go ahead."

Marina nods, and she and Katie share a brief hug before going off to the shelter to join Rhonda and Jing.

Cole watches them go, his brows knitted together, then turns to look at me. "Can I ask you something?" he says, his voice low.

I nod, my heart suddenly in my throat. Maybe someone *did* notice my slip when I was talking about Arielle. "Uh, yeah, sure. What is it?"

He doesn't say anything for a few seconds, giving time for my anxiety to build. "Feel free to tell me to fuck off," he finally says, "but … when you came out, was it anything like Katie's experience?"

I let out a relieved breath. "No, it wasn't. I never told my parents, but I think they knew anyway. At least, they never mentioned it to me. Meanwhile, when I told Arielle, she just rolled her eyes and said 'Really? I'm *shocked*,' so she could obviously tell. Most of my friends didn't really care—or, at least, they didn't treat me any differently, which was good enough for me."

"I'm glad to hear that." He slumps his shoulders and leans back against the log. "Really, I mean it. Nobody should ever be treated differently just because of who they love, or what gender they are."

I nod my agreement; I just wish everyone felt the same way. "Why do you ask?"

For a moment, he just stares at me, his eyes burning with reflected firelight. "I guess I wanted to—" He seems to catch himself, coughing into his hand. "I was just curious, I suppose." He gives me a smile that would have made me weak in the knees if I wasn't already sitting down, but it fades away a heartbeat later. "By the way, I appreciate your honesty. You're a great guy, and I really am looking forward to getting to know you better once all this is over."

I look away before he can see the tears that have come to my eyes. "Thank you," I tell him, my voice wobbling a little bit. "I'm looking forward to getting to know you too, Cole."

When I look up again, his smile has returned. "Anytime," he says. "I guess that's really all I wanted to say, so I might as well go to bed too." He stands up and brushes sand off his legs before walking over to me, pausing long enough to gently squeeze my shoulder. "Good night, Ry."

CHAPTER 10

DAY 14

I wake up just after sunrise the next morning, my eyes bleary and my mind feeling like it's full of fog. Careful not to rouse my tribemates, I make my way out of the shelter and sit by the fire, or what remains of it after I banked it last night, and make myself a cup of tea. I sip it as I look out over the ocean, focusing on the sound of the waves rolling in.

Normally, I wouldn't be up this early, but I slept even more poorly than usual. I couldn't stop thinking about my conversation with my tribemates last night, and sleep was the furthest thing from my mind until the wee hours of the morning. I knew that Katie and Marina had personal issues outside of the game, but I didn't know the depths of them until last night. I'm glad that they were willing to open up to me, but part of me is afraid that'll just make it all the more painful when and if I have to get rid of them. I mean, I barely knew Joe or Ashley, and I didn't enjoy voting them out. How much will it hurt if I eventually have to stab Katie in the back, or Marina or Rhonda?

The problem is that I need my alliance to stick together for at least the next few votes. If we don't, the Sikas will outnumber us at the merge, and none of us Merus will have a shot at winning. I need my alliance to trust each other, and that means we need to know each other, to *like* each other. I just wish the idea wasn't so enticing, particularly when it comes to Cole. The truth is that ever since my parents died, I've had trouble getting close to people, and Arielle's recent troubles have only made it harder. What's the point in opening myself up to someone if they're going to be taken away from me? And this time it'll be even worse, because there will be someone to blame—either my alliance will be mad at me for voting them out, or vice versa.

As much as I like the three women, I think they'd understand if I were to vote them out. But Cole just seems so easy-going, so ready to accept what the world has to throw at him, in a way that almost perfectly complements my own anxious nature. If he got voted out, maybe he'd accept it with grace and a grin, or maybe he'd take it even harder than the others would. All I know is that the closer I get to him, the less I want to find out which it would be, for my own sake as much as his.

And that scares me, because the only way I can avoid sending him home *and* still have a chance at winning the game is to sit next to him at the final two, and I don't think I can beat him, not if the others are feeling even half of the effect that he has on me.

I'm so caught up in my own thoughts that when I hear someone clear their throat behind me, I almost jump ten feet into the air.

"Sorry if I startled you, chile," Rhonda says, sitting down across from me. She busies herself with making coffee before glancing up at me, a light frown creasing her face. "You all right, honey? You look like somethin's botherin' you."

I shake my head, as if I can make all my worries fly away. "I'm fine," I tell her. "I guess I was just thinking, and I got distracted."

"Oh?" she says, one eyebrow raised. "Anythin' I can help with?"

I open my mouth to respond, then pause to consider my words. I may hate it, but this is a game, and anything I say can and will be used against me later. "Does it ever get to you?" I finally ask. "The fact that we have to get to know each other and then vote each other out, I mean. It feels … *wrong*, in so many ways, but that's what we have to do if we want to win, right?"

Her quizzical expression fades to a sympathetic one, and she leans forward. "Of course it bothers me," she says gently. "I think it'd get to anyone, except maybe for someone who's *truly* heartless, and that definitely ain't you." She sighs deeply. "You may not believe it, but I could barely sleep the night Ashley went home. I just kept thinkin' about the fact that she went home because of me. Sure, it was five of us that wrote her name down, but I was the one to suggest it, wasn't I?" She shakes her head. "I tell myself that we all knew what we signed up for when we came out here, and that deep down all of us want the same thing: to make life easier for the ones we love. You got your sister, Cole has his momma, I've got my son. Even if we ain't always perfect along the way … well, we're doing it for the right reasons. And if that ain't enough, then I don't know what is."

We sit in silence for a few moments after that while I ruminate on what she said. "Thank you for putting it into perspective," I say eventually, taking her hand and squeezing it gently. "Do you actually tell yourself that? Or were you just being rhetorical?"

"Oh, I most certainly do," she replies, her voice firm. She gives me a wink, the corners of her mouth turned up slightly. "And sometimes, I even believe it."

DAY 15

Our seventh immunity challenge, on day fifteen, isn't held in the same place as the others. Instead, the motorboat takes us to a large rectangular platform floating about a hundred feet from shore. The platform has purple and blue mats, as well as a podium, so I'm guessing this is where the challenge will begin.

Also in the ocean, perhaps ten feet away from us, float two smaller platforms, each holding something that looks like a hollow cylinder topped by a funnel. The cylinders are made of rings connected by struts, so we can see through them to the shore. Like the mats, one is painted purple, and the other is blue. The platforms they're standing on must be tethered to the seafloor because they don't move with the waves. Beyond those, about halfway to the beach, there are two markers, about the size of basketballs, bobbing on the surface of the water. There are also a few other rafts, but I assume they won't be part of the challenge because they have cameras set up on them.

As usual, we're all silent during the motorboat ride from our beach, but this time I think we'd all be quiet even if we were allowed to talk. We all know the merge—the end of the tribe phase and the beginning of the individual phase of the game—will come soon. Unless there's a twist, at that point all the remaining players will come together and live on the same beach, as one big tribe. After that, all the challenges will be for individual immunity rather than tribal immunity, meaning that instead of one tribe being immune and the other going to tribal council, everyone who's left in the game will go to tribal, with only one person having immunity at any given time. That will continue until there are only two people left; at some point, the people who are voted out will join the jury, meaning they'll be able to vote one of the two remaining people to win. It's a massive shift in the game, and getting all the way to the end will require correspondingly massive shifts in our thinking.

More importantly, this challenge could be our last chance to get an advantage over the other tribe. Usually, but not always, the tribes merge when there are ten people remaining. Assuming the pattern holds, that means we've got two more tribal challenges left. Since the two tribes are even right now, if we win both challenges, we'll be up six to four when we merge, and we can just get rid of the Sikas one by one. But if we lose them both, then *we'll* be the ones at a disadvantage. We all know the stakes, and I don't doubt the other tribe does too.

Alex is waiting for us when we arrive, with two burlap sacks next to him. Once both tribes are on our respective mats, the cameras turn on, and he gives us his TV smile. "Welcome to today's immunity challenge," he says. "First things first: I'll take back the idol." He takes the wooden idol from Cole and places it on the podium. "You are once again playing for immunity. However, before we get to today's challenge, there's a twist."

I hear collected groans, as well as a few cheers, from both tribes. I don't say anything, but my heart begins to speed up, and my mouth goes dry.

Outwardly ignoring our reactions, Alex bends down and picks up one of the sacks at his feet. "Inside this bag are six rocks: four purple and two blue," he says, hefting the sack. "Meru, each of you will reach into the bag, without looking, and draw one of the rocks. Those of you who draw a purple rock will remain on Meru, while the other two will join Sika immediately." He points to the sack at his feet. "Sika, your bag holds four blue rocks and two purple rocks. As with the other tribe, the two of you who draw the purple rocks will join Meru. We're going to do this *before* the immunity challenge, so you will compete with your new tribemates."

He pauses to let it sink in, and I frown as my mind runs through the implications. Based on the numbers, I'm guaranteed to lose at least one of my alliance members, and possibly two. If it's the latter, Jing might take the opportunity to team up with the newcomers, making it three on three against me and whoever else is left. And that's if I don't switch to Sika myself, which is a one in three chance—if that happens, I'd be going into a situation where it's four against two at best. Either way, I'm going to have my work cut out for me.

Apparently, Alex isn't done yet, because he reaches into a pocket and pulls out what look like two rolled-up pieces of parchment, one tied with blue string and the other with purple. "There's one more little thing I need to tell you about," he says, holding the scrolls for us to see. "Instead of a reward, both tribes will receive a clue to a hidden immunity idol that we've hidden at your camp."

My heart starts beating even faster as soon as he says the words "hidden immunity idol," and I doubt I'm the only one. The show introduced the concept around season ten, and it quickly became a fan favorite. Basically, the producers hide a small totem or bracelet at each tribe's camp, and whoever finds it can use it to negate all the votes cast for them at a single tribal council. It's not game-breaking, since each idol can only be used once, and whoever finds it has to choose when to use it. Still, anything that keeps you in the game even a day longer is powerful, and we'll all have to take it into account if we want to stick around.

"Now, some of you will know that this is not the first time we've done something like this on *Marooned*," Alex continues.

"However, there is one big difference this year: unlike in past seasons, this idol must be played *after* the votes are cast, but *before* they're read. That means there's a whole other layer of strategy to consider, because if you play the idol and nobody voted for you, it was wasted. Conversely, if you *don't* play the idol and you get voted out, you'll have missed the opportunity to save yourself. But there will be plenty of time for you to consider that later." He hefts up one of the sacks and walks over to us. "Now, let's find out our new tribes. Don't peek or reveal your rock until I've told you to—we'll wait until everyone on both tribes has drawn their rock, and then reveal them together."

He goes down the line one by one; I'm fifth, so by the time he gets to me, there are only two rocks left to choose from. I pick one without looking, as Alex instructed. I'm not sure who I want to leave our tribe—I mean, preferably no one, but it doesn't seem like that's an option—other than that, I *don't* want it to be me. *Come on, let it be purple.*

Alex moves on to Marina, who takes the last one, while the rest of us stand with our fists clenched. Then it's Sika's turn, and Alex repeats the process for the six of them. Most of them look anxious, but the young Black woman has a thoughtful expression on her face as she reaches into the bag.

Finally, after what feels like an eternity of waiting, Green Hat draws his rock, and Alex steps back. "Everyone will reveal on three," he says, as we all lift our fists, holding them out in front of us. "One … Two … *Three.*"

On three, I open my hand, revealing a purple rock, and breathe a huge sigh of relief. *Good. That could have been much worse.*

My relief is short-lived, however, as I remember that *somebody* had to switch. I scan up and down the line of my tribemates, looking for the telltale blue rocks. The first one I see is held by Jing, which isn't ideal, but it isn't the end of the world either. I'd rather lose one of my allies than two, even if it means Jing has a chance to team up with the Sikas.

When I see that Cole has the other blue rock and my heart drops. *That really sucks.* I may not want to sit next to Cole at the end, but I can't deny that I'll miss his presence at camp. I don't know any of the Sikas, but I doubt any of them will be nearly as good at cooking as him, and that's not even mentioning the fact that he's just generally a good guy to be around. *Maybe it'll be good to get a break from him for a little while.* For some reason, that thought feels as hollow as the buoys bobbing out in the ocean.

My train of thought is interrupted when Alex clears his throat. "Looks like Cole and Jing from the Meru tribe will be swapping with Alina and Juan from the Sika tribe," he says. "You four, please trade your insignias and move to the correct mats."

At Alex's indication, Cole and Jing step away from the rest of us, taking off their necklaces and exchanging them with Alina and Juan—the frizzy-haired white woman with large glasses and the muscular Hispanic man from my boat on day one. *Don't worry about Cole*, I tell myself sternly as the two newest members of our tribe come and join the rest of us. *Focus on getting yourself through the next few tribal councils.*

For better or worse, I don't have very long to dwell on my emotions because Alex wastes no time getting down to the immunity challenge. "For today's challenge," he says, "two members from each tribe will swim out to a marker, where they will dive down and release five buoys, then work together to bring them back to the mat. Once you've retrieved all five buoys, another member of your tribe will attempt to throw the buoys into the container." He gestures to the large stationary cylinder. "The remaining three tribe members will be stationed in the water near the container, collecting any missed shots and returning the buoys to the platform. The first tribe to land all five buoys in their container wins immunity. Understood?" He waits for us to nod. "All right. I'll give you a minute to strategize, and then we'll get to it."

Gathering together, the new Meru quickly decides to send Katie and Marina to release the buoys. Juan will be our thrower, and Alina, Rhonda, and I will collect the stray shots. I'm a bit apprehensive about someone I don't know taking the most pivotal role, but Juan seems confident, and he's performed well in the other challenges. Plus, he and Alina are first in line to go home if we lose, so I suppose he has an incentive to do well.

In short order, everyone on both tribes is ready. Marina and Katie line up at the front of the platform, ready to dive in. On the other side, Jing and the young Black woman are going for Sika.

Once everyone is set, Alex raises his hand in the air. "Castaways: ready … set … GO!" he shouts.

The four swimmers immediately dive in and begin to make their way out to the markers, while the rest of us cheer them on. Katie and Marina reach their marker first, but only barely. Katie takes a deep breath and dives down, and fifteen seconds later, five purple buoys pop up to the surface. Katie surfaces a few seconds after that, shaking water out of her hair, and she and Marina begin corralling the buoys. Meanwhile, Jing pops up for air without her tribe's buoys, costing her precious seconds as she dives down again, allowing Marina and Katie to open up a bit of a lead.

However, Jing gets her buoys on the second try, and by the time Marina and Katie have managed to gather all their buoys together and begin making their way back to us, the two Sikas are less than a minute behind. It takes some time for both pairs to corral their buoys and get them all back to the platform, the lead constantly changing as one tribe or the other loses a buoy in the waves and has to go back for it.

After what feels like forever, Katie and Marina reach the platform, and the four of us help them get both themselves and the buoys out of the water. Once the two swimmers and all five buoys are on the mat, Alex shouts, "Meru, you're good!" and Rhonda, Alina, and I dive into the water, while Juan gets ready to shoot.

As I'm swimming away from the platform, I hear splashes behind me. *Sika must be right on our tail.* I glance back at the platform to see Cole stepping up to shoot for Sika. Some emotion I can't quite place twinges in my brain, but I stomp it down just as quickly as it comes and pick up my speed. *Focus, Ryan.*

Once the three of us reach the cylinder, we begin treading water while Juan starts shooting the buoys as though they're basketballs. His first few shots miss, and there's a delay as we go collect the missed shots and throw them back to the platform. Meanwhile, Sika cheers as Cole lands his first buoy. Barely ten seconds later, they start cheering again as Cole makes another shot. "You can do it, Juan!" I shout, almost saying Cole, but catching myself just in time. "You got this!"

Thankfully, Juan makes his next shot, briefly raising my spirits and cutting Sika's lead to one, but Cole quickly lands his third and fourth buoys. After a few misses, Juan lands his second, but he just can't keep up with Cole's pace, even though Cole's shots are fewer and far between now—he only has one buoy left, and if he misses, he has to wait for his tribe to return it before he can shoot again.

And then, while Rhonda and Alina swim out to retrieve one of Juan's shots, Cole steps up and shoots. His buoy arcs through the air, landing perfectly in the funnel and quickly sinking down into the cylinder. He raises his hands in triumph, the rest of his new tribe cheering as Alex shouts, "Sika! Wins immunity!"

As soon as he does, Juan tosses his own buoy away, his shoulders slumped. But I only have eyes for Cole, who celebrates with his tribe, an expression of immense relief on his handsome face.

CHAPTER 11

DAY 15

The motorboat ride back to our beach feels longer than usual. It's never fun to lose a challenge, but this time is especially nerve-wracking because there are so many unknowns. Had the tribe switch not happened, we all would have voted out Jing, barring some sort of miracle on her part. But now, with both the tribe switch and the idol, there are way more possibilities to consider, and I have a feeling this afternoon is going to be much more stressful than it might have otherwise been.

Of course, that was probably the reason the producers decided to shake things up in the first place. It may be terrible for us, but I'm sure it's great viewing for the audience back home.

But before we can get to the drama, we need to do some housekeeping, so as soon as we get off the motorboat, the six of us gather together in front of the shelter so we can introduce ourselves to our new tribemates. Katie, Marina, Rhonda, and I go first, briefly telling the newcomers where we're from and what we do for a living.

Then it's Juan's turn. "It's nice to meet you all," he says. He looks maybe forty years old, with short black hair and a matching mustache, and he has a tattoo of a dragon running down his back. "I'm from Arizona, and I'm a construction worker."

He turns to his fellow Sika—well, former Sika—who blinks rapidly a few times. Her glasses give her an owlish look, and if I had to guess, I'd say she's my age or a few years younger. "My name's Alina," she says, a Boston accent showing even in those three words. "Um, I guess you already knew that. What else, what else … oh, I live in Rhode Island, and I'm a CPA. Well, technically, I'm studying to be a CPA, but I've been working as an accountant for a couple of years, and I took the exam a week before I left for Samoa, and they probably already released the results. And even if they haven't yet, then—" She stops talking abruptly and takes a deep breath. "Sorry," she continues. "I tend to babble when I get nervous, as Juan already knows. I'll shut up now."

"It's okay," I tell her, grinning lightly. "We won't bite. I promise."

She gives me a relieved smile. "Thanks for that," she says. "But, uh, before I forget, should we look at the clue we got to the hidden immunity idol?"

Oh, right. I had almost forgotten about that in all the craziness. Rhonda pulls the clue out of her pocket—Alex gave it to her before we left the challenge—and undoes the string, revealing a parchment similar to the ones we use to vote at tribal council. "Y'all ready?" she says. She waits for us to nod, then clears her throat. "*If safety is what you seek,*" she reads, "*then look down low, not up high. But as you draw closer to me, just remember to stay dry.*"

We all stand quietly for a moment, pondering the clue and what it might mean. "High and low … that could refer to the tides, right?" Alina eventually offers. "Maybe it's somewhere near the ocean."

"That would make sense," Katie agrees. "And 'look down low, not up high' could mean that it's hidden somewhere that's only exposed at low tide—a cave or a rock or something, I don't know."

Alina's eyes light up, and she starts to respond, but Juan clears his throat. "Why don't we worry about the idol later?" he says, giving Alina a meaningful glance. "We did just get here, after all. Surely we have more important things to do right now."

Her eyes widen, and she nods. "Oh, yeah, that makes sense. I'm sure the idol isn't going anywhere anyway." She gives us an awkward smile. "Maybe we could take a tour of the camp instead? I'd love to see where I'm going to be living for the next few days."

Rhonda and Marina nod their agreement, but Katie and I share a look, and it's obvious we're both thinking the same thing. *We have to find the idol before they do.*

Still, no good will come from running off by ourselves, so we take Alina and Juan on a quick tour of our camp. Truth be told, there isn't much to see, and it doesn't take long for us to show them the shelter, well, and firepit.

The tour might just feel short because my mind is occupied the entire time. *Where could the idol be*? Alina and Katie's deductions make sense, but it almost seems *too* easy, like we're missing something important. Then again, I'm sure the producers want us to find it—what's the point of hiding the idol if it never gets found?—so, maybe I'm overthinking it.

If I wasn't already suspicious that finding the idol is priority number one for Alina and Juan, the fact that they both immediately make up an excuse to go walking down the beach as soon as we get back to the shelter would do it for me. Rhonda, Katie, and Marina immediately go to follow, but I quickly corral them before they can all wander off in different directions. "Listen, we need to think about this strategically," I say, in hushed tones. "Obviously, it would be best if one of us finds it, but if one of *them* finds it, we at least need to know about it, so we can plan accordingly. So I say instead of splitting up and going off on our own, we tail them. We can search too, as long as we're careful not to take our eyes off them."

"Won't they realize we're following them pretty quickly?" Marina asks, frowning. "I don't know about you, asere, but I'm not very stealthy."

"I don't think it matters if they see us," Katie says, her brows knitting together in thought. "Actually, it might be better that way—if they know we're watching them, they might be distracted."

"Are we all agreed, then?" I ask, waiting for the three of them to nod. "Ok, great. In that case, Marina, you and Katie follow Alina. Rhonda and I will follow Juan."

With that, we hurry off after the former Sikas. Rhonda and I catch up to Juan as he ambles down the beach less than a minute later. He and Alina must have had their own short strategy session, because they're walking in completely opposite directions. Rhonda and I stay about twenty-five feet back from him, close enough to see if he finds anything, but not so close that he can feel us breathing down his neck. We keep our voices low, chatting about our favorite foods and movies and other inconsequential things, partially in case Juan overhears us, but also because most of our attention is focused on watching him and looking for likely hiding places at the same time. As Katie suggested, we don't really attempt to hide our presence, but we don't advertise it either.

To Juan's credit, he does an excellent job of pretending he's not being followed—and he obviously knows, because only someone who's completely deaf and blind wouldn't realize we're here. The tide hasn't reached its lowest ebb yet, so at first, he pauses to bask in the sun or stand in the waves, clearly trying to give the impression of someone who's just enjoying a walk on the beach and is definitely *not* looking for an immunity idol, hidden or otherwise. But as time passes and we reach low tide, he starts to openly search more, stopping every so often to examine a conspicuous rock or hollow. Meanwhile, Rhonda and I do the same, although through unspoken agreement, we make sure that only one of us is searching at any given time, the other watching Juan.

After doing this for about an hour, Juan apparently decides that he's had enough, because he abruptly turns around and begins walking the way we came. He passes Rhonda and me with a small smile and a shake of his head, but doesn't say anything.

The walk back to camp is much the same as the walk out, although there are a few new places to check that weren't exposed by the receding tide when we came by earlier. As we get closer to the camp, I wonder if Juan is going to keep searching or give up once we reach it. I hope it's the latter. My legs are tired from walking, not to mention all the swimming I did during the challenge.

I get my answer when we approach the camp and Juan immediately heads straight to the shelter and lies down. Rhonda and I sit by the fire pit, keeping an eye on him in case he gets back up. But he just lies there with his shirt laid over his eyes, which is fine by me.

About half an hour after that, Alina returns, with Marina and Katie in tow. She goes to the shelter to wake Juan, and they begin talking to each other, keeping their voices low. Hopefully, they're commiserating over the fact that neither of them found it.

Meanwhile, Marina and Katie join us at the fire. "I swear, that woman is as slippery as an anguila," Marina says, pinching the bridge of her nose. "You turn around for one second, and she's gone. I don't know how she does it."

I share a glance with Rhonda. "I'm pretty sure Juan doesn't have it," I say, as Rhonda nods her agreement. "But you think Alina might?"

Now it's Katie and Marina's turn to glance at each other. "Well, we didn't *see* her find anything," Katie replies. "But like Marina said, there were a couple of times we lost sight of her, so who knows? If I were betting on it, I'd say no, but I wouldn't want to stake my life on it."

We're all silent for a moment, presumably thinking about how we can find out whether Alina found it. Then Rhonda leans forward, gently biting her bottom lip. "You know," she says, her voice quiet, "we could just go through her bag."

My first instinct is to laugh and, apparently, I'm not the only one, because Marina giggles. "Good one, Rhonda," she says. "You almost had me there."

Rhonda's expression doesn't change. "I was dead serious, honey. I ain't saying we should steal it, just that we should look for it. Like Ryan said earlier, if they have it, we gotta know about it."

Marina looks at Rhonda as though she's seeing her for the first time. "Are you chiflado? We can't do that!" She pauses for a moment. "Wait. *Can* we do that?"

"I don't see why we couldn't," Katie says, her brow furrowed in thought. "Honestly, it's not a terrible idea. Rhonda's right—it's not like we'd be stealing anything."

Marina shakes her head vigorously. "Nope, count me out. If you three want to do this, I won't stop you, but I am *not* going through her personal stuff."

Rhonda accepts this with a nod, then turns to me. "What about you, Ryan? You must have some thoughts in that head o' yours."

She's not wrong, if I'm being honest with myself. On the one hand, the idea of going through Alina's personal items doesn't really appeal to me. I can't imagine I'd be happy if someone went through my stuff, even if the only things I really have out here are a few pieces of clothing and a canteen. At the same time, this isn't a normal situation, and I don't want to lose the game because I wasn't willing to put up with a little invasion of privacy. Could I really look Arielle in the eye and tell her I was sent home because I refused to look in someone else's bag? Plus, it's not like I owe Alina anything—I barely know her, and she has no reason to trust me, or any of us besides Juan.

But all of that is immaterial, because there's one glaring problem that none of us seems to be acknowledging. "It won't work," I say with a sigh. "Even if she did find it, there's no guarantee she put it in her bag. For all we know, she's got it in her pocket, or she hid it out in the woods somewhere only she can find it. Besides, she seems pretty chatty, but if she finds us going through her stuff, she'll clam up immediately."

Rhonda's shoulders slump down, and she leans back. "That's a good point," she says. "An' now that I think about it, it might be too late anyway. For all we know, they found it before we caught up to them. Or maybe they picked it up while we were giving them the tour of our camp. Oh sure, we probably woulda noticed, but 'probably' and 'maybe' ain't gonna cut it here. No, I think we just gotta assume that one of them has it."

"Well, if we think it's more likely that Alina has it," Marina says, "why don't we just vote for Juan? That way, if she plays it tonight, he'll go home anyway."

Katie shakes her head. "I don't think that's a good idea. What if she gives it to Juan before tribal? It's not safe to pile our votes on either of them. We need to figure out a way to make sure that one of them goes home no matter what."

Once again, we're silent, pondering the problem before us. The fact that the idol has to be played after the votes are cast, but before they're read, really throws a wrench into things. If it were *before* the votes were cast, this would be easy—should one of them play it, we'd just all vote for the other. Now we can't do that, because if we choose wrongly, none of our votes would count. *Then whoever the two of them vote for would go home.*

But that thought gives me an idea, and my heart begins to beat faster as I think through all the permutations. "I might have a solution," I say. I look up, fixing Katie with a steady gaze. "What happens if there's a tie between two people at tribal?"

She frowns, presumably trying to figure out how the idol fits in with a possible tie. "There's a re-vote, but the people who are tied can't vote, and everyone else can only vote for one of them. Then, whichever of them gets the most votes the second time around goes home."

Perfect. I was pretty sure that was true, but it's good to have confirmation. "In that case," I say, "I have a plan that will ensure one of them goes home, whether or not they have the idol."

Three sets of eyes stare back at me beneath identically raised eyebrows. "Well, by all means, do share this magical plan with us," Rhonda says.

"Okay. Okay. I think this should work. No, it *will* work." I lean forward, suddenly feeling way more energized than I should, considering that I'm currently both food- and sleep-deprived. "All right. Here's what we're going to do …"

My stomach flutters as we walk into tribal council later that night. I haven't been this nervous since the very first tribal I went to, nearly two weeks ago. *This plan is going to work*, I tell myself. If only my body would listen.

In an attempt to distract myself, I think back on the last few hours. My alliance tried their best to poke holes in my plan, but it held up despite their concerted assault, and it didn't take long to convince the three of them to go along. It's not foolproof—there could always be another unforeseen twist—but it's pretty damn close.

I had thought that Alina and Juan might use the hours before we left to try to convince one or two of us to vote with them, but apparently, they figured finding the idol was the better strategy, because they spent most of the time searching. Once again, the four of us followed them, although with much less urgency than before. We didn't see anything, but they could have managed to find it right under our noses when we weren't looking. Or maybe Rhonda was right, and they found it very early on, before we started following them the first time.

Either way, there wasn't as much schmoozing as I thought there would be. Juan did sidle up to me about fifteen minutes before tribal and ask me how I felt about the rest of my tribe, but I stuck with my usual strategy of being polite but non-committal, like I did with Beck and Jing in days past, and he took the hint. I didn't want to blow him off completely—there was always the chance he'd reveal something he shouldn't—but I also didn't want to seem too eager. I'm sure he and Alina did the same with the others, but I'm not worried about them flipping. At this point, I trust them about as much as you can trust anyone in this game.

Now, as we take our seats on the tribal council set, I'm ready to just get it over with so I can stop worrying. *As long as I go back to camp at the end of this, I'll be happy.*

Fortunately, once we're all set and the cameras are on, Alex wastes no time getting down to business, pointing to Alina. "What was the feeling like joining a new tribe?" he asks. "Did you feel welcomed?"

"Um, on a personal level, I definitely felt welcomed, I guess," Alina responds. Her voice is steady, but when she reaches up to adjust her glasses, her hand trembles a bit. "I mean, these four"—she gestures to my alliance—"are very nice, so don't get me wrong about that. But at the same time, it definitely felt like Juan and I were newcomers. Like we were intruding on their camp, in a way. It almost reminded me of being in high school and trying to sit at the cool kids' table, you know?" There's some scattered chuckling at her analogy. "Like, sure, they were polite and everything, but it was clear that they wanted you gone as soon as possible."

Alex nods. "Rhonda, as one of the 'cool kids,' do you agree with Alina's assessment?"

"Well, first of all, ain't nobody called me *cool* in at least twenty years, so thank you for that," she says, eliciting even more laughs. "And to your question, if I were back home in Georgia, I'd be appalled if someone came to my house and didn't feel completely welcome. But out here it's different, 'cause at the end of the day, only one of us can win, and everyone else is just in the way. So, I apologize to these two if they felt left out, but I certainly don't *blame* them for feelin' that."

Alex has some more back and forth with Rhonda on the subject of the new tribe members, bringing in Juan and Katie to get their opinions too, before turning to me. "Ryan, obviously the tribe swap was a big twist," he says. "But it was only one of the twists that you all faced today. Was there any talk of the hidden immunity idol at camp?"

"You could certainly say that," I reply, grinning despite myself. "Like you said, it's a big twist, and it has the potential to turn this game on its head, so of course we'd be remiss if we didn't talk it over. Where it might be, who might have it, that sort of thing."

Alex nods again. "So, Marina, what do you do to make sure that it's not *your* game that gets turned on its head?"

"Well, that's the question, isn't it, Alex?" she replies, laughing. "I mean, you can talk and plan until your teeth fall out, but at a certain point, it's out of your hands, and you just have to vote and cross your fingers that it all goes well."

Alex smiles. "Couldn't have summed it up better myself," he says. "Speaking of which, it is now time to vote. Ryan, you're up."

I get up and walk over to the voting booth, feeling strangely calm. *Maybe it's like Marina said—it's out of my hands at this point.* When I reach my destination, I walk over to the table, pausing only to uncap the marker before writing down "ALINA" in big letters on the parchment. *It's up to the other three to make sure everything goes according to plan.*

Once we've all voted, there's the usual delay while the producers and Alex decide what order to show the votes in to maximize tension. Even though there are only six votes in the urn, it takes a little while longer than usual; hopefully, that means we were successful. If we did it right, there will be quite a bit of drama for the producers to pick over.

Eventually, Alex comes back with the urn and places it on the podium. "If anyone has a hidden immunity idol and you want to play it, now would be the time to do so," he says.

I watch Alina and Juan out of the corner of my eye. My plan should work even if one of them plays the idol, but I'm curious as to whether they managed to find it despite our efforts. Actually, it might be better if they *do* play it—then it would be one less thing to worry about going forward.

But neither of them moves or says anything, and after waiting for a few seconds, Alex nods. "In that case, I'll read the votes," he says, opening the urn. "Once the votes are read, the decision is final, and the person voted out will be asked to leave immediately."

He reaches into the urn and pulls a parchment out, turning it to reveal my handwriting. "First vote: Alina.

"Juan.

"Ryan.

"Juan.

"Ryan. That's two votes Ryan, two votes Juan, one vote Alina, one vote left."

He reaches into the urn, the entire set dead silent, and pulls out the last parchment. He looks at it for a moment, then shows the six of us what it says: "Alina."

I let out a deep sigh of relief. *So far, so good.* I would have preferred not to get any votes, but ultimately it won't matter, not tonight.

"The votes are tied," Alex continues. "According to the rules of *Marooned*, we will now have a revote. Alina, Juan, and Ryan: you cannot vote. Marina, Katie, and Rhonda: you *can* vote, but *only* for one of the other three." He points to my left. "Marina, you're up first. Take the urn with you when you go into the voting booth."

He hands the urn to Marina, who walks towards the hut as I lean back in my seat and look up to the sky. I suppose I'm not quite out of the woods yet. My alliance could still choose to stab me in the back, as unlikely as that seems. But so far, everything is proceeding according to my plan. *Just one step left.*

Once Marina gets back, Katie goes to vote, then Rhonda, the latter clasping my shoulder and giving me a brief smile as she sits back down.

This time around, Alex returns very quickly with the urn. "Again, once the votes are read, the decision is final, and the person voted out will be asked to leave immediately," he says. "I'll read the votes.

"First vote: Juan."

He pulls the second parchment out of the urn and slowly opens it, looking at the name written on it. "The seventh person voted out is …" He reveals the vote to us. "Juan. That's two, that's enough. Please hand me your insignia."

Juan stands up and takes off his necklace, handing it to Alex.

"Juan, your time in this game has come to an end," Alex says, snapping the token on Juan's insignia in half. "It's time for you to go."

DAY 16

I've barely had time to make myself tea on the morning of day sixteen when Neema drags me off to do a confessional. As I walk with her, I think back to the night before. It's never fun coming back from tribal: everyone is always relieved that it wasn't them going home, but also upset that it had to be *someone*, especially if it was one of their allies. Last night was no different. Alina, of course, took Juan's leaving the hardest, and she was much more withdrawn than she had been when we first met her hours before. Meanwhile, the four of us were happy that our plan worked, although we tried to temper down our enthusiasm so as not to alienate Alina.

Now, as Neema gets me set up and has me sit down on the beach next to a tidal pool, I feel a smile spreading across my face almost involuntarily. *We really pulled it off!* I mean, I was pretty sure it would work, but years of watching this show have taught me that there's *always* a chance something can go wrong.

Apparently, Neema has noticed my upbeat expression, because

her first question to me is, "So, Ryan, I'm guessing you're pretty happy with how tribal went down last night?"

"Yeah, you could say I'm pretty happy with it," I reply, still smiling. "I mean, nothing against Juan—he seemed like a nice guy. But we're coming up to the merge, and I need to make sure to keep as many trustworthy people as I can around."

"Is that why you chose to target Juan over Alina? Do you think she's more trustworthy?"

I shrug. "Not really. Juan just seemed like he'd be a bit more of a threat in challenges going forward, and that will really matter once we get to the individual phase of the game. Plus, Alina's more talkative, and we figured she might let something slip about the other tribe's dynamics that we can use to get an advantage. In the end, though, I would have been okay with either of them going home."

"It seems like you had a plan going in to ensure that would be the case, even if one of them found the hidden immunity idol. Can you detail what the plan was and how you pulled it off?"

"The plan was to force a tie. We couldn't just pile all our votes on one of them and hope for the best, because if we chose wrong, one of us would go home. So instead, we forced a tie—that way, if one of them played the idol, it would have been two to two, and on the revote we'd just vote for the other one. The only way it could have gotten messed up would have been if one of the four of us flipped or voted for the wrong person, but obviously that didn't happen."

Neema nods; she's not really showing it, but I can tell from her faint smile that she's impressed. "Given that neither of them played the idol last night, do you think it's still hidden out there somewhere? Or do you think someone found it and is waiting to play it?"

I pause to think about it for a moment. "I would guess that nobody's found the idol yet, although I suppose it's possible that Alina found it and just got lucky last night. I doubt it, though. If I were in her situation, and I had the idol, I definitely would have played it."

"What about the other members of your alliance?" Neema

prods. "Do you think one of them has the idol?"

"I'd like to think that if they did, they would've told the rest of us. But, again, I suppose it's possible someone found it and just kept quiet about it."

"If you found the idol, would you tell your alliance about it?"

I open my mouth to say *yes, of course I would tell them*, but I stop myself before the words come out. Would *I tell them*? "I … guess I haven't really thought about it," I say slowly, tapping my finger against my thigh. "I mean, yeah, maybe I would tell them if I found it. But there would be advantages to keeping it hidden, so there's a chance I would keep it a secret."

Neema nods again and moves on to another subject, but I answer on autopilot, still thinking about the idol. On the one hand, I do trust my alliance, and I'd like to believe they'd be honest with me if one of them found it. But on the other hand, whoever finds the idol will immediately have a target on their back. I don't think my alliance sees me as a threat, but we all know that only one person can win this game, and I don't want to give anyone a reason to vote me out.

CHAPTER 12

DAY 17

As we walk into the challenge area just before noon the next morning, the sun is promising yet another warm day. As usual, Alex and the other tribe are waiting for us as we walk in and take our spot on the purple mat. "Sika, getting your first look at the Meru tribe," Alex says. "Juan voted out at the last tribal council."

I look over at the other tribe to gauge their reaction to this news. There are some frowns and shaking heads, but nobody looks particularly surprised. The two former Merus react differently: Jing gives a brief smile, while Cole grins widely and clenches his fist at his side. It still feels strange seeing the two of them standing on the other mat, and I let my eyes rest on Cole for a bit longer than strictly necessary before returning my attention to Alex. As much as I've enjoyed not having to constantly police my own thoughts and actions for the last couple of days, I'd be lying if I said I didn't miss him.

Alex waits for the reactions to die down, then says, "Once again, you are playing for immunity. Sika, I'll take back the idol." He proceeds to do so, placing the idol on the podium. "You'll also be playing for reward," he continues. "Instead of immediately returning to camp, the winning tribe will be taken to a different island, where we've set up a barbecue feast—ribs, chicken, potato salad, cold drinks, and brownies and ice cream for dessert. Sound like something worth playing for?" He pauses while we all cheer and clap. "All right. In that case, let's get to it.

"For today's challenge, you'll work together to dig up a ladder that we've buried in the sand. You'll then carry the ladder to a tall pole, where one tribe member will climb up and get a key while the others hold the ladder steady. Next, you'll use the key to unlock a chest containing bags of puzzle pieces. Finally, two tribe members will use the puzzle pieces to complete a three-dimensional tree puzzle. Sika—you have one extra member. Who's going to be sitting out?" He points to Sika, and Green Hat raises his hand. "All right, Randy sitting out for Sika. I'll give both tribes a minute to strategize, and we'll get started."

After a short delay to decide who will be performing which portions of the challenge, and so Neema and Steve can give us our walkthrough, we're all set. As he's done so many times before, Alex raises his hand in the air. "Castaways: ready … set … GO!" he shouts.

On the last word, all ten of us, excluding Green Hat—Randy, apparently—rush out to two rectangular areas of sand marked by flags at the corners, and begin searching for our ladders. My tribe starts in the middle, using our hands to dig. It isn't long before Rhonda unearths a purple-colored rung, but the ladder is tall enough that even once we know where it is, it still takes a while to get it all the way out. I shovel sand as best I can, feeling like a dog trying to dig up a bone.

Eventually, we've got enough of the ladder uncovered that we can lift it out of the hole we've dug, shaking the last bits of sand off it. Shouts from the other tribe indicate that they've done the same. We carry our ladder over to the next station, leaning it against the pole as Marina climbs up to grab the key while the other four hold it steady. As soon as she's back down, we run to the chest, and Marina unlocks it.

Once she's done, Alina and I step forward, taking as many pieces as we can carry and sprinting them over to where we'll assemble the puzzle. When Alex said we'll be making a tree puzzle, I wasn't quite sure what he meant, but when I saw it during the walkthrough, it made sense: the base is a piece of wood cut to look like the trunk of a tree, with branches sticking out of them, and the pieces are shaped like leaves, with indentations to match protrusions on the branches of the tree base.

While we're carrying the second armload of pieces over to the "tree," I quickly spare a glance over to the other tribe. It looks like they're a little bit ahead of us, but just barely, so I put my head down and focus on the task at hand. *Come on, Ryan. You can do puzzles in your sleep.*

Finally, Alina and I have all the pieces over to the base, and we begin assembling the puzzle. It's hard at first—there are just so many leaf pieces that it's hard to find the right one to match any given branch. We place one, then another and another, slowly but surely working through the pile of unplaced pieces. Still, it feels like each one takes forever, and I start to get nervous. *We need to go faster*! Pausing for the barest of seconds, I quickly glance over to see how the other tribe is doing, hoping that we're at least not *too* far behind.

When I see their puzzle, I almost do a double take. I thought Alina and I were moving slowly, but we're a good ten pieces ahead of Sika—a substantial lead, considering there are only thirty or so pieces total. *Did they fall behind earlier*? No, they were right alongside us; I could hear them unlocking their chest and dropping their puzzle pieces on the ground. Besides, the two Sika puzzlers are moving at an unhurried pace, which they wouldn't do if they knew they had to catch up to us. *Are they* trying *to lose*? I mean, it certainly looks like it, but that can't be true. *Why would they want to—*

And then it hits me like a ton of bricks. *They* are *losing on purpose!* I freeze, mentally kicking myself. *I should have seen this coming*! They have to know that if we lose, Alina is going home, and they'll be down six to four when we merge. *Of course they want to throw the challenge*!

Suddenly, I feel lightheaded, and there's a ringing sound in my ears. *It's not too late! I can stop building the puzzle and hope that they don't notice. I can—*

But then Alina places another piece, and I realize that even if I sat down and ignored the puzzle, she has every incentive to keep going. It might take her twice as long, but that wouldn't matter, since Sika isn't going to give her any competition. I'd only be delaying the inevitable.

So with a nauseous feeling in my stomach, I get back to work on the puzzle, wanting to just get it over with. When Alina places the last piece and Alex shouts out, "Meru! Wins immunity!" my tribemates celebrate behind me, but it's all I can do not to break down and cry.

As Alex promised, instead of taking us back to our tribe camp, the motorboat takes us to a different beach, where a table laden with food and drink awaits. In other circumstances, I might be excited, but now all I can think about is what I know will happen at tonight's tribal. I load up my plate mechanically—I may be upset, but I'm not going to pass up this opportunity to eat—while doing my best not to show how I'm feeling. Either the others haven't realized that Sika threw the challenge, or they haven't realized the implications, because they all seem happy and carefree. I'm not going to tell them just yet. *No need to ruin the party for everyone else.*

Fortunately, while we're eating, the conversation is light-hearted, sticking to things like how this food compares to what we have at home, how much better it is than our usual fare—that sort of thing. I still jump in and add something every now and then, but for the most part, I remain silent. *Hopefully, the others think I'm just focused on eating as much as I can.*

Apparently, I didn't fool everyone, because when we get back to camp, Rhonda immediately pulls me aside. "You all right, chile?" she asks, her voice thick with concern. "You were a million miles away durin' the reward."

"Not really." I pause, gathering my thoughts, and take a deep breath. "Did it seem to you like the other tribe kinda just … *gave up* once they got to the puzzle?"

"To be honest, I wasn't really watchin' them. I was focused on you and Alina. I guess I saw their puzzle after Alex called the challenge, and it did seem like they shoulda done better. But why …" She frowns deeply. "Now, hold on just a minute. You don't think they lost on *purpose*, do you?"

"That's exactly what I think. I'm betting they decided before they even left their beach that Cole needs to go home tonight."

"Still, that don't explain why you're so upset. We all knew that Cole and Jing were vulnerable over there, but you wanted to win just as much as the rest of us."

"I'm upset because I should have thought of it first!" The

words tumble out of me, true in their own way, if not necessarily the whole truth. "If we had done the same thing, maybe we could've figured out a way to let them win. Then Alina would be going home, and we'd have the advantage. Now, if we merge tomorrow, there will be five of them and five of us, and who knows whether Jing will still want to be on our side?"

Rhonda's frown dissipates as she steps forward and hugs me. "Oh, honey, you can't do everything by yourself," she says. "Besides, if they really were set on losin', do you think they would have just changed their minds if we just sat there and twiddled our thumbs? Naw, we'd all still be sittin' there, trying to make the other tribe break first. And I don't know about you, but I'd have been mighty pissed if I lost out on that barbecue."

I smile despite myself. "That's true. It would have been a sad challenge if *both* tribes were trying to lose."

"You're damn right it would be." She laughs, but it fades away quickly. "And as for what happens at the merge … well, we don't know what's going to happen tonight, much less in the next two weeks. It's like you and Katie love to say—anything can happen in this game." She lightly punches my shoulder. "All I'm sayin' is, don't count us out just yet."

The rest of day seventeen is absolute torture for me. Rhonda must have told Katie and Marina about our discussion on the beach earlier, or maybe they deduced it for themselves. Either way, they're just as subdued as I am that night, when we should be celebrating the fact that we're not heading to tribal council. The only one who doesn't seem quite as funereal is Alina, although she's not exactly jumping for joy either. I can't blame her for being relieved. Had we lost, she'd probably be going home tonight.

And despite what I told Rhonda, the fact that we lost our chance to go into the merge with a numbers advantage isn't really what's bothering me. I mean, it's not *ideal*, but Rhonda was right when she said that nobody knows what could happen in the next few days. Assuming we do merge tomorrow, we'll be even at five, at worst. That isn't great, but also, isn't the end of the world either.

No, the worst part is that I *should* be jubilant, because this is the perfect opportunity to have Cole go home without getting a single drop of blood on my hands. I know the Sikas are going to target either him or Jing, because they wouldn't have thrown the challenge if they weren't absolutely sure they could get rid of one of them. Of the two, Cole is the obvious choice—no disrespect to Jing, but Cole is a much bigger threat than she is. If the Sikas find out that he's part of our alliance and Jing isn't, they'll almost *have* to get rid of him.

And yet, even though I should be positively giddy right now, all I can think about is how much I'll miss Cole, and all the countless talks and smiles and jokes and glances we could have shared for the next few weeks. *That's exactly why he needed to go home*, I tell myself. *If he can make someone like me feel this way, then how could I possibly beat him at the end?*

But knowing that doesn't make me feel any better, and I go to sleep earlier than usual that night, feeling like the weight of the world is on my shoulders.

DAY 18

I sleep in later than usual the next morning and wake to the sound of a motorboat. For a moment, in my half-awake state, I'm a little confused—we just had an immunity challenge yesterday. *Could there be another twist?*

And then it hits me, and I sit up so fast it's like I've been possessed. *It's the merge*! The boat must be bringing the Sikas to our beach—usually, the producers pick one or the other tribe's camp, so we don't have to start from scratch.

I get up, now fully awake, and walk down to the beach to greet my new tribemates. Alina, Rhonda, Katie, and Marina are already waiting there. "We made it," Katie says softly. "I thought I was going to be the first one voted out, but here I am at the merge."

I take her hand and squeeze it; she gives me a brief smile

before returning her attention to the boat. At first, it's just a speck on the horizon, too far away to make out individual faces. As it draws closer, I can see there are six people on the boat—the five Sikas plus the captain—but the boat goes up and down with the waves, making it hard to see any one person for long enough to identify them. I keep an eye out for Cole or Jing, hoping to see the former, even though I think it's unlikely.

And then Marina reaches up to shade her eyes with one hand and squints. "I don't believe it," she says. "Is that …?"

She trails off just as the boat crests a wave, leaving her question unasked. But I know exactly what she was going to say, because standing towards the front of the boat is Cole, his blond hair flying in the wind, his wide smile unmistakable even from here. For a bare second, I wonder if it's a mirage, if I'm so desperate to have him back that I'm just seeing what I want to see.

And then Rhonda lets out a big, "Whoop!" and Katie waves and calls out his name, and I know he's real. A feeling of relief crashes into me like a wave, leaving me weak all the way down to my toes. *I can't believe they didn't vote him out last night!* The unexpected strength of it almost bowls me over, so powerful I feel like I'm going to collapse to my knees, and it's only through intense effort that I remain standing. A tear of joy streams down my cheeks, then another, and I'm sure I must look like an idiot, but I don't care. Right now, all that matters is the fact that Cole is back, happy and healthy and *here* with me, where he belongs.

CHAPTER 13

DAY 18

That sensation of joy and relief and *completeness* sustains me for a few moments longer, completely washing away all the anxiety I've been feeling for the past day or so. The contrast is breathtaking, and, for a second, I feel like I'm on top of the world. *I'm so happy he's back.*

But the feeling recedes, leaving a deep sense of confusion behind. *What the hell?* I mean, yeah, he's my ally, but I doubt I'd be reacting like this if it were Katie, or Marina, or even Rhonda. *Why do I care so much?* There's no reason for me to be this happy, this *excited*, that Cole's still here. *Unless—*

Then it hits me like a ton of bricks, and a heavy pit forms somewhere deep in my chest. *Unless I'm starting to fall for him.* Now that I'm thinking about it, it makes perfect sense: it's the reason why I was so upset yesterday at the thought of Cole going home, why I've been so reluctant to get rid of him in the first place, even though I *know* he's a threat. Hell, it even explains why I didn't want to get to know him at the beginning of the game. Part of me must have known that if I got too close to him, I'd start to have feelings for him. I thought I was immune to his charms, but I was wrong.

The feeling of heaviness in the pit of my stomach grows, and suddenly it feels difficult to breathe. *Oh, this is very,* very *bad.* If this is how I'm reacting now, barely halfway through this game, can I really trust myself not to fall head over heels in love with him over the next two weeks? I still think he needs to go home if I want to have any chance of winning, but will I be able to pull the trigger when and if the time comes? "Maybe I should just vote him out now and save myself the heartbreak," I mutter, keeping my voice low so the others don't hear me.

But it doesn't take very long to realize that I couldn't do that even if I wanted to. For better or worse, I need him—and Marina and Katie and Rhonda too—at least for the next few votes, or I'll be dead in the water. The first priority has to be getting rid of the Sikas and getting my alliance to the final five. If we don't stick together, we'll all be sitting ducks, just waiting for the Sikas to take us out one by one.

No. I just have to focus on the game. And I *definitely* can't let anyone, especially Cole, find out I see him as anything more than an ally, because if they do, they might use it to their advantage. Besides, it's not like anything will come of it anyway. Cole hasn't given me a single indication that he's interested in men at all, let alone *me*. I can't imagine the embarrassment of getting rejected on primetime television while the whole world, including Arielle, watches. All I can do is act like everything's normal, no matter how much I may feel otherwise.

All this goes through my head as the motorboat slows down and comes ashore. Soon, it stops, and the five newcomers—Cole and four I don't recognize, meaning they must have voted out Jing last night—jump off the boat, while the five of us who are waiting walk out into the surf to greet them. I intentionally put on a big smile; thankfully, it isn't *too* difficult to act happy. I *did* just make the merge with my alliance intact, and that's something to celebrate.

When we reach Cole, Rhonda, Katie, Marina, and I wrap him up in a big hug, while Alina does the same with her former tribemates. "Boy, am I glad to see you guys," Cole says, one arm wrapped around me and the other around Katie. "It feels like it's been forever."

"What happened over there last night?" Rhonda asks, grinning. "Not that we ain't happy to see you too, but I woulda guessed they'd send you home, not Jing."

Cole glances over to the Sikas—well, the former Sikas, I suppose—before turning back to us. "I'll tell you all about it later," he says, his voice low. "For now, let me just enjoy how good it feels to be back." He turns to me, his eyes shining as bright as the midday sun. "I know it's only been a few days, but I've missed you so much."

By the time we all make our way back to the shelter a few minutes later, there's a table spread with food and drinks waiting for us. The producers must have been waiting for us to go down to the shore so they could set it up, although who knows where they were keeping it before that. We take our seats at the table and begin eating our sandwiches and fruit, trying and failing to maintain table manners as we do. I may have eaten yesterday, but when you don't know when you'll be eating real food again, you take every single opportunity to get some fuel in you. Meanwhile, the five who didn't win the last reward are even more ravenous, having not eaten a full meal since before the game started two and a half weeks ago.

Once we've devoured enough to take the edge off our hunger, we go down the line and introduce ourselves to our new tribe-mates. Marina goes first, then me, Katie, and Rhonda. Then it's on to the former Sikas. Of course, I've met Alina, but I've only seen the other four at challenges and on the very first day, so I'm excited to meet them.

First up is Green Hat, otherwise known as Randy. His facial hair has grown from a goatee to a beard, giving him even more of a scruffy look. He tells us that he lives in Mississippi and that he's a trucker. "I'm sure y'all are very surprised to hear that," he says to general laughter, his Southern accent even deeper than Rhonda's. "But seriously, I'm lookin' forward to gettin' to know y'all."

Next is the young woman with long braids in her hair, who pauses eating a ham and cheese sandwich to introduce herself. "Nice to meet you all," she says. Her brown eyes sparkle with intelligence, and she gives us a cautious smile in between bites. "I'm Tamika, and I used to be a competitive swimmer, but now I'm a grad student in New York."

After her is a man who appears to be about my age, or maybe a couple of years older, named Ashraf. "I work in cybersecurity," he says, frowning lightly as he peels an orange. Like Alina, he wears glasses, although his are thicker than hers. "I was born in Pakistan, but I moved to the U.S. more than a decade ago, and now I live in Silicon Valley."

Lastly, there's a tall, willowy white woman with shoulder-length dirty blond hair, who tells us her name is Jennifer. "But you can call me Jenny," she says with a quick, high-pitched laugh. If I had to guess, I'd say she's ten or fifteen years older than me, perhaps in her late thirties or early forties. "I'm a farm vet out in Minnesota, so this"—she gestures to the beach—"is all completely new to me."

"Well, it sure is nice to meet y'all," Rhonda says, her inner Southern gentlewoman making an appearance. "And welcome to our home. Although, I suppose it's your home too, now."

Randy perks up. "Oh, that reminds me," he says, taking a small bag out of his pocket. "Steve—the producer, I mean—gave me this. Said it's our new insignias."

He opens the bag and takes out a necklace with a red token dangling from it, passing it down to the other end of the table. When I get mine, I slip off my old one and put it in my pocket before putting on the new one. It'll be a good souvenir, assuming I'm allowed to bring it home.

"We also have to pick a name for our new tribe," Randy continues. "Pendin' the producers' approval, of course, just in case one of y'all was fixin' to pick something naughty."

We all share a laugh; I sincerely doubt any of us would want to do that even if they'd let us. Millions of people are going to watch this show when it airs, and none of us wants to look stupider than we already do.

"What about Sefulu?" suggests Jenny once the laughter dies down. "It means 'ten' in Samoan, and there are ten of us. It'll be kind of like a reminder that we're all one tribe now, even though we were separate before."

Nobody has a better suggestion, so we agree to tell the producers that we've decided on Sefulu. Everyone seems happy with it, even though they must have all realized the obvious irony. There may be ten of us now, but it won't be long before we're down to nine, and I intend to make sure that it's one of the former Sikas who goes home next.

After everyone's had a chance to finish eating and disperse

around the camp, I quietly go up to the other members of my alliance one by one and ask if they'd like to join me for a swim in the ocean. Fortunately, they all catch on pretty quickly, and soon enough we're all gathered in a loose circle about thirty feet from shore, far enough away that our voices won't carry but close enough that we can see if any of the Sikas try to eavesdrop on us.

"So tell us, Cole, how'd you do it?" Marina asks. "I thought you were for sure going home last night."

"To tell you the truth, I thought I was too," Cole says, rubbing the back of his neck. "I mean, don't get me wrong, I'm glad I'm still here. But it was a mess."

"I'm glad you're still here, too," I tell him, forgetting myself for just a second. *Keep it together, Ryan*! "I mean, I'm sure we all are," I add hastily.

Cole grins at me. "Thanks, Ry," he says. "I appreciate it." His cheeks flush red, and he looks away before clearing his throat. "Anyway, as I was saying, they definitely threw that last challenge. They kept talking about how they needed to get rid of the big threats before the merge, and it was pretty obvious that they meant me. The only one who would even talk strategy with me at all was Tamika. The rest of them were polite, but it was clear they were keeping me at a distance. I figured I was a goner after we lost.

"But when we got back to camp, Jing flipped out. I guess she figured all the talk about voting me out was just a smokescreen in case she had an idol or something. In any event, she spent that whole afternoon trying to convince them that they needed to vote me out. She didn't even try to hide it from me. She just kept saying that if they didn't get rid of me, they'd be making a huge mistake, and that she'd gladly work with them once we got to the merge. In the end, I think the four of them just decided that she seemed *too* eager and got spooked. She ended up writing my name down, but everyone else, including me, voted against her."

There are a few seconds of silence as we digest that information. "That's crazy," Katie finally says, shaking her head. "I mean, I'm not complaining. But Jing didn't really seem like the kind of person to freak out like that."

"I ain't surprised," Rhonda says quietly. "This game messes with your head until you don't know which way is up anymore."

We nod in agreement; this game makes every single one of your instincts go haywire. "Who do you guys think they're going to target tomorrow?" I ask, more to change the subject than anything else.

"It could be any of us, verdad?" Marina says. "Sounds like they're not going to turn on each other. At least, not immediately. So that means it's going to be one of us."

Katie nods her agreement. "They'll probably try to get rid of whoever they see as the biggest threat. But you could make an argument for any of us. Cole's obviously the strongest physically, but Ryan and I are fairly smart, and Marina and Rhonda are good social players."

The others fall silent, and I frown as I ponder my own question. *What would I do if I were them?* The most important thing is winning immunity challenges, and if previous seasons are anything to go by, most of the challenges moving forward will rely more on physical strength than smarts. Like Katie said, Cole is the strongest of us, and I doubt it'll take the Sikas more than a second to come to the same conclusion, if they haven't already.

But on the other hand, the Sikas have gotten a chance to know Cole in a way that they haven't with the rest of us. Sure, he was only on their tribe for four days, but that's an eternity in a game like this. They might think they have a chance to work with Cole later on down the line. There are just too many factors to consider, too many unknowns to be sure of anything.

Evidently, I'm not the only one who's come to that conclusion, because Marina turns to Cole. "What about the hidden immunity idol?" she asks. "Cole, you were over there for a few days. Do you think one of them found it? If you know who did, maybe we can put a target on their back."

He shrugs. "I think so, but I'm not a hundred percent sure. As soon as we read the clue, everyone ran off and started searching. Then later, I saw Ashraf showing something to Jenny, but I couldn't see what it was, and when I got closer, they just pretended like they were just chatting. But the four of them gave up searching pretty soon after that, which was pretty suspicious." He lowers his eyebrows in thought. "Maybe it was a ruse to make me think they found it so I would stop looking myself. Either way, nobody played one at tribal last night, but that doesn't really mean much. I'm guessing you guys didn't find yours?"

The other four of us shake our heads. "And we're pretty sure Alina hasn't found it either, so it's probably still out there," I add. Or one of the others is lying and has already found it, but it's not like they'll come clean now if they haven't already. "If only we had some idea of where to search."

Katie perks up. "Cole, do you remember your tribe's clue? Maybe if we have two clues, that'll help us find it."

"Oh yeah, that's a smart idea!" he replies. "Hang on, let me think." He closes his eyes for a few seconds, then says, "I don't remember exactly what it was, but it was something about looking up in the trees. *Look up in the trees, you'll see me wave in the breeze?* I don't know, something like that."

Katie, Rhonda, Marina, and I share a look. "Yeah, I don't think that's gonna help us," Rhonda says. "Sorry, honey. It was a good thought." She lets out a sigh. "Maybe we should just forget about the darn idol. Who knows if they even found theirs? Like Cole said, it could have all just been a ruse."

"I think we need to assume that they do have it," I say. "And I mean *all* of them, not just one of them, because whoever found it might give it to someone else before tribal council."

"Even if that happens, what can we do about it?" Marina asks. "Sure, if we all vote for the same person and they guess correctly, somos fula. But we don't have the numbers to split the votes, like we did when we got Juan, so we might as well take the chance. It's a one in five shot."

Katie clears her throat. "I might have a solution," she says, biting her lip. "We just have to convince them that we're putting all our votes on one of them, so they play the idol for that person. But in reality, all five of us vote for someone else."

We all consider Katie's plan for a few moments. "Honestly, that's probably our best bet," I eventually say. "We'd have to be careful not to be too obvious about it, but I think we could pull it off."

"Cole, you saw Ashraf showing something to Jenny, right?" Katie asks. "Maybe we pretend to target him, just in case he doesn't feel like giving it to someone else."

"That makes sense," I agree. "But there's one more problem. Even if we get rid of the idol, we're still tied." I focus all four of them with a steady gaze. "That's why we need to get one of them to flip and vote with us if we can. Cole, did you get an idea for which one would be most likely to turn on the others?"

He thinks about it, then nods slowly. "If I had to pick one, I'd probably say Tamika. She didn't seem to like the other three very much. Plus, she was the only one who was willing to talk to me about the game."

It's not much to go on, but I have a feeling it's the best I'm going to get. "All right. Here's what I'm thinking: Cole and I will try to convince Tamika to flip and vote with us. Marina, Katie, and Rhonda, you three do your best to plant the seed that we're voting all for Ashraf, and if you can, try to figure out who they're going to vote for. That work for everyone?"

There's a chorus of nods and yeses. "Sounds good to me," Cole says. "Is that everything, or should we get started now?"

I nod decisively. "We all know what we have to do," I say, trying to project a confidence I don't quite feel. "Let's get out there and do it."

CHAPTER 14

DAY 18

Over the next few hours, the five of us try our best to implement our plan without giving away our strategy, or even the fact that we *have* a plan, to the other tribe. I'd be shocked if they didn't assume we're up to something, but if we're lucky, they won't know the details until it's too late. And we could use that luck. At the same time, everyone tries to go about their day like it's normal, for the most part. The chores still have to get done, even if the next two days could decide our fates. Meanwhile, I keep my eyes open for a chance to talk to Tamika.

I get my chance later in the afternoon of day eighteen, when she announces she's going to go collect firewood to stockpile. "Anyone want to come with me?" she asks.

"I will," I reply, trying not to sound too eager. "I'm not doing anything at the moment."

She nods, and we each grab a machete—fortunately, the powers that be let Sika bring theirs over with them, so we now have two instead of one—and head into the woods.

I lead Tamika over to an area where there are a lot of trees with older, dry branches. "You said you're a grad student, right?" I ask, reaching down to pick up a piece of fallen wood. "What do you study?"

"That's right," she responds. "I'm doing my master's in education."

"Oh, that's awesome! Does that mean you want to be a teacher, then?"

She smiles and grabs another stick. "That's the idea. I've actually got a job lined up at a school in the city for when I graduate."

"Well, in that case, congratulations. My sister is a teacher too."

"Oh, really? What does she teach?"

"Middle school English," I tell her. "Seventh grade. I wouldn't recommend it—apparently the kids are terrors at that age."

"So I've heard," she replies with a laugh. "Don't worry, I'll be teaching elementary schoolers. I'm sure they'll have their own struggles, but I'm still looking forward to it."

We continue to talk about our personal lives as we go about our task, one of the ever-present cameramen trailing us constantly. I learn that she has twin brothers who are about my age—one is in the Army, while the other is in med school at Stanford. I tell her more about Arielle, leaving out her recent health issues, of course. I still haven't told anyone about those. It's small talk, but that's all I need right now: a chance to connect with Tamika, to build a relationship that could get me a little farther in the game.

After a while, we finish collecting and return to the camp, depositing the firewood near the shelter. "I could use a break," she says, taking a swig from her canteen. "Want to come sit on the beach with me?"

I don't really have anything better to do, so I agree, and we continue our conversation, moving on to talking about our respective cities and how they compare to each other. She seems both intelligent and personable, and the conversation flows naturally. *It's a shame one of us will probably have to vote the other out eventually.*

But then, seemingly out of nowhere, she cuts off mid-sentence and looks past my shoulder, her expression quickly changing from an amused grin to a light frown. I turn to see the other four Sikas huddled with each other. They're far enough away that we can't hear exactly what's being said, but they're obviously discussing strategy. None of them is looking in our direction, and we've kept our voices fairly low, so I doubt they even know we're here.

I clear my throat lightly. "You know, if you want to join them, I won't be offended," I tell her. "I've taken up enough of your time already."

She shakes her head. "Thanks for the offer, but I'll pass," she says, grimacing. "I don't think that's such a good idea."

I lay back in the sand and close my eyes, pretending to bask in the sun, as though I don't have a care in the world. "You don't have to pretend," I say, keeping my voice light. "We may be on the same tribe now, but I know that doesn't mean we're on the same side."

"Trust me, you're not the problem," she says, with a snort. "To tell you the truth, it's not that I don't want to talk to them. I think *they* don't want to talk to me."

"Oh?" I crack open my eyes, willing myself to act normally. "Why is that?"

She gives me a long sideways look, as though she's considering how much to tell me. "Let's just say I don't get along with them."

"Wait, really? How come? I've only known you for a few hours, and I'd say you're pretty easy to get along with."

She pauses for a long moment that stretches on for what feels like an eternity, her eyes searching mine. Finally, just when I'm starting to wonder if I've pushed too far, she sighs and looks down. "It's been like that since day five," she says. "When we went to tribal council the first time. The four of them acted like it was my fault that we were there at all. That was after the challenge where we had to throw the sandbags up onto the poles, remember? I knocked Randy's off, and they kept saying that was what lost it for us. Hell, they probably would have voted *me* out if Lauren hadn't all but quit, and they didn't need me for the swimming challenges." Her lips curl into a sneer. "When we got back to camp afterwards, Randy told me I was lucky that I didn't go home. Ever since then, he's acted like I should be down on my knees thanking him, and the rest of them fall all over themselves doing whatever he says."

"Ugh, that sounds terrible. At least you made it to the merge—if nothing else, you've got some fresh faces to talk to."

"That's true." She lowers her voice, keeping her eyes on the four Sikas. "Between you and me, I'm pretty sure I was the next to go if we hadn't swapped tribes. Randy never came out and said it, but I bet he was gunning for me to go home."

In a flash, an idea crystallizes in my brain. "That would explain some things."

Tamika turns her gaze on me instantly, eyebrows raised. "Oh?

What kind of things?"

I sit up, trying to pretend as if I've just remembered who I'm talking to. "Nothing," I reply hastily. "Just forget I said anything."

She shakes her head. "Uh-uh. If you know something, I want to hear it." She leans forward and lowers her voice. "If you're worried that I'm going to run over there and tattle on you, I promise I won't. I don't owe them a single thing, least of all my trust."

"Well …" I bite my lip, pretending to consider her words before apparently coming to a decision. "You didn't hear it from me, but Cole said Randy pulled him aside after tribal council last night and asked him whether he'd be willing to vote you out next. He figured Randy was just trying to see if he'd flip on us, so he didn't really think anything of it, but maybe Randy was actually being serious."

For the second time, Tamika stares at me without speaking for seconds that feel like hours, while I silently will her to believe my lies.

Eventually, she nods, her expression inscrutable. "Well, you've certainly given me a lot to think about," she says, her tone as guarded as her expression. She gets up, holding her hand out to me. "Come on. We should probably get back to work."

Tamika and I continue to collect firewood for another hour or so after that. Unlike before, we're mostly silent, which is fine with me. I've laid out the bait, and now I just have to wait and hope she bites. I feel a little bad for lying to her, but we all knew what we were signing up for. *And anything that keeps me in the game is a good thing right now.*

Other than the ethical grayness of it, I'm pretty happy with how our conversation went. There's more work to do—I just planted the seed in her mind, but it still has to grow if I have any hope of getting her on our side. Of course, as soon as we get back to the shelter, I make sure to tell Cole about his made-up conversation with Randy last night, just in case Tamika decides to follow up with him. A little while later, I see the two of them whispering together on the beach, Cole looking apologetic and Tamika angry, and I hide a smile. *Maybe we* can *pull this off.*

To make things even better, a little while after that, Marina pulls me aside and tells me that she thinks she, Rhonda, and Katie successfully convinced the Sikas that we'll be voting for Ashraf, although they didn't make any headway in figuring out who they're targeting. "Not that it really matters much," she says, frowning. "But still, it would be nice to know."

I nod, still hopeful that the Sikas will try to get one of us to vote with them. They'd have to at least tell us a name to write down, and even if it's a lie, it would give *some* indication of what they're thinking.

But to my surprise, as the day passes, none of the Sikas approach me to see if I'm willing to flip on my alliance. At first, I figure they're excluding me for some reason, but when the five of us reconvene after sunset and compare notes, that notion is dispelled. "I got no clue what they're up to," Rhonda grumbles. "Alina and I chatted—or rather, *she* chatted, and I listened—in the shelter for nearly two hours, and she didn't say a single word about the next tribal council."

"Same for me," Katie says. "I talked to Jenny and Ashraf, and neither of them said anything about who they were voting for, or even asked me if I'd be willing to join them."

"How about you, Cole?" Rhonda asks. "You'd think if they were gonna try to flip someone, it would be you."

Cole frowns. "Randy did ask me whether I was tight with you guys, and Jenny told me she thought we could work together down the line, but that was it." He looks at me, his eyes flickering with reflected firelight, and I have to remind myself not to get lost in them. "What do you think, Ry? Are we missing something important?"

I pause to think about it before responding. "I don't know," I reply slowly. "I mean, maybe they're just waiting to see who wins the next challenge, or they could be biding their time to see if we crack. Or maybe they think it doesn't matter if we flip because they have the idol, and they're convinced they'll play it right."

Rhonda shakes her head. "I don't like it," she announces, crossing her arms over her chest. "But I guess there ain't much we can do about it right now, other than keep tryin' to convince

Tamika to vote with us."

I nod my agreement. Our plan to get Tamika to flip might not succeed, but right now it's all we've got. But then, even if she does desert her tribe and all five of us stay loyal, it still might not be enough, because if the Sikas play their idol correctly, it won't matter if we have more votes than them. That's assuming they even have the idol in the first place. *There're just too many permutations to consider.*

More than anything, I wish I knew what the Sikas are up to. There is not a single shred of doubt in my mind that they have a plan, too. I'm sure I'll find out what it is sooner or later, but the longer it takes, the more likely it is that they'll take over the game and vote us out one by one.

DAY 19

Ten tall poles, perhaps two feet in diameter and fifteen feet high, and each painted brightly in a different color, await us in the challenge area the next morning. Each pole has several rings carved around the diameter, perhaps footholds or handholds. I have a guess as to what the challenge might be, but I might be wrong. Either way, I just need one of my allies to win, or at the very least, for Ashraf and Randy to lose. The former because it would mess up our plan to flush his idol, and the latter because I'm hoping we can convince Tamika to flip and vote him out.

Alex is there already, watching as we all file in and stand on a single red mat. Next to him is the usual podium where he puts the idol for us all to see, but this time it's covered by a burlap sack. "You ready to get to today's immunity challenge?" he asks, giving us that TV grin that he does so well. "First things first, I'll take back the idol."

He takes the large idol from Marina, but instead of putting it on the podium, he sets it down on the ground. "You are no longer playing for tribal immunity. Instead, you'll be playing for this." He pulls the cover off the podium with a flourish, revealing a large necklace made of colorful feathers and carved wooden beads linked together on a string. "From now on, you'll be competing for individual immunity. If you're wearing this, that means you're safe, and you cannot be voted out at tribal council. Sound like something worth playing for?" As usual, he waits for us to cheer. "In that case, let's get to it.

"For today's challenge, each of you will be assigned to one of the poles you see behind me. All you have to do is hold on to the pole for as long as you can. You may not stand on top of the pole, but otherwise, you can pick any spot you want to hang on to it. If at any point you fall off, or any part of your body touches the ground, you're out. The last person left standing wins immunity."

It sounds incredibly simple, which is reinforced by the fact that there's no walkthrough. Instead, we're randomly assigned to our poles, and once Alex gives the okay, I climb up as high as I can, positioning my feet into one of the carved rings. It can't hurt to have some wiggle room in case I slip.

Once we're all in position, Neema signals to Alex. "I'll count to three, and the challenge will begin," Alex says. "Three, two, one … we're on."

For once, his pronouncement is met with dead silence, as all ten of us concentrate on staying where we are. It quickly becomes clear that it's not going to be as easy as it sounds. Even if we weren't all malnourished, the pole is just wide enough that my arms start to hurt almost immediately, and it's impossible to get a good foothold in the shallow rings. Meanwhile, the sun beats down on us, unrelenting in its heat, making me thirsty almost from the second the challenge begins. I do my best to focus, hoping that everyone else is suffering more than me.

About fifteen minutes in, I hear a scraping sound off to my left, and I look up in time to see Rhonda drop off her pole. She takes a seat on a bench off to one side of the area. Alina follows shortly thereafter, leaving the rest of us to hang on for our metaphorical lives. I can't speak for everyone else, but I started feeling stiff as a board five minutes in, and it's only getting worse. Every so often, Alex announces how much time has passed or makes some comment about how we're all looking, but for the most part, we compete in relative silence.

Then, just as my back is starting to really hurt, Ashraf slides down his pole, and his feet touch the ground, putting him out of the challenge. Less than a minute later, Randy drops too, and I breathe a quiet sigh of relief. My arms burn like they're on fire, but I continue to hang on. Half an hour passes, then forty-five minutes. The ones who are already out cheer us on, but I try to tune them out. *Do it for Arielle.*

Just after the forty-five-minute mark, Marina drops, immediately followed by Tamika, leaving just four of us in the challenge: me, Cole, Jenny, and Katie. Every single one of my limbs feels like it's about to fall off, but I dig in and hold onto my pole as though it's the only thing keeping me alive.

The pain in my arms and legs builds and builds until finally, just after an hour and fifteen minutes, I can hold on no more. I slowly drop to the ground, taking a second to unclench my muscles before I walk over to the bench. About ten minutes later, Cole drops too, shaking his arms with a pained expression on his face as he comes over to join us. With him out, that just leaves Katie, who has barely moved since the beginning of the challenge, and Jenny, who has slid down so that she's only a foot or two above the ground. As much as I hope my ally wins, I have to give props to Jenny for lasting this long. *They must both be in so much pain right now.*

And then, just after the hour-and-a-half mark, seemingly out of nowhere, Katie slides down and drops off her pole, ending the challenge. "Jenny! Wins immunity!" says Alex, raising his hands in the air triumphantly.

The rest of us clap, some of us less eagerly than others, as Jenny steps down from her pole, a huge smile on her face. Instead of handing us the tribe idol, Alex has Jenny come over to him so he can place the immunity necklace around her neck. I cheer and clap with the others, but I'm already thinking about what happens tonight, and how I can make sure I live to see another day.

During the motorboat ride back to camp, I ruminate on how I should approach Tamika when we get back. We only have a few hours left before tribal, so I don't want to wait *too* long. But on the other hand, if I approach her immediately, that could seem pushy. Besides, if the other Sikas find out what I'm doing, it would give them more time to try to come up with a counter-strategy. If she does vote with them, and it ends up being five to five, then presumably it would still be tied on the revote, and I don't know what happens then. I'd much rather have it be six to four. The only question is how I can best ensure that happens. *Should I talk to her immediately or try to wait until later?*

But all that worrying turns out to be for naught, because we've barely gotten off the boat before Tamika asks if she can speak to me privately, her voice taut and her eyes narrowed. I agree immediately, even though my stomach starts to churn at the sight of her expression. Hopefully, she isn't mad because she figured out that I lied to her.

We walk down the beach, just the two of us and a cameraman. As soon as we're out of earshot of the rest of the tribe, she turns to me. "You were right," she says, her nostrils flaring. "Randy and the others were trying to get me out."

I breathe a huge sigh of relief internally while doing my best to keep a straight face. "Are you sure?"

She nods, her lips flattened into a thin line. "I talked to Cole yesterday, and he told me all about his and Randy's little conversation after the last tribal. How Randy shook his hand and told him not to worry, 'cause I was the next to go."

Wow, I had no idea Cole was such a good actor. The handshake was a perfect detail to add. It sounds exactly like something Randy would do. "I hope you're not upset with Cole for not telling you before. He's a good guy, I promise."

She waves a hand dismissively. "Oh, don't worry about that. I'm not mad at him, or you either. You didn't have to say anything to me, but you did. Randy, on the other hand …" She wrinkles her nose, as though she's just smelled something distasteful. "Oh, of course *he* denied it when I confronted him this morning, but if I didn't already know he was lying, his shit-eating grin would have given it away. And did you hear him clap when I fell off the pole today? He tried to play it off like it was a mistake, but I just *know* he was waiting for me to fail."

I didn't hear anything like that at all, but I was pretty focused on not falling myself, so maybe I just missed it. "I wondered about that," I lie. "I thought maybe I was hearing things, but I guess I was wrong."

"He probably doesn't even care if I heard, 'cause he believes I'll just fall in line and do what I'm told. He thinks he can just use me until he doesn't need me anymore and then cut me loose." Her eyes lock onto mine, her gaze flinty and cold. "Well, he's wrong. I'm gonna get him before he gets me, and that's a promise."

There it is: the opening I've been waiting for. "Why don't we vote him out tonight?" I ask, trying to sound like this is an idea that's just come to me. "He doesn't have immunity, and if he thinks he's safe anyway, he won't even see it coming. It'll be a perfect blindside."

She frowns. "Who else would vote for him? I'm pretty sure the rest of my tribe doesn't want him out just yet, and I don't want to let him know that I'm turning the tables on him if it's too early. Then he'll get rid of me for sure."

"I think I can convince my alliance to vote for him without too much trouble." That much, at least, is true. An understatement, if anything. "It'd be six against four, and you wouldn't have to deal with him anymore."

She looks at me, her eyes narrowed, not saying anything, while I try not to wilt under the pressure. It's obvious that she knows what this would mean. I keep quiet too, afraid that if I try to push her, then she'll bolt. My heart pounds against my ribs as the silence stretches uncomfortably. *Please*, I silently will her. *I need you on our side.*

Finally, after a few long moments, she sighs. "I'll do it," she says. "But I have one condition."

My pulse slows down somewhat, but not completely. "What is it?"

"I want you to promise me that you won't vote me out at six," she says, holding out her hand. "And I won't vote you out then either. After that, anything goes. But I'm not flipping on my alliance just so I can be on the bottom of yours."

I bristle on the inside, although I make sure to keep my expression neutral. I don't blame her for wanting me to make that promise, but I'm not sure it's one that I can keep. I'm not even sure if it's one that I *want* to keep.

On the other hand, if I don't take this deal, I might not even make it to the final six in the first place. And if it turns out I can't hold up my end of it … well, I'm not here to be honorable, I'm here to win a million dollars.

So, with little outward hesitation, I grasp Tamika's outstretched hand and seal our new deal with a handshake, even as I hope that it doesn't come back to haunt me.

CHAPTER 15

DAY 19

Tamika and I rejoin the others shortly thereafter. As soon as we're back at the camp, I make a beeline for my alliance. I need to tell them the good news as soon as possible, just to make sure we're all on the same page.

Thankfully, three of them—Marina, Rhonda, and Katie—are gathered together near the shelter, chattering quietly with each other. With a quick look around to ensure no one is listening in—besides one of the ever-present cameras, of course—I join them. "I've got news," I tell them, suppressing a smile. "Where's Cole? He should hear this, too."

Rhonda shrugs. "No clue," she says. "He said he was going to the well to fill his canteen, but that was a little while ago."

"Should we wait for him?" Marina asks. "I'm sure he'll be back soon."

I think about it for a few moments, then shake my head. "No, it's fine. We can fill him in later." I look around again. "Not here, though. Let's go walk down the beach a bit."

My three allies nod their agreement, and we start to walk away from the camp, towards the ocean. I don't know where the Sikas went, but they could be back at any moment, and I don't want them to overhear what I'm about to say. If they find out that Tamika has agreed to flip on them, they could try to convince her otherwise. Or, even if she resists, she could slip up and let them know that we're targeting Randy. If they really do have a hidden idol, and they manage to play it correctly, it wouldn't matter whether Tamika flips.

It turns out I wasn't the only one who had the same thought, because as we turn a corner, I see the Sikas, minus Tamika, off in the distance, having their own conversation. Cole is with them too, listening while Randy talks, the latter gesturing in the former's direction. They're way too far away for me to tell what they're saying, but whatever it is, it looks intense. I swallow over a lump in my throat that wasn't there just a moment ago. *Are they trying to flip him*? If they were going to try to convince one of us, he's the obvious choice. Maybe he even feels like he owes them for keeping him over Jing, especially if—

Despite the warmth of the sun, an icy feeling comes over me. *Especially if they made some kind of deal with him*. At first glance, it seems unlikely, but I've only known Cole for a short time. *Who knows what he would have done to stay in the game*? Now that I think about it, the story he told us about Jing going home seems a little *too* fishy. *Maybe he thought it was the only way he could stick around.* The thought of Cole betraying us like that hurts, like a knife stabbed into my heart, but I'd be an idiot if I didn't at least consider the possibility. *He would never do that to us, would he?* After all, didn't I tell myself I'd do anything for Arielle, even if it meant stabbing my allies in the back?

Cole glances in our direction and almost does a double take. Randy looks up and, upon seeing us, stops talking immediately. Nodding to Cole, he walks away, as though the discussion was finished, the other Sikas trailing behind. If anything, my suspicion only grows upon seeing the abrupt end to their conversation.

Meanwhile, Cole comes over to join us. "Hey guys," he says, with a smile that seems slightly forced. "What's up?"

Rhonda looks to me, waiting for me to nod ever so slightly before responding. "Ryan has news," she says, her voice as even as ever. "But we didn't mean to interrupt y'alls conversation."

Cole shakes his head. "Nah, it's fine. They were trying to get me to tell them who has our immunity idol, but I think I did a good job of stonewalling them." He shrugs. "Anyway, what's the big news?"

Once again, the other three look to me, and I only hesitate a moment before responding. This plan won't work without Cole, and I just have to take the risk of telling him if I want to have any chance at success. "I talked to Tamika earlier," I tell them. "She said she's willing to vote for Randy tonight."

A wide smile crosses Cole's face; it certainly looks real. "That's great!" he exclaims. "I knew you could do it, Ry."

The other three are grinning too, although perhaps a shade less than Cole. "How did you do it?" Katie asks. "I saw you two talking when we got back, but I couldn't hear anything."

I quickly explain how I managed to convince Tamika, keeping my voice low just in case the Sikas are listening in. There's not much to tell, so it doesn't take very long, but I try to give as much detail as possible, just so they can't accuse me of leaving out key information later.

When I finish, there's silence for a moment as they digest the information. Then Rhonda looks at me, her lips pursed. "Do you think we can trust her?" she asks. "I don't mean to throw cold water on y'all, but for all we know, she could just be sayin' what she thinks we want to hear. Could even be the whole thing's a ruse, and she really has been workin' with them all along."

I shrug. "The thought had crossed my mind," I tell them. It's true—sometimes I feel like I've spent every waking moment out here thinking through different possibilities, and when I start to feel overwhelmed, I just remind myself that I'm doing this for Arielle. "But I don't really think we have a choice. If she's lying, there's not much we can do about it anyway."

"He's right," Katie says, nodding. "We've done the best we can to make sure everything's in our favor; now all we have to do is wait."

Rhonda sighs deeply. "Yeah, I suppose y'all are right. We'll find out one way or the other soon enough." She shakes her head. "Well, I guess we should probably be gettin' back to camp. We don't want the others to get *too* suspicious."

She turns to go, and I move to follow her. She's got a point—if we're gone too long, the Sikas might start to wonder where we've gotten off to. But before I can get more than a couple steps away, Cole reaches out and grabs my arm. His touch is light, but it feels like an electric shock passing through me, and I try my best not to react outwardly. "Can I talk to you, Ry?" he asks, his voice even lower than before. "Just for a minute."

I nod, suddenly unable to breathe, let alone speak. Marina looks at me, one eyebrow raised, but I shake my head ever so slightly. Whatever Cole has to say, I want to hear it.

Once we're alone, Cole stares at me for a long moment, then sighs and looks away. "I … wasn't entirely honest earlier," he says quietly. He looks at me again, his bright blue eyes burning with an intensity that I've rarely seen in them. "The Sikas want me to vote with them. But I would never, *never* do that. I guess they think they have a chance to convince me since I lived with them for a few days, but they're barking up the wrong tree." He pauses, his hands fidgeting at his sides. "You believe me, right?"

"I do," I say automatically, even though I'm not sure whether it's true. If he *were* going to flip on us, and we really did catch him in the act, it would be in his best interest to do some damage control. On the other hand, it's not his fault that he got switched to the Sikas, and it's natural that they'd want to at least talk to him to see whether flipping is a possibility.

In a way, all of that is irrelevant, because even if I didn't believe him, I wouldn't want him to know. Suddenly, a part of me wishes I could just be candid with him, not just about this but about everything. I wish I could tell him how I feel about him, even if it wouldn't change anything, even if he were to reject me immediately. I *hate* having to constantly think about every single word I say, wondering if the next thing I say is the one that's going to send me home.

But then, before I can make a complete fool out of myself, cold hard reality slaps me in the face. I may not like having to police every word and action and thought that runs through my mind, but that's what I have to do if I want to win. Arielle gave up so much for me when our parents died, and this is the least I can do to repay her.

Fortunately, my lukewarm response is good enough for Cole, because he lets out a breath and gives me a small smile. "Thank you, Ry," he says. He reaches out as though to grab my hand, then awkwardly pulls it back. "I knew I could count on you."

I nod and give him a reassuring look, even though my insides are roiling. *I'll have time to be open and honest when I've won.* In the meantime, I just have to make it through this tribal council, and the one after that, and the one after *that*, until I can finally drop this façade and stop worrying over every little thing.

My heart pounds like a drum as we walk into tribal council later that night. As always, Alex is waiting for us, his expression neutral as we file in and take our seats. "First of all, congratulations to all of you on making the merge," he says, nodding to us before turning to Cole. "Cole, what were your feelings when you stepped off that boat and saw your former tribemates again?"

"Honestly, I was mostly just relieved," Cole says, the corners of his mouth turned up as he gives a slight shake of his head. "I know I was only gone for a few days, and I'm glad I got a chance to know the others, but it still felt like I was coming home."

Alex nods and turns to his left. "Katie, what were your thoughts when you realized that you've made it to the next stage of the game?"

"I mean, obviously, it was a good feeling to know that I've gotten this far," Katie replies, tapping her fingers on her leg. "At the same time, there's a lot farther to go, and I have a feeling it's going to require a huge shift in how we all think about this game. I just hope I get the chance to keep going and live to see another day."

"Well, we know there's one person who isn't going home tonight. Jenny, I'm guessing it must feel nice to have immunity?"

"You could say that," Jenny replies, relief evident in her tone. "You never know when it could be you, and it's certainly nice to have that security that it won't be tonight."

Alex gestures to Ashraf. "Ashraf, do you think it'll be you going home tonight?"

"Oh, I suppose it's always a possibility," he says. He leans back in his seat, a small smile on his lips. "But I'd say it's unlikely. From a statistical perspective, if nothing else—after all, nine out of the ten of us will still be here in the morning."

Next, Alex turns to Tamika. "Tamika," he says, "what are you basing your vote on tonight?"

She pauses for a moment before responding. "Tonight, I'm basing my vote on who I can trust," she finally says, her gaze locked onto Alex's. "That, and who can get me furthest in this game. Those are factors for any vote, but I think they're especially important tonight."

Alex smiles, seemingly pleased with Tamika's answer. "Truer words were never spoken." He points to Jenny, who's seated all the way at the end of the row. "And with that, it is time to vote. Jenny, you're up."

She goes and votes, followed by Marina, then Cole, and so on. When it gets to my turn, I walk to the voting booth, write down RANDY on the parchment in large letters with no hesitation, and hold it up to the camera. "My vote is for Randy," I say, my voice steady. "Nothing against you personally, but this is my best chance to stay in the game, so you have to go."

Then I carefully fold the vote, place it in the urn, and return to my seat. My heart beats a steady thump-thump-thump in my chest as I wait for the voting to finish and Alex to go get the urn. *This has to work*, I tell myself over and over again. *This* will *work*.

Finally, Alex comes back and puts the urn in its usual place on the podium. "If anyone has a hidden immunity idol and you want to play it, now would be the time to do so," he says.

For a moment, no one moves, and I wonder if I've miscalculated. Then, after a few more interminable seconds, Randy holds up his hand. "One moment, Alex," he says, reaching down for his bag. He grins widely and laughs. "I swear I've got it here somewhere."

My heart immediately leaps into my throat and stays there, even as I try to keep my expression as blank as possible. This could just be a bluff—maybe he wants to see if he can get a reaction out of us, so whoever actually has the idol knows whether they need to play it for themself. *Please, let that be true.*

But then he pulls out something that looks like a bracelet with blue and green glass beads on it, and my heart almost stops. He stands up and walks over to Alex, every step thudding in my ears as I realize that my game might be over. "I know Jenny's already safe tonight, but I'd like to increase our odds," he says, handing Alex the idol. "I'm playing this for Ashraf."

As soon as he says Ashraf's name, relief washes through me, and I close my eyes and let out a quiet sigh. *That was close.* Then I remember that I need to try to hide how I'm feeling, just in case there's another surprise waiting in the wings, so I reopen my eyes and try my best to still my expression. The rest of my alliance, including Cole, is clearly thinking the same thing, because they all have stone-faced expressions. Still, the tells are there if you know what you're looking for—the way the corners of Katie's mouth are twisted up ever so slightly, or the way Rhonda's hand lies lightly on her chest. Tamika, on the other hand, has her head down, looking at the ground, so I don't know what she's thinking.

Meanwhile, Randy takes his seat and shakes Ashraf's shoulder, both of them grinning widely, like they've just won the Super Bowl. Jenny and Alina look happy too, the former even clapping her hands together in excitement. *We'll see how long their good humor lasts.*

Once we're all settled again, Alex holds up the idol that Randy just handed him. "This is a hidden immunity idol," he intones. "All votes cast for Ashraf will not count. As usual, once the votes are read, the decision is final, and the person voted out will be asked to leave immediately. I'll read the votes."

He reaches into the urn and pulls out one of the parchments, staring at it for a second before turning it to show us. "First vote: Randy."

I glance to my left just in time to see Randy and Ashraf's faces drop. Their smiles are replaced by confused expressions so quickly that it would be funny if it wasn't so … okay, I guess it's a little funny, although I doubt the Sikas would agree.

Meanwhile, Alex continues to read the votes. "Next vote: Marina. That's one vote Randy, one vote Marina.

"Randy.

"Marina.

"Randy.

"Marina. We're tied, three votes Randy, three votes Marina.

"Randy.

"Marina.

"Randy. That's five votes Randy, four votes Marina, one vote left."

I let out a quiet breath. Five votes for Randy means Cole truly didn't flip, that he was telling the truth the entire time.

But I'm not out of the woods yet, because as Alex said, there's still one vote left, and it could determine the course of the rest of the game. I reach out and take Marina's hand in mine, giving it a light squeeze. *It all comes down to Tamika now.*

Alex reaches into the urn with exquisite slowness, opening the last parchment. "The ninth person voted out is," he says, flipping the vote around to show us the name written on it. "Randy."

I let out a huge sigh of relief and hear four others as Alex motions to Randy and says, "Please give me your insignia."

Randy stands up and walks over to Alex, looking shell-shocked as he hands the latter his necklace. "Randy," Alex says. "Your time in this game has come to an end." He snaps the red token in half, then gestures to the path behind him. "It's time for you to go."

CHAPTER 16

DAY 20

When I wake up the next morning, the sky is dreary and gray, but thankfully, it isn't raining. I go sit by the fire with Katie, Cole, and Tamika and boil some water—the coffee from our challenge reward a week ago is long gone, but there's still a bit of tea left. I glance at Cole, who has his own mug, ignoring the feeling of warmth that's starting to come over me every time I look at him. I still feel bad for doubting him yesterday, but what's done is done, and it's not like I ever openly accused him of anything. No, what's really important going forward is how to keep myself from getting even more emotionally attached to him than I already am. He notices me looking and winks at me, and I feel my neck flush. *Easier said than done.*

Trying to distract myself, I reflect on what happened after we got back from tribal council last night. My allies and I tried our best not to gloat, but the sense of relief and satisfaction was palpable. There was a lightness to our voices that wasn't there earlier, like we'd all faced the firing squad and came away with our lives. I'm willing to bet I wasn't the only one who thought we were done for when Randy stood up with his idol.

Meanwhile, the three who were in the minority didn't seem upset or angry so much as stunned. I guess they really did believe we were targeting Ashraf, or maybe they thought Cole would vote with them. I certainly don't think they expected Tamika to flip, if the occasional glares they gave her as we sit around the fire were any indication.

Now, in my half-asleep state, it takes me a little while to notice that Ashraf, Jenny, and Alina are nowhere to be found. I can only assume that they went off to strategize and try to figure out how they can dig themselves out of the hole they're in. I'm not particularly concerned, since, with the numbers the way they are, they'd need two people to flip to their side to have any chance. But that doesn't stop me from feeling vaguely disquieted. It could just as easily have been me in their position had a few things gone their way instead of ours.

Right then, the three of them walk out of the woods, talking to each other in low voices, their expressions grim. Alina looks over in our direction before gesturing to the other two, who immediately stop talking. Then, with a nod, Jenny walks over to where we're sitting, while Ashraf and Alina head over to the shelter.

"Morning, everyone," Jenny says as she approaches us, her grim expression replaced by a smile that doesn't quite reach her eyes. "Ryan, would you mind coming to the well with me? We should probably make sure we're full up on water in case it starts raining."

"Sure," I reply, giving her an equally fake smile. We've got more than enough water right now, but that's beside the point. The only question is why she waited until now instead of doing this two days ago. "Let me just grab everyone's canteens."

A short time later, we're on our way, walking down the familiar path to the well, trailed as always by one of the cameramen. "I'm sorry if you and I got off on the wrong foot," Jenny says once we're a good distance away from the rest of the camp. "I know I can be a bit brash at times, and that sometimes rubs people the wrong way."

In truth, I have no idea whether she's brash or not, because this is the first real conversation we've had since we met. "Don't worry about it," I assure her. "I'd rather you speak your mind if that's what you want to do."

"That's good to know. To be honest, I think you and I could work well together if we put our minds to it."

And there it is. "I wouldn't be opposed to that," I lie. "After all, you can never be too sure in this game."

She nods. "That's exactly what I'm saying. You never know when someone will stab you in the back. I mean, just look at what happened with Tamika last night. Your group seems tight, but can you really trust them all not to turn around and vote you out once it's down to the final five or six?"

"I have considered that possibility," I admit. It's true—I'd be a fool not to consider it—but I still trust my alliance far more than I trust Jenny, my recent Cole drama notwithstanding. "I'd hate to be blindsided like that."

"So then why not go after one of them before they can do it to you? You'd have the three of us to fall back on if you did, and it would give you a leg up on the others."

Just then, we reach the well, and I take a moment to pretend that I'm considering her suggestion. "Let's say I do vote with you three at the next tribal," I say, as I fill one of the canteens. "If you had your way, who would go home next?"

"It has to be Cole." She leans toward me, her chin held high. "We all know he's a physical threat. But if you really think about it, you'll realize he's playing a great social game too. Everyone likes him, and he hasn't made any enemies. If he gets to the end, he'll win in a landslide, and we'd have no one to blame but ourselves."

I do my best to keep a straight face while she talks, despite the unease that roils somewhere deep in my chest. I can't deny that what she's saying is true. I've had many of these same thoughts myself. But now is hardly the time to break up my alliance, especially considering all the effort we just spent to get an advantage over the Sikas. And after yesterday, I almost feel like I owe Cole the benefit of the doubt, at least for a little while.

Still, I have to at least *pretend* like I'm open to the idea, if only to get more information from her. "Why didn't you all vote for him last night?" I ask, keeping my tone as neutral as I can. "I'm not saying it's impossible now, but surely that was your best chance."

"Well …" She looks around, even though it's clear nobody besides us and the cameraman are in earshot, and lowers her voice. "To tell you the truth, we thought about it. It's just that … well, no offense, but we figured he was the most likely to flip on you guys. We thought that if we could convince anyone, it would be him. Obviously, we were wrong, but we had to try."

It takes some effort not to roll my eyes. I had been wondering if the Sikas had some deeper strategy that wasn't immediately obvious to me, and it seems that wasn't the case. Or, at least, Jenny isn't willing to share it with me just yet. "That makes sense," I respond. "Well, you've given me a lot to consider. I'll need some time to think about it."

"Of course. That's all I ask." She gives me a smile as she fills up the last canteen. "Should we get back to camp? We don't want anyone to get suspicious."

I'm about to agree when something catches my eye, and I look down. One of the rocks that makes up the outside of the well is loose, and there's a patch of beige that looks out of place among the gray rocks. Normally, I'd ignore it, but it's the same color as the cloth that Randy pulled out of his bag last night. *Could it be …?*

I quickly look back up, my heart suddenly racing. "You go on ahead," I tell her, trying to keep my voice normal. "I think I got a rock stuck in my shoe. I'll catch up with you in a bit."

I go down on one knee, fiddling with one of my sneakers, and thankfully, she nods and walks away without questioning me. Once she's turned the corner and is out of sight, I quickly move the loose stone, revealing a cloth-wrapped parcel, tied up with dark-brown string. I grab the parcel and slip it into my pocket.

Then, I do my best to smooth my features before jogging up to meet Jenny, hoping beyond hope that she hasn't realized that I just found a hidden immunity idol.

I only stay in the camp long enough to make an appearance before I make an excuse and go off down the beach, trailed as ever by a cameraman. My mind is racing with possibilities, and I want to open this parcel immediately and make sure it is what I think it is. Finding a secluded spot, I look around to ensure none of my tribemates are nearby before pulling the parcel out of my pocket and untying the strings, my hands shaking as I do.

When I see what's inside, I let out a huge breath that I didn't know I was holding. There in my lap sits a bracelet with purple beads, similar to the one I saw in Randy's hand last night. It looks unimpressive, like the sort of thing you could buy for five dollars at a D.C. gift shop, and yet I can't stop smiling.

With the bracelet is a piece of parchment, folded up several times to fit in the parcel. I unfold it to reveal a message:

Congratulations! You've found a hidden immunity idol. This idol will negate all votes cast against you or one other person of your choice at a single tribal council. This idol must be played after *the votes are cast, but* before *they are read. The last opportunity to play it will be when there are five people remaining in the game. Choose wisely, and good luck.*

I read the parchment once, twice, three times, making sure I've gotten all the information I can out of it. Then I put it in my pocket, resolving to burn it later when nobody is looking. I don't want to take the chance that one of my tribemates will find it and discover my secret. Meanwhile, I turn the idol in my hands over and over again, still grinning like a loon. *I can't believe I found it!* It's been five days since we got the clue. But then, we were all looking near the ocean, and I found it at the well, essentially the complete opposite end of our living space. *What did the clue say again?* I don't remember the exact language, but it was something like "look low, not high, and as you draw closer, remember to stay dry." *How could that …?*

Then it dawns on me, and I smack my forehead with my palm. *Draw, as in draw water from a well. Of course*! And "look low, not high" was meant to be taken literally—the idol was just a few inches off the ground. "I'm an idiot," I mutter, shaking my head. "I should have figured this out days ago."

But that doesn't really matter. Now I have a hidden immunity idol, and since Randy played his last night, it's the only one in the game. For a second, I'm tempted to tell the rest of my alliance, if only so they know they don't have to worry that one of the Sikas found it. Plus, we can all share a laugh about how we completely misunderstood the clue.

On second thought … If I tell them, I can't un-tell them. And having the idol will put a target on my back. Maybe not right now, but definitely once the numbers start to dwindle. I don't know what I'd do if the positions were reversed, but I'd at least consider voting out whoever had it once we're down to six. *No, it's probably better to keep this to myself for now.* Maybe I'll tell Rhonda or whoever later on, but not until I'm *sure* I can trust them. It bothers me that I'll have to lie to my alliance, even if it's by omission. And that's not even counting how I lied to Jenny about wanting to work together just now.

I stare out into the water, still idly turning the idol in my hands. This game just keeps getting more and more complicated, and I have quite a few decisions to make.

By the time we get to the challenge area a few hours later, the cloudy weather has progressed to a drizzle. It's not full-on rain, like on day four, but enough to make us all wet and cold and miserable. Hopefully, there's some sort of reward to go along with immunity today. Not that I'm likely to win, but it's nice to have something to look forward to.

Today, the challenge area has nine balance beams, each painted a different color. At the near end of each beam is a barrel, and at the far end is something that looks like a gate made of wood and rope. Past that is a single large, stepped structure with three levels. Each level is about ten feet high, and there are nine ropes hanging from the second level down to the first, and another nine hanging from the third level down to the second.

Alex is waiting for us as we file in and take our places on the red mat. I swear he must be part robot, because he's still smiling despite the rain. "Are you ready to get to today's challenge?" he asks. "First things first—Jenny, I'll take back immunity."

He pauses while Jenny walks over to him and turns around so he can unclip the necklace, then places it on the podium. "Once again, you are playing for immunity at tomorrow night's tribal council," he continues. "You are also playing for reward.

"The winner of today's challenge will stay overnight at a spa, where you'll be treated to a full-body massage and a hot shower. After that, you'll have dinner and get a good night's sleep in a nice, soft bed. This is a chance to rest and recharge, which could be just the thing you need to give you an advantage in this game. Sound like something worth playing for?"

We all cheer and clap loudly at his pronouncement, myself definitely included. Sleeping in an actual bed and not just on a pile of bamboo logs sounds sublime, and that's not even counting the real food and all the spa treatments.

Alex nods, apparently pleased with our enthusiasm. "In that case, let's get to the challenge," he continues. "You'll each fill up a bucket with water, then carry your bucket across a balance beam, making multiple trips, using the water to fill a second, larger bucket. Once you've filled up the second bucket, a gate will drop. You'll then use ropes to climb all the way up to the top of the platform. The first person to reach the top wins immunity and a reward." He pauses to let it sink in. "I'll give you a minute to prepare, and then we'll get to it."

Nothing in Alex's description or the obligatory walkthrough makes me feel any more confident that I'll actually win this challenge, but as I line up at the beginning of the course, I'm willing to give it my best shot. Immunity would be nice, but real food and a good night's sleep sound like just what I need.

I look up just in time to see Alex raise his hand. "Castaways," he intones. "Ready … set … GO!"

At the last word, I sprint off to where my first bucket waits, quickly filling it with water from the barrel. Once that's done, I make my way to the balance beam, moving a little slower so I don't spill any of the precious water. The fewer trips I have to make, the better chance I have at winning. I manage to get across the balance beam without falling, although occasionally I slip or misplace my foot, and some water spills.

When I get to the other end, I run to pour what's left in the second bucket. Splashing noises from my left and right indicate that at least some of the others have made it across, too. Picking up the pace slightly, I make another trip, and another and another. As the second bucket fills up, it grows heavier, making it sink lower and lower each time. On my fifth trip, it finally reaches the tipping point, and my gate begins to lower. I hear a shout off to my left, and quickly glance over to see that Alina's gate is lowering too. To my surprise, we're the only ones who've gotten this far. *Maybe I* can *win this*!

I only get a second to bask in my lead, because my gate finally drops. As soon as it does, I run over to the stepped structure, and I grab the rope and begin to haul myself up, using my hands to pull while my feet scrabble against the wall, trying to find purchase. It's slippery, and I'm hardly the strongest person out here, but I persevere, and eventually I make it to the second level.

As I run to the next rope, I see frizzy hair out of the corner of my eye, which means Alina is still right with me. Panting hard with exertion, I grab the second rope and pull myself up. My arms are starting to hurt, and my legs are already cramping, but I push through the pain. *Keep going, Ryan! Just a little further!* I'm halfway up to the third level, so close I can almost taste it, even as I struggle to climb faster, each additional foot becoming an ordeal as I reach for the top.

And then I hear a scraping sound off to my right, and almost involuntarily, I turn to see Cole seemingly flying up the wall, his muscles taut as he pulls himself up. A pit forms in my stomach, and I redouble my efforts, pushing myself harder and harder. *You can do this*!

But just before I reach the top, I hear Cole haul himself over, immediately followed by Alex shouting, "Cole! Wins immunity and reward!"

My limbs suddenly feel like jelly, and I barely have enough energy to heave myself over the top of the wall, just a few seconds before Alina does the same. Cole is on his feet already, his arms raised in triumph, but instead of congratulating him, I just collapse onto my back, too exhausted to even sit up.

After we've all had a chance to recover, we make our way back to the large mat at the beginning of the challenge. Once we're all ready and the cameras are on, Alex points at Cole. "Cole, come get your necklace," he says. Cole goes over to him, grinning widely as Alex clasps the immunity necklace around his neck, the rest of us clapping politely.

Alex waits for the applause to die down before he continues. "Cole, along with immunity, you've also won a reward." He gestures towards the rest of us. "Choose one of your tribemates to join you."

Hope flares in my chest, temporarily getting rid of the ache in my sides from climbing those ropes. *Pick me*, I silently plead. *Come on, Cole. I need this.*

Cole looks at each of us in turn, his eyes seeming to linger on me while my anticipation grows higher and higher. Then, with a small shake of his head that seems almost apologetic, he turns away from me. "I'll take Tamika," he says. "She deserves it."

Tamika lets out a loud *whoop* and runs over to join Cole, and the hopeful feeling in my chest snuffs out like a candle. I know choosing Tamika is the best move from a game perspective. As military as it sounds, she deserves a reward for her voting with us last night. Plus, it means the three Sikas will have less time to try to convince her to rejoin them.

At the same time, that doesn't mean I'm *happy* with it, and I look down at the ground to hide my pained expression.

But then I hear Alex say, "Cole, choose one more person to join you on the reward," and I look back up, the flame of hope suddenly burning again.

This time, Cole doesn't hesitate. "It was a close contest, and it's only fair that I take the person who came in second," he says, grinning at me. "Get over here, Ry."

I practically run over to where he's standing, not giving him a chance to change his mind, whispering my thanks as I reach him. He spreads his arms out wide, and I hug him, feeling more than a little self-conscious. *How are his arms this strong after three weeks of barely eating?*

With no more fanfare, Alex tells the rest of the tribe to head back to camp, while Cole, Tamika, and I wait for a motorboat to come to take us to the spa. Once the boat comes, we all clamber on, eager for some rest and relaxation. Tamika and Cole both have wide grins as they stare ahead, looking for a glimpse of our destination as the boat skips across the jewel-blue sea, their eyes sparkling with anticipation. Cole catches me looking at him and winks; I look away, but not before I see his cheeks suddenly turn red, as he presumably remembers we're not supposed to communicate with each other on the boat.

But as we pull up to a new island with pristine white beaches and several low wooden buildings flanked by palm trees, my primal need to shower and sleep and eat like a real person drives away all thoughts of Cole, if only temporarily. We pull up to a dock and get off the boat, immediately greeted by three smiling attendants with colorful clothing and leis, in addition to the obligatory camera crew. They lead the three of us to changing rooms with individual shower stalls so we can wash up, Tamika peeling off to go to one room while Cole and I go to another. We strip down while the water heats up, and I purposefully avoid looking in Cole's direction, since I doubt he'd appreciate me checking him out while he's naked.

But any residual awkwardness I'm feeling only lasts for a moment, because as soon as the first touch of the hot water from the shower hits my skin for the first time in nearly three weeks, I'm basically in heaven. I've accumulated more sand, dirt, and grime than I care to admit, and after washing myself down with real soap, I feel like a new man.

After drying myself off with a thick cotton towel, which is probably the cleanest thing I've seen in twenty days, I'm taken to a patio facing the ocean, where Cole, Tamika, and I are treated to hour-long massages. I swear the woman who does mine has magic fingers, because she makes all the tension and stress that's built up from sleeping on bamboo logs every night disappear.

"I could get used to this," Tamika sighs at one point. I couldn't possibly agree with her more.

Just when I'm starting to feel like a pile of clean, extremely relaxed goo, the massage ends, and one of the attendants gives me a fluffy white bathrobe to slip into. Finally, we're led to a large, open room whose main feature is a table piled high with sandwiches, salads—both of the vegetable and pasta variety—and warm brownies for dessert. The three of us eat as though we haven't seen food in days, which … isn't that far from the truth. None of us is self-conscious about our lack of manners. We all realized long ago that you never know when your next meal might be coming, so it's better to gorge yourself and look uncouth rather than be polite and hungry.

After we've all eaten our fill, we lean back in our seats, too stuffed to do anything but sit there and talk. "Thanks again for bringing me, Cole," Tamika says, her eyes closed. "I needed that."

"Same for me," I add. "I owe you one."

Cole flaps a hand at us. "Don't mention it," he says, grinning. "I'm just happy I got to bring you two along. Immunity is nice and all, but all this would have sucked if I were by myself."

Tamika cracks open her eyes and looks at Cole and me in turn. "I hate to talk shop, but speaking of immunity, have you guys thought about who you want to go home next?"

"I mean, it has to be one of the other three Sikas, right?" I ask. "I don't want to give them a chance to regroup."

"Of course," Tamika says with a nod. "But which one first?"

I shrug, unwilling to be the first one to throw out a name, and she turns to Cole, who bites his lip. "You know them best," he says. "Which one would you pick?"

She pauses for a moment. "Well, there are arguments for all of them," she says thoughtfully. "Alina's smart, but she's sneaky too, and if we let her get too far, she might just slip through the cracks until it's too late. Ashraf isn't much of a social or physical threat, but that might mean it's *more* likely he makes it to the end if we don't get him now, because everyone will want to sit next to him at the final tribal council. Jenny's definitely the best of the three at challenges. She did win one, after all, and if she wins a few more, we'd all be screwed."

That was a good analysis, which just makes me even more glad that Tamika is on our side now, instead of working against us. "There's something else to consider," I add. "Jenny came up to me this morning and tried to convince me to vote for Cole." I turn to address him. "Obviously, you don't have to worry about anything tomorrow night. But the point is, she's targeting you, and if you don't win the next one, she might push even harder to get rid of you."

Cole frowns. "I'm not surprised. Even when I was on the Sika beach, I got the sense that she didn't want me around. I don't know if I said something to her that she didn't like, or if I just rubbed her the wrong way, or what." He lets out a sigh. "I guess what I'm trying to say is that I don't have a problem with getting her out before she can get me."

I look at Tamika, who shrugs. "Fine with me," she says. "I'm not really dying to see her gone, not like I was with Randy, but I'll gladly write her name down too. Better her than me."

I nod. "Sounds like we're agreed, then. We'll have to talk to the other three when we get back and get them to sign off too, but I can't imagine they'll be against it."

Tamika claps her hands together. "Well, that was easy," she says, then yawns widely. "Now, if you boys will excuse me, I know it's still early, but there's a bed that's calling my name, and I'm not gonna ignore it." She gets up to go as we wish her good night.

Then it's just me and Cole—well, plus a camerawoman, but I've gotten so used to being filmed by now that her presence barely registers. Cole, however … being with him always makes me feel self-conscious, even at the best of times. But now, with just the two of us in a highly romantic setting and nothing else to distract me … well, there's a chance that I'll just die of embarrassment. Suddenly, I want him so badly that it's a wonder he can't feel the desire coming off me in waves. I try to push down that feeling, but it's difficult, like I'm trying to push a mountain down with my bare hands.

It certainly doesn't help that he looks clean and comfy from the shower, giving his flawless skin a healthy glow that I haven't seen since the first few days. He's grown a bit of a beard in the past three weeks, and it's a bit scraggly, but it looks good on him—I suspect anything would look good, if it was on him—and I'd give almost anything to feel it under my hand as I gently cup his face, and to see him smile and know that it's meant for me and me alone. I know it'll never happen, and that it would be a disaster if he had even the slightest inkling that I'm thinking these things about him. But that doesn't mean I can't dream about what it would feel like to have him kiss me, for him to whisper sweet nothings in my ear and tell me that he—

Cole chooses that moment to speak, snapping me out of my reverie. "Thanks for telling me about Jenny targeting me," he says, his blue eyes locking onto mine. "I figured she might, but it's good to have confirmation."

I shake my head, feeling like I've just awoken from a dream. "Don't mention it," I tell him. I can feel my cheeks reddening; hopefully, he thinks it's from the massage. "We're allies, right? We have to look out for each other."

He moves his hand slightly towards me, hesitates for a bare second, then gently pats me on the shoulder. "I mean it," he says softly. "I'd like to think that we're more than just allies, and I …" His eyes flick to the camera, then back to me so rapidly I'm not even sure I saw them move. "I trust you, Ry. And I just want you to know how much I appreciate you."

My mind short-circuits as I try to come up with a meaningful response that doesn't give away anything. "Really, it's nothing," I say, my throat suddenly dry as a desert. *How can he break me so thoroughly with just a gaze, a touch, and a few kind words*? "I trust you too, and I'm glad we got to meet each other."

Cole's gaze holds mine, and he licks his lips, looking nervous. "Listen, Ry …" He hesitates, tapping his fingers on his leg. "Can I ask you something?"

My heart starts to beat faster, the pulse pounding in my ears like a drum. If we were in a Hallmark movie, now would be the perfect time to declare his undying love for me, to hold me close and never let go. "Of course," I reply, my voice higher than usual. *Keep it together*! "What is it?"

His eyes dart quickly to the camera again before returning to me. "You don't have to answer this if you don't want to, but …" He takes a deep breath. "Is something the matter with Arielle?"

Whatever I was expecting him to ask, it wasn't *that*, and a shard of pain spikes directly into my chest. I've thought about Areille so many times since coming out here, and I figured I was used to the emotions thinking about her brings: pressure to win for her, and fear that I might lose and go home empty-handed. Above all, though, is guilt for leaving her alone, even though I know it's for the best.

But hearing Cole ask about her, his voice full of sympathy, somehow magnifies those emotions, makes them more *real*, and now I can't hold them back anymore. Before I know it, I'm crying, letting out all the sadness and anxiety and worry that have built up, all the tears that I could never let myself show because any weakness could be fatal in this game. For a bare moment, I feel completely alone, even though I know in my head that I'm being watched even now by the unrelenting eye of the camera, as I have been almost every second of the last few weeks.

And then Cole wraps his arms around me and presses my head against his warm chest, and just like that, I feel a little better. "I'm sorry," he murmurs. "I didn't mean to hurt you."

I look up into his eyes, still a bit teary. "It's all right," I tell him, my voice still shaky. "I just … how did you know?"

"Come on, Ry. I may not be as smart as you, but even I notice things sometimes." He gives me a light, easy grin that fades just as quickly as it came. "It's clear that you love her, but whenever anyone asked about her, you'd get this faraway look in your eyes. It's obvious *some*thing is wrong, even if I didn't know the details. If you don't want to talk about it, you don't have to. I just figured that if you *did* want to talk about it, I could give you a chance to do that."

I shake my head again. "No, it's fine," I reply. From a game perspective, I'm still not sure whether it's a good idea to tell him. But I think that if I don't, I might burst. "Hang on, let me just …"

Taking a deep breath, I gently unwrap myself from his arms and scooch away a bit—still close, but far away enough that we're not touching. If I'm going to do this, I don't want to be distracted by how nice it feels to be held by him.

"You already know that our parents died when I was sixteen, and that Arielle basically raised me after that," I continue, willing myself to look him in the eye. "But what I didn't tell you is that she was diagnosed with breast cancer two years ago. Thankfully, the doctors caught it early. They said she had a good prognosis, because she was young and otherwise healthy, but even so, that moment of hearing she was sick, that she might …" I trail off and I swallow before I resume. "Well, it was hard for me, and I can't even imagine how it must have been for *her*. I tried to stay strong, but deep down I was terrified. I just kept thinking that I couldn't lose her, too. She started treatment pretty much immediately, and even though she never complained once, I could tell it was taking a toll on her, and that almost broke my heart. She did so much for me after our parents died, and there wasn't a single thing I could do to make her better." My voice gets small, barely above a whisper, and I look down. "I just felt so … so *helpless*."

Cole takes my hand in his and gently squeezes it. "I'm really sorry," he says, his voice as gentle as his touch. "I'm guessing she's better now, or you wouldn't be out here?"

I nod and look up again, wiping my cheek with my other hand. "The treatment worked, and she was officially declared cancer-free six months ago. She'll have to have tests for probably the rest of her life, but that's a small price to pay. The real problem is—"

For the second time in as many weeks, I remember who I'm talking to, and I catch myself before I give away too much. "The problem is that I don't know how she's doing while I'm out here," I add, somewhat lamely. "I mean, I'm sure she's fine on her own, and she insisted that I come out here as soon as I got the call from casting. But it still hurts not knowing."

Cole sighs. "Oh, Ry," he says, squeezing my hand once again, harder this time. "I can't imagine how difficult it must be for you to go through this game with that hanging around your neck."

Part of me wishes I could tell him the whole truth. But this is still a zero-sum game, and even though I trust him, I can't take the chance, so I just shrug. "I'll see her in a couple weeks, and until then I'm just going to do my best to focus on the game."

"I guess that's the smart move. We do have a lot of game left to play, don't we?" He lets out a breath and leans back. "To tell you the truth, I'm really not looking forward to what happens when we get down to the final six. I've been trying not to think about it too much, but I guess I'll have to at some point. Assuming I don't get voted out first, that is."

Pain stabs my heart once again, but this time it's at the thought of Cole being voted out. I know he'll have to go at some point, but that doesn't mean I have to *like* it. "I can't say I haven't thought about it," I admit. "But there's so much that could happen between now and then."

"Ugh, don't remind me. After that scare with the hidden immunity idol last night, I'm ready for anything." He frowns, furrowing his eyebrows. "Speaking of idols, what do we do if Jenny or one of them finds the one that was hidden at our beach? Katie told me about how you split the votes to get out Juan but I'd rather not take the chance if we can avoid it."

Maybe it's because I feel bad for lying by omission about Arielle, but suddenly I feel an overwhelming compulsion to ease his mind. "We don't have to worry about that," I say, making a split-second decision. "They're not going to find the idol."

He gives me a quizzical look. "What do you mean? Did someone find it already?"

I take a deep breath before I continue. What I'm about to say could completely mess up the game for me, even more so than the truth about Arielle, but it's too late to back down now. "Yes," I tell him. "I found it this morning."

"Are you serious?" He breaks out into a wide smile, and he reaches out and shakes my shoulder lightly. "That's awesome! Where was it?"

Despite my trepidation, I return his smile with a small one of my own; his enthusiasm is contagious. "It was hidden behind a loose rock on the outside of the well. We must have walked by it a million times. Really, anyone could have found it. I just got lucky."

"Sometimes you just need a little luck in this game." He leans forward, his eyes alight. "Have you decided what you're going to do with it yet?"

"Not really. Hopefully I won't need to use it for a while, but you never know." I pause, nervous again. "Listen, could you do me a favor and not tell the others that I found it? I'll tell them eventually, but for now I just want to try to figure out what I'm going to do with it."

"Don't worry, I'm not telling anyone." He mimes zipping his mouth shut. "It'll be our little secret."

CHAPTER 17

DAYS 21-24

We both go to bed soon after that. The allure of sleeping in a real bed under a real roof in a temperature-controlled room is too much to ignore. Even though I didn't tell Cole everything about Arielle, I still feel like a weight has been lifted from my shoulders. That, plus the fact that I've got a full belly for the first time in three weeks, helps wash away some of my anxiety. I sleep like the dead and wake up feeling more rested than I have in a very long time.

Once Cole, Tamika, and I are all awake, we're herded out of the spa and onto a motorboat so we can return to camp. It almost physically hurts to get on the boat. I am *not* looking forward to sleeping under the stars and eating nothing but white rice again, and from Tamika and Cole's longing glances at the spa as we pull away, I'm guessing they're feeling something similar. At least we've only got two weeks until this whole ordeal is over, if we're lucky.

As the boat races over the cerulean ocean, I cast my mind back to the previous night and my discussion with Cole. In retrospect, I probably shouldn't have told him about the idol—or Arielle, for that matter. Even if he doesn't actively spread my secrets around, he could still let something slip accidentally. Or, in the worst-case scenario, he might just decide on his own that I'm a threat and corral the others into voting for me, without technically breaking his promise to keep quiet.

And yet, as I glance over at Cole, his blond hair streaming in the wind, I realize that I'm certain he won't intentionally break his vow of silence, let alone try to get rid of me. Maybe I'm just being naïve, but I believe him when he said he trusts me. Of course, that doesn't mean he won't let my secrets slip, inadvertently or otherwise. But I'm willing to take that chance if it means I can cement our bond. *I just have to hope it doesn't come back to bite me later.*

Thankfully, when we get back to the beach, it's relatively easy to put thoughts of Cole out of my mind and focus on the game again. The first order of business is to get my alliance to agree to vote out Jenny, so over the next few hours, I make sure to speak to Katie, Marina, and Rhonda, both separately and as a group. At first, I'm a little worried they might be upset that Cole took me on the reward over them. I doubt I'm the only one who saw the value in bringing Tamika along, but I bet all three of them would have liked to have been in my place.

But when I bring up our plan to get rid of Jenny tonight, all of them are okay with it. "Oh, you don't have to convince me," Rhonda says with a dismissive wave of her hand when I ask her what she thinks. "It's gotta be one of those three, and it might as well be her." Katie and Marina agree too, with a minimum of fuss, to the point that I wonder if it's all going *too* easily. But after all the stress of the days immediately before and after the merge, I'm not about to look a gift horse in the mouth.

On the other side, Jenny, Ashraf, and Alina have surely figured out that we're targeting one of them, and it quickly becomes clear they aren't going down without a fight. I swear, every time I sit down, one of them asks if they can talk to me privately, where they inevitably throw out another reason or two why I should vote with them. The only reason I get a break is that there are three of them and six of us, so they just don't have the numbers to individually corral each of us at all times. Which, now that I think about it, is also the reason they're in this position in the first place.

As expected, since Cole won immunity, they're forced to change targets. This time, they've apparently settled on Katie. "Just think about it," Ashraf tells me, a note of pleading in his voice, as we ostensibly collect firewood. "Not only is she at MIT, but she's studying *nuclear engineering*. Do you really want to go to the end with someone that smart? If we let her get to the final tribal council, she'll talk rings around whoever she's sitting next to." I politely refrain from mentioning that the same logic could be used against me, and instead just make noncommittal noises. *No need to put the idea in his head.*

Now that I think about it, they could be telling the others to vote for me instead of Katie. If that's the case, I wouldn't like it, but I'm not particularly worried. Even if they manage to convince Tamika to vote with them, which I think is rather unlikely, it would *still* be five to four against them. They'd have to flip *another* one out of my alliance, and I'm just not seeing that happen at this point.

Plus, I have the hidden immunity idol, so even if they did turn on me, I can still save myself. While I'd rather not use it so soon after finding it, I would gladly play it if it means I'll stay in the game. I don't think it'll come down to that, not tonight, but you never know.

In the end, it doesn't matter because there are no surprises that night at tribal council, and Jenny is voted out with six votes. As expected, the remaining three go to Katie. Alex almost seems disappointed as he reads the votes, perhaps hoping for a last-minute change to make this episode more exciting when it airs, but I'm just relieved that the six of us stuck together and our plan was successful.

There is one slight change to the proceedings tonight. Before Alex takes Jenny's insignia, he informs her that she'll become the first member of the jury, the group that will watch the remaining tribal councils and vote for the winner at the end. I'm a little bit concerned that I didn't really build a connection with Jenny, since it means I might be less likely to get her vote at the end, but it's too late now. Besides, it's not like most of my alliance was any better, so maybe I'll be the lesser of two evils.

Of course, none of it will matter if I don't manage to survive this next week and a half and earn my spot in the final two. That's still a big if, but at least now I'm one step closer than I was before.

The next few days are comparatively calm from a game perspective. With Jenny gone, there are only two of the Sika alliance left, and the rest of us spend some time on day twenty-two and the morning of day twenty-three debating which of them should go next. Like Tamika said at the reward, there are good reasons to vote out both of them—Alina is smart and not half bad at challenges, and Ashraf could fly under the radar all the way to the final two if we're not careful. All six of us have our own opinions, but nobody is dead set on getting one or the other out first. I personally would rather get rid of Alina now, but I don't push very hard. I have a feeling I'm going to need to save all the social capital I possibly can for when the two of them are gone, and it's just the six of us left.

Which, if I'm being honest, isn't something I'm looking forward to. It'll be nice to be that much closer to winning the million, but I've come to know my alliance, including Tamika, pretty well over the last few weeks, and I genuinely like all of them. It's sad to think that the best-case scenario is that I stab four of them in the back so I can make it to the final two. That would hurt, but it would be infinitely preferable to being stabbed in the back myself. *At least I have Rhonda, and maybe Cole, on my side.* Although, one or both of them could be lying to me, which would make it hurt even more—especially if it's Cole who ends up being the one to shatter my hopes and dreams. I think I can count on him, but trust only goes so far when you're competing for a million dollars. For all I know, he could wake up tomorrow and decide he wants me gone once we're down to six. And even if he doesn't, the others might.

But I have a few more days before I have to worry about any of that. The most important thing right now is making sure the two Sikas go home, which means the debates continue. By the time our next immunity challenge rolls around, we've just about settled on sending Alina home. None of us really thinks that Ashraf has a chance to get much further in the game, but Alina could win a few challenges, and who knows what could happen then. It's much better to get rid of her sooner rather than later, to avoid giving her the chance to shake things up.

Then she proceeds to immediately validate our concerns by winning the challenge on day twenty-three, officially making all our discussions over the last day and a half completely pointless. It feels almost anti-climactic to have the decision taken out of our hands, but we always knew it was a possibility. "Look on the bright side," Katie says with a shrug once we get back to the beach. "At least now we all know who to vote for tonight."

That afternoon, Ashraf and Alina try to convince some of us to flip once more, but their efforts are even more doomed than last time, since they'd need to convince three of us, and it's clear their hearts aren't really in it. As usual, I politely hear them out and agree to nothing. No reason to antagonize them when they're about to be on the jury.

Ashraf is voted out that night, which I'd like to think comes as a surprise to absolutely no one. This time, the two of them target Cole, but I doubt that even they believed their votes would be anything more than throwaway ones. Cole is annoyed to see his name written down, and Alina is obviously sad to see her alliance member go home, but everyone else seems okay with how it turned out. I wouldn't say any of us really had anything *against* Ashraf, but somebody had to go, and better him than any of us.

We wake up the next morning to full-on rain, which means there isn't much strategizing going on despite being stuck in the shelter. It's hard to think about the game when you're just trying to conserve your energy and not freeze to death. At one point, Cole turns to me, his voice pitched low. "You know, it's times like these when I kinda wish I were back home," he says.

"Honestly, same," I reply, my teeth chattering. "But this is what we came out here for, right?"

"If you say so." He gives me a grin that fades away quickly. "Ry, you'll stay in touch, won't you? After we get home, I mean."

"Of course I will," I tell him, my heart beating faster. "Why do you ask?"

He opens his mouth to respond, then closes it. "No reason," he eventually murmurs. "I just don't want you to forget about me."

Without thinking about it, I wrap an arm around his shoulder and give him a quick side hug. "Like I'd ever do that," I reply. "You're unforgettable."

He laughs quietly. "Thanks, Ry. I appreciate that."

We settle back into silence, and there's a hollowness in my chest that wasn't there before. I haven't really thought about what happens when we all go home in ten days or so, but now that I *am* thinking about it, I find myself less than enthused. Being around Cole all the time hasn't exactly been the best thing for my mental health, yet I really am going to miss him. Sure, I'll probably visit him once in a while, but it won't be the same. At least out here, I get to see him smile, cheer him on in challenges, and just generally know that he's *there*, close enough to touch. I can even tell myself that things would be different if we weren't competing for a million dollars.

I shake my head at that last thought. *We're going to go our separate ways soon enough, and I might as well get used to that now.*

I just wish the idea didn't feel quite so devastating.

DAYS 24-25

Thankfully, the rain trails off in the afternoon and fully stops just before sunset, giving us a chance to build a fire and dry off before bed. "My kingdom for a towel," Tamika says, shivering as she holds out her hands. "Or, better yet, a dryer. But I'll take what I can get."

I sit next to her, with Marina on my other side, trying to glean some sort of warmth from the flickering flames. Now that I don't have to worry about dying of hypothermia, I have a chance to think about our next immunity challenge, which I assume will be tomorrow. I'd love to win, but mostly I just want Alina to lose. If she's immune at the next tribal council, my alliance will have to turn on itself a few days early. Then I'd have to consider who I want to vote for, and, more importantly, how to make sure nobody else is voting for *me*.

I spend a good portion of that night and the morning of day twenty-five thinking about those two things. If Alina does win, the easy choice is Tamika. I like her a lot, and she did save us at the merge, but I only met her a week ago. Sure, I haven't known the others for much longer than that, but in this game, two and a half weeks truly make a difference. I did promise Tamika that I wouldn't get rid of her at the final six, but technically, that doesn't mean I can't vote her out *before* that. Granted, she'd probably still hold it against me, and I'd basically be ensuring she doesn't vote for me if I make it to the final two. But then, if I don't vote her out, whoever goes in her place might not look too kindly upon me either.

In the end, all my musing comes to naught because Cole wins the challenge. Even though I lost, I'd be lying if I said it's not a relief that I don't have to worry about voting out one of my alliance yet. It's clear I'm not the only one, since I swear there's a collective sigh of relief over the usual polite clapping when Alex puts the necklace around Cole's neck.

When we get back to camp later that day, I expect Alina to put up a bit of a fight. But apparently she's decided that her position is hopeless, because she spends her last afternoon relaxing on the beach. I can't say I blame her. This game is hard enough on our mental health already.

In that vein, tribal council that night is a rather relaxed affair. The only one who seems upset is Alex, whose questions to us seem more pointed than usual. I'm sure that the six of us eliminating the minority alliance one by one by one won't make it easy for the editors to create exciting, unpredictable episodes that the audience will rave about, but he'll just have to deal with it. Besides, he has to know that things are about to get a lot more dramatic once the minority alliance is gone and the rest of us have to turn on each other.

In any event, we get to the voting much quicker than we usually do, and there are no surprises when the votes are revealed. Cole gets one vote, I assume Alina's, but the other six are against her. She has a tiny smile on her face as Alex snaps her insignia, and when he finishes, she turns to wave at us. "Good luck, guys," she says. "I'll see you on the other side."

Then she walks down the ramp, leaving the rest of us behind to face the next battle. *And then there were six*, I think, as we all stand up and take our leave, heading to the motorboat that will take us back to camp. *Now it gets really tough.*

CHAPTER 18

DAY 25

"Cheers to us," Katie says as we sit by the fire later that night, raising her canteen in the air. "Final six. Who would have guessed we'd be the last ones standing?"

"I'll second that," Marina says, laughing. "Before we came out here, I thought I'd be happy if I just made it past the first few days. Now here I am, still in it with less than a week to go."

Cole and Tamika voice their agreement, but Rhonda shakes her head. "Speak for y'all selves," she says, a hint of a smile creasing her face in the firelight. "I always knew I'd get this far."

Katie rolls her eyes, but she's smiling too. "Of course you did," she says playfully, before turning to me. "What about you, Ryan? Did you ever think you'd make it this far?"

I pause for a moment. "I don't know," I finally say. "Obviously, I hoped I would. But the pessimist in me knew I could easily be voted out first."

"Like that would ever happen," Rhonda says, with a snort. "There was no way I was ever gonna let you go home first, not over the other alliance. Oh, I liked Jing, I suppose, but the other three were, shall we say, not my favorite people in the world. Especially Ashley."

Tamika turns to Rhonda, a questioning look on her face. "What did you have against her, exactly? I know she was the first one voted out, but I don't think I ever heard the whole story."

Cole jumps in before Rhonda can respond. "Oh, now you've done it," he says, grinning. "I hope you're not planning on doing anything for the next hour or so, Tamika."

Rhonda nods while the rest of us chuckle. "I know we're all tired, so I'll try to give you the short version, and that's God's honest truth," she says, leaning back and forming a steeple with her fingers. "To answer your question, Ashley was a nice enough girl, but in the three days she was with us, she did not one bit of work around camp. I don't think she ever picked up a single piece of firewood, cooked a grain of rice, or did anything but lie around the shelter all day. In fact, she …"

I tune Rhonda out as she continues to list Ashley's deficiencies. I've heard all of this several times before—for that matter, I *lived* all of it not three weeks ago—and I don't think I'll be missing much if I don't hear them again. Instead, I think about my answer to Katie's question, namely, whether I thought I would make it this far. What I said wasn't *wrong*, but it wasn't the full truth either. Back home, part of me knew that it was unlikely that I'd be sitting here at the final six, just from a statistical perspective. After all, two-thirds of the contestants we started with are gone, either home or to the jury. I'd like to think that I have a good grasp on my own strengths and weaknesses, and while I may be smart but I'm not exactly the strongest or most physical person out here, and that was always going to be a disadvantage.

But another part of me was absolutely certain that I'd not only make it this far, but much further. That was the part that understood that I *have* to win, that refused to even consider the possibility of failure. Because if I fail, I'm failing not just myself, but Arielle too, and I *can't* fail her, not after all she's done for me. I knew from the moment I got the call from casting that the hardest part would be getting to know people before turning around and voting them out, but I told myself that I wouldn't let personal feelings get in the way of my winning the million.

Now, as I look at my alliance—my *friends*—laughing as Rhonda continues to complain about Ashley, I know that it's going to be even tougher than I expected. It's not just my feelings for Cole, although that's certainly a part of it. No, the truth is that I've gotten to know these five people pretty well over the last month, and it's going to hurt me personally to vote them out, whether or not they know it's coming. I'll still do it, because the only way I make it to the final two is to send four of the others home. I may hate that, and it's just the way this game is played, and there's nothing I can do about it. As much as I love my alliance, they mean nothing to me compared to Arielle.

And yet, as my gaze falls on Cole, his blue eyes sparkling in the light of the fire, something stirs deep within my chest, and I can't help but wish that it didn't have to be this way.

DAYS 26-27

The vibe at camp feels like a textbook example of mutually assured destruction. It's obvious from the increased fidgeting and occasional nervous laughter that my tribe has come to the same conclusion I have: someone has to go next, and it's going to be someone we all know and love. Nobody's come right out and said it, or tried to throw someone else under the bus—at least, not to me—but we all know it's coming. I could try to jump-start the process, but even if I could pick a name to throw out there, the next immunity challenge could shake everything up, considering how few of us there are left. If I try to target someone and they win the challenge, that would be a pretty big setback.

Of course, that doesn't mean I'm not going to *think* about who I want to go, and I'm sure the others are doing the same. Personally, I don't want to get rid of Cole or Rhonda just yet. Of the five remaining, I'm closest to them, and I think they're the most likely to take me to the end if we get there, although I'd at least consider voting for either of them if it came down to them or me. Katie and Marina are both options, as much as I love them. I certainly wouldn't *enjoy* voting either of them out, but I'd still do it, with much less hesitation than Rhonda or Cole.

And then there's Tamika. On paper, she's the easiest choice. The big sticking point, at least to me, is that I'd be breaking the promise I made to her before the merge vote if I were to vote for her. That doesn't mean I won't do it, because honor only takes you so far in this game. But I'd prefer another option.

At least I'm not the only one who seems to be feeling the pressure, because the six of us are far more subdued than usual as we arrive at the challenge area on day twenty-seven. Like the one on day fifteen, we start in the ocean, although the floating platform where we all gather is closer to land than it was then. In between the platform and the shore are six markers, each a different color. Past those, on the beach itself, there are six wooden logs, all parallel to the shoreline and perhaps a few inches above the sand. Beyond them is a large platform with six wooden tables, each the size of my office desk.

Alex is waiting for us when the motorboat drops us off on the platform. "Welcome to your next immunity challenge," he says once we're all in position and the cameras are on. "Cole, I'll take back immunity."

Cole takes off the necklace himself and hands it to Alex, who takes it and places it on the podium. "Once again, you are playing for immunity at tonight's tribal council," Alex continues. "You are also playing for reward. The winner of today's challenge will have a protein-packed lunch delivered to them at camp: steak, veggies, mashed potatoes, and, best of all, warm chocolate chip cookies and milk for dessert. We're getting down to the wire, and eating a full meal might just give you the edge you need to win the next few challenges and get you that much closer to winning the game. Sound like something worth playing for?" As usual, he pauses while we all cheer and clap. "In that case, let's get to it.

"For today's challenge, you'll swim out to markers, where you'll dive down and retrieve a bag of wooden letter tiles. You'll then make your way to the beach and dig under one of the logs until you can squeeze underneath it. Finally, you'll use the tiles to solve a word puzzle. The first person to complete their word puzzle wins immunity and a reward." He pauses for a moment to let it sink in. "I'll give you a minute to prepare, and then we'll begin."

A few minutes later, we're all set. I take a deep breath. I could really use that food. *Not to mention immunity tonight.*

Once he gets the okay from production, Alex raises his hand in the air. "Castaways," he shouts, "Ready … set … GO!"

On the last word, all six of us dive into the water and begin swimming to our markers. The waves push me up and down, the currents swirling around me as I struggle forward. It's hard work, and I do my best to make long, even strokes, like I was taught when I was a kid.

After a little while, I get into a groove, and I can almost believe I'm making good time. But when I stop and take a quick breather, I see Tamika far out ahead of me. Katie and Cole are a few lengths behind her, and I can't see Rhonda or Marina, which hopefully means they're behind me for the moment. *Come on, Ryan, push!*

Tamika reaches her marker first and dives down well before I reach mine. When I get there, I take a deep breath and swim down, using my hands to follow the rope that attaches the marker to the seafloor. After a few seconds, I come to what feels like a large clip attached to a large bag, and I unhook it while my lungs scream for air.

As soon as the clip is undone, I flip myself over and push upwards, taking the bag with me, surfacing just in time to see Marina dive down for her own bag. Rhonda is slightly behind her, while Cole, Katie, and Tamika are all still ahead of me. I begin swimming towards the shore again, hopeful that I can make up some time when I get to the word puzzle.

Unsurprisingly, Tamika reaches the shore while I'm still a good thirty feet out, running up to her wooden log and dropping her bag of letter tiles before she begins digging in the sand. Cole gets there next, then Katie, each of them digging out from under their own logs to make a gap large enough that they can fit through.

When I finally reach the shore, I begin digging under my own log, trying not to despair at the fact that I'm falling further and further behind. Salty water streams down my hair, into my eyes, making it hard to see, but I just dig harder. Less than a minute later, I hear a shout from Tamika and look in her direction just long enough to see her successfully push herself under her log. I quickly look away, focusing on my own digging. *Just a little more.*

I dig and dig and dig, and after a couple interminable minutes, I think I've made a gap large enough to fit through. I get on my back and slide my head under the log, then push with my legs so that my shoulders go under, then my stomach. It's uncomfortable, and it's a close fit—I probably would have had to go back and dig more if I hadn't lost so much weight in the last twenty-seven days—but I make it. "I can do this," I mutter, more to myself than anyone else.

Pushing the last of my body under the log, I stand up and grab my bag. Tamika and Katie have already reached their tables, but Cole is still digging, his back covered in sand—he must have tried to fit under, gotten stuck, and tried again. Hope flares in my chest. *Maybe I have a chance*!

I run up to my table and dump my letter tiles on it. There are slots in the table to fit the tiles, with gaps every so often that are meant to be spaces between words, with eight words total. Two tiles are already fitted in for me—a comma between the second and third word, and an apostrophe in the fourth. I begin moving my tiles around, seeing what letters I have, trying out different combinations as quickly as I can. The fourth word has two letters following the apostrophe, so it's probably 'you're.' I slot in those letters, hoping I'm right. *One word down, seven to go.*

But before I can even figure out a second word, I hear Tamika shouting for Alex, and my heart drops. I keep working just in case Tamika is wrong, even though I know it's probably over.

"Tamika thinks she has it," Alex says, off to my right. "Say it, Tamika."

I glance over to Tamika, who looks exultant. "You win, and you're not going home tonight!" she shouts.

Alex nods, dashing any remaining hopes I might have had. "Tamika! Wins immunity and reward!"

As soon as I hear him say it, I put down the tiles I'm holding, then go over to congratulate Tamika on her win, trying to put on a happy face despite the mounting feeling of dread that's stirring deep in the pit of my stomach.

When we get off the motorboat at our tribe beach a half hour or so later, Neema directs Tamika, along with Marina and Katie—Tamika chose the latter two to share the reward with her—to a clearing, where their meal presumably awaits. Meanwhile, Rhonda, Cole, and I go to camp, where we build up the fire and make our own lunch of boiled rice and coconut. The spices we won on day five are long gone, so the rice is bland, but it's better than nothing. At first, we eat in silence. I think we all know we'll have to discuss strategy at some point, but nobody wants to be the first one to throw out a name.

We've mostly finished eating by the time someone cracks. "So, what are you boys thinkin' for tonight?" Rhonda asks, eyeing us as she eats the last of her rice. "I got some thoughts, but I want to hear y'all's opinions too."

Cole slumps his shoulders. "It sucks that we have to vote someone out," he says, his tone defeated. "It has to be either Marina or Katie, right? I'm not voting for either of you, and Tamika is immune. It's not like we have many options."

I'm not surprised to hear him throw out those two names. If he *did* mean to vote for me or Rhonda, he probably wouldn't say it to our faces. "I'm with Cole," I say, shrugging. "I love Katie and Marina, but it has to be one of those two."

Rhonda shakes her head. "Y'all are right. Can't say I'm happy 'bout either of them goin' home, though. They're both fine young ladies." She sighs. "Still, better them than us, I s'pose."

"I'm not going to disagree with that," Cole says, while I nod my agreement. "Do either of you have a strong feeling between the two of them?"

Rhonda taps her lip with a finger. "If I had to pick," she says slowly, "I'd probably say Marina. Katie's smarter than all of us, except maybe you, Ryan. But I don't think that's gonna help her much over the next few days. Marina, though … she ain't pissed anyone on that jury off, least as far as I know. And besides, she's got three young kids at home. If she gets to the end, she'd get a lot of votes, that's for sure. Heck, even *I* might vote for her at the end if she's up there and I'm not." She shakes her head. "No offense to you gentlemen, but I'd rather take my chances with one of y'all."

"That sounds good to me," I say. "What do you think, Cole?"

He lets out a long sigh. "I guess I'm fine with Marina too," he says, running his fingers through his hair. "I'm not happy about it, but I'll write her name down. Better her than us."

"Excellent," Rhonda replies. She puts down her mug—now that we're well out of coffee and tea, we're using them as bowls for our rice—and stands up. "Well, now that we've gotten that settled, I think I'm going to go for a swim and try to wash off some of this sand. If y'all will excuse me…"

She walks away, leaving Cole and me by ourselves, the two of us silent. I can't speak for Cole, but I, for one, am still thinking about what's going to happen tonight. I don't doubt that the three on the reward are having a similar conversation, debating which of us they'll target tonight. Maybe if I had a bigger ego, I could convince myself that they're throwing my name out there, but it has to be Cole. He's already won two individual immunity challenges, and he's got to be favored to win most of the rest. Besides, he hasn't made any enemies. He even got to be on the same tribe as Jenny, Alina, and Ashraf for a few days, so he might be more likely to get their votes in the end.

I glance up at him, my stomach roiling. *Maybe I should just get rid of him now, while I still can.* We're getting close to the end of the game, and if I want to win, there are surely better options than sitting next to him at the final two.

And yet, that thought doesn't ring as true as it might have even a week ago. Sure, Cole has his strengths—but then, so does everyone else out here, including me. Maybe I'd lose to him if it came down to the two of us, but maybe I wouldn't. I could say the same about each of the other four. Besides, I still need to get to the final two if I want to have *any* chance of winning, and I trust him more than anyone out here except maybe Rhonda.

Or at least that's what I tell myself, and if the little voice buried deep in the back of my head says that the real reason I won't even consider getting rid of him is that because I know it would hurt *him* if I stabbed him in the back … well, I've done my best to ignore that voice so far. Why stop now?

The six of us are completely silent except for our footfalls on the wooden planks as we walk into the tribal council set later that night. The silence isn't unusual—we're on camera, but only so production can get some cool shots of us walking in, and we're not allowed to talk, just like when we're on the motorboats to and from challenges. But this time, the silence feels heavy, like a weight has descended upon us. No matter what happens tonight, someone we all know and love is going home. Even though the five that remain will be one step closer to the million, it'll still hurt to vote out one of our own.

To be honest, I'm still not fully convinced that *I'm* not the one who'll be joining the jury in a few hours. Sure, I think everyone is on board, but they could just be humoring me. I don't even know if I could blame them if they got rid of me. I'd be upset—devastated, even—but I know it wouldn't be easy for them, just like it won't be easy for me to vote for Marina. And at least it would be because they think I'm a threat to win.

Once we've all sat down on one of the six stools, Alex takes his own seat across from us. "So, Tamika," he says. "Let's talk about today's immunity challenge. Do you think you needed to win immunity tonight in order to stay in the game?"

"I don't know if I *needed* it, but it sure doesn't hurt," Tamika says with a chuckle. "It's been said before, but you never know what might happen in this game. Having that certainty, even if it's just for this one tribal, is definitely a good thing."

Alex turns to his right. "Rhonda, given that Tamika is immune, tonight you're going to have to vote for someone that you've lived with for nearly a month. Does that make it more difficult for you than voting out, say, Alina or Jenny?"

Rhonda nods. "You could say that. Don't get me wrong—I told you at the very first tribal council that I expected every vote would be difficult, and that's God's honest truth." She leans forward. "But tonight will be even harder, because I consider each and every one of these people a friend, and I don't want to hurt any o' them. I'll still do it, because if it ain't one of them, it's me, and I ain't ready to go home yet."

Alex accepts her answer and moves on to Cole, then Marina,

then Katie, asking them questions in turn. Their answers are honest, but cagey. I'd expect nothing less at this point in the game, when a single word can turn everything on its head.

Finally, Alex turns to me. "Ryan, let's say whoever you vote for tonight is the person who goes home. What would you want to say to them before they go, if you got the chance?"

I think for a moment before I respond. "I guess I'd just want to tell them that I'm sorry," I finally say. "My vote isn't personal, and I hope we can still be friends when all this is over. I don't know if they'd want to hear it, but that's what I'd say."

"A fair response." Alex points to Tamika, sitting at the end of the row. "And with that, it is time to vote. Tamika, you're up."

Tamika goes off to the voting booth, followed in turn by Cole, Katie, Marina, and Rhonda. I go last, and when I reach the table with the parchment, I pause to take a breath before writing Marina's name down. "Marina, it's been a pleasure getting to know you," I say as I hold up the parchment to the camera. "I just don't want to sit next to you at the final tribal council, so you have to go. Like I said, nothing personal."

Then I place the parchment into the urn and return to my seat, suddenly ready to get this over with.

Once everyone's voted, Alex gets the urn, placing it in its usual spot on the podium. "If anyone has a hidden immunity idol and you want to play it, now would be the time to do so," he says.

Nobody moves, which is entirely unsurprising to me, considering I'm the only one with an idol. For a brief moment, I consider playing it for myself. But nothing I've heard tonight has really made me think it's me, and I would love to save it for the next tribal, so I keep it in my pocket.

"In that case," Alex continues, "I'll read the votes. Once the votes are read, the decision is final, and the person voted out will be asked to leave immediately."

He takes a parchment out of the urn and opens it before revealing it to us. "First vote: Marina.

"Cole. That's one vote Marina, one vote Cole.

"Marina.

"Marina."

He reaches into the urn, pulling out the next parchment slowly. "The thirteenth person voted out, and the fourth member of our jury, is …" He reveals the vote to us. "Marina. That's four, and that's enough. Please hand me your insignia."

Marina stands up, a rueful smile on her lips, walks over to Alex, and hands him her necklace.

Alex takes it from her, then snaps the red token in half, and says, "Marina, your time in this game has come to an end. It's time for you to go."

But instead of going, Marina turns back to us briefly. "Good luck, guys," she says. "I love you all."

Only then does she walk down the ramp behind Alex, leaving the five of us behind.

CHAPTER 19

DAY 28

There are no celebrations when we return to camp a little while later, even though we all should be happy that we made it to the final five. Rhonda may have been the one who said tonight's vote was harder than usual, but we were all thinking it.

And yet, instead of mourning, we still sit around the fire and talk, like we usually do after tribal council. If only to assure ourselves that this isn't a dream, and we are all really still in contention for the grand prize.

Well, everyone besides Cole, that is. He seems unusually withdrawn, speaking only when one of us asks him a direct question, and his answers are short. The rest of the time, he just sits there with a distant look in his eyes, his gaze occasionally flicking to me or to the lone night cameraman. I'm not a mind reader and it's clear what he's thinking: he's gotten votes at the last four tribals, and even though he's managed to stick around, it could easily be him next time. I wish I could reassure him that he won't be going home anytime soon, if only to cheer him up.

But I can't bring myself to do it, because it would be a lie. There are no guarantees in this game, and we both know that. Pretending otherwise would just be silly. So instead of trying to comfort him, as much as I want to, I leave him to stew in his own thoughts. Hopefully, he'll be better in the morning.

When Katie says she's going to bed a little while later, and Tamika and Rhonda decide to join her, he doesn't even react, still silently staring into the fire. It hurts me to see him like this, but I can barely keep my eyes open, and I don't think there's anything I can say that will make him feel any better. I reluctantly go to the shelter too, adjusting my pack under my head to try to get slightly more comfortable.

I'm awakened what feels like a heartbeat later by someone gently shaking my shoulder. *Is it morning already*? It certainly doesn't *feel* like morning. My thoughts are fuzzy to the point where I wonder if I'm dreaming, and I feel even more tired than I did when I went to bed. *Who woke me up*?

Still more than half asleep, I open my eyes, only to find that it's still the middle of the night. There's a gray shadow standing over me, and I blink a few times until it resolves into Cole, his face lit by soft moonlight. Instantly, I come fully awake, a million questions running through my mind. *Is he okay? Why did he wake me up? What's going on*?

Before I can voice any of them, Cole gently places a finger over my lips. "Sorry for waking you up," he whispers, his voice barely audible above the sound of the waves. "I wanted to talk to you, but I was hoping for some privacy. And, well…" He gestures away from the shelter, towards the fire, at something I can't see. "Now's probably as good a chance as we're going to get."

Frowning, I sit up, careful not to nudge Rhonda or Katie. *Privacy? What is he talking about*? I follow his outstretched arm with my eyes, but there's nothing out of the ordinary. *What am I supposed to be—*

And then I see what he's pointing at. The lone night cameraman, the one who stays with us overnight, is leaning against a tree, his camera set down next to him, his chest rising and falling with slow, even breaths. In fact, now that I'm more awake, I think I can even hear him snoring.

"He fell asleep a little while ago," Cole whispers. "I figure this is our chance to talk without worrying about the whole world watching us."

I nod, my curiosity piqued, even though I'm still incredibly perplexed about this whole thing. What does he want to talk about that he doesn't want anyone to hear? Why all the secrecy?

It seems I'll have to find out, because he gives me a quick smile, then turns on his heel and carefully makes his way out of the shelter. I follow him, doing my best not to make noise or wake any of the others. Rhonda grunts as I pass by her, and I freeze, wondering how I'm going to explain this to her when I don't even know what's going on myself.

But she turns over without opening her eyes, and after a few seconds, I keep moving. *That was close.*

Once I'm out of the shelter, Cole leads me down the beach a ways, then sits down and leans against a log, gesturing for me to sit down too. I notice that we're a good distance from the cameraman, but still able to see him, so we'll know if he wakes up. *What in the world is happening*? I don't know, but the whole situation seems absurd, and once again, I question whether I'm still asleep and this is just a strange dream.

But then Cole looks at me, his handsome features clear in the light of the full moon, and somehow I *know* this is real, even if he does look like a dream come true.

Suddenly, I'm blushing, and I force myself not to look away. "So," I say quietly, "are you going to tell me what this is all about?"

He nods, then turns his gaze back to the ocean, rubbing the back of his neck with one hand. "I'm really sorry for all this cloak-and-dagger stuff," he says, his voice louder than it was in the shelter, but not by much. "Like I said, I wanted to tell you something, and I didn't want the others to overhear us."

I wait for him to continue, more curious than ever, but he doesn't say anything. "And?" I prompt him after a full minute has passed. "What is it?"

He's silent for a few moments more, moonlight reflecting in his eyes as he stares off into the sea. "Tonight's tribal was a wake-up call," he says, his voice distant, as though he's talking to himself. "I know I've gotten votes before, but tonight felt different. Like it was the first time where I *really* felt like I could be going home." He looks down, but not before I see a single tear running down his cheek. "I tried not to show it, but when we were talking with Rhonda while the others were on reward, I was so nervous I was almost shaking. I thought you two were just humoring me, and that Marina was convincing Tamika and Katie to write my name down as we spoke."

He sniffles, and before I can stop myself, I take his hand in mine and gently squeeze it. "Hey, come on," I say, trying to keep my tone light. "We've been allies for almost a month now. There was no way I was gonna let you go home."

He looks up and gives me a smile, and I have to fight the urge to kiss him. "I knew you'd have my back," he says. "To be honest, that's pretty much the only reason why I didn't completely freak out. I trusted you, and I don't regret it at all." His smile fades as quickly as it came. "But it could be my turn at the next tribal council, or the one after that. And you've been so open with me, about Arielle and the idol and everything, but I haven't really returned the favor. So, I guess I realized that I didn't want to leave without telling you the truth, which is …" He trails off, and when he speaks again, his voice is even quieter. "That I'm bi."

A wave of conflicting emotions washes over me—happiness that he's willing to open up to me and sadness that he felt like he had to keep it a secret until now. Beneath those, buried deep yet rising with every millisecond, is hope. *Does this mean I have a chance?*

But I only think along those lines for a few seconds before I make myself stop. This doesn't change anything, and I can't let myself believe otherwise, because if I do, I'll only get hurt. "Thank you for telling me," I say, ignoring the sharp pain in my chest. "I'm glad you feel comfortable enough with me to talk about it."

He shakes his head. "I'm sorry, Ry. I should have told you earlier. I almost did, when I saw how everyone reacted to you and Katie, and then again when you told me about your sister that night at the spa." He looks away and sighs. "But I'm not really out at home. My mom knows, and a couple of my best friends, but that's it. I wanted everyone else to find out from me personally, instead of seeing it on the show."

"You have nothing to be sorry for." I give his hand another squeeze. "Everyone should be free to come out when they're comfortable. You don't have to apologize to me."

"Thanks for that. Really, I appreciate it." He looks back at me and gives me a grin that quickly turns into a grimace. "You might want to hold that last thought, though. There's more, and I don't know if you're going to like it."

My heart starts to race, and I don't dare let myself wonder what he's about to say. "What is it?"

"I … well, I guess I just wanted to tell you that I really like you, Ry," he says earnestly, his voice twisting slightly upwards when he says my name. Even though his words are hesitant, his eyes are locked onto mine, the certainty in his gaze visible even in the dark. "In a romantic way, I mean. You're smart and funny and cute and just overall *amazing*, and I thought that maybe…" He glances away again, but only for a fraction of a second. "I was hoping that maybe there's a chance you like me too?"

Silence fills the air like a heavy fog as I stare back at him wordlessly, my mouth open wide in shock. This has to be a dream, because there's no way any of this is real, that it could be happening to *me,* of all people. But Cole certainly *looks* real, his eyes full of hope and the corners of his mouth turned up slightly, and the log I'm sitting on and the sand between my hands all feel real, and that means I have to say *something*, anything, before he takes it back, before he tells me it's all a joke.

And yet my mouth refuses to cooperate, as though it's been disconnected from my brain, and the silence stretches on and on for what feels like forever, but is probably only a few seconds. After waiting for a few more expectant moments, Cole's face drops, and he holds up his hands, as though he's defending himself from me. "Look, forget I said anything," he says, all in a rush. "It was a silly thought, and I shouldn't have put you on the spot like that. Just forget about it, and we can—"

The mixture of shame and regret I hear in his voice finally cuts through the invisible bonds keeping me from reacting, and without giving myself a chance to think about what I'm doing, I close the distance between us and kiss him on the lips. It feels good—it feels *incredible*—but for a single heartbeat, he doesn't move, and I start to wonder if I've made a huge mistake.

Then, to my eternal relief, he's kissing me back, his lips warm and as soft as silk. He pulls away just for a moment, gives me a wide, affectionate smile, then presses his mouth against mine once more. I cup his face with one hand, his beard rough against my palm. We kiss hungrily, like lovers who have just reunited after being apart for years, and I love every second of it. I've wanted this for so long, and the reality is far better than I ever imagined in my wildest dreams.

Eventually, Cole pulls away again, just barely, his forehead less than an inch away from mine. "I've wanted to do that for a while now," he whispers; I swear I can *hear* the grin in his voice, even if I can't see it. "I've had a crush on you since we first met back on day one."

I laugh, feeling as light as a feather, and kiss him again, just because I can. "I could say the same to you. You looked so damn handsome on that boat. I had to stop myself from throwing myself at you."

"Wait, really?" He leans back a bit more, enough that I can see he has one eyebrow raised. "Then why did you avoid me for the first few days? I thought you hated me up until, like, day five."

I gently stroke his cheek with my thumb. "I'm so sorry, Cole," I tell him, my voice low. "I didn't mean to hurt you. I think deep down I was afraid that if I let myself get too close to you, you'd distract me when I needed to focus on winning the game. I thought I was doing a good job of hiding it, but I guess I was wrong."

"Well, I suppose I can forgive you, given the circumstances." He leans in and kisses me again. "Seriously, though, I'm not upset. I'm just grateful you were willing to take a chance on me. I wouldn't have wanted to go home thinking you hated me."

I blink away a tear or two. "I *never* hated you," I tell him, letting my forehead rest against his. "Not for a single second. You're the sweetest, most incredible guy I've ever met. I just didn't want to give you the chance to break my heart."

He wraps his arms around me, and I gladly let him pull me close as I lay my head on his shoulder. "It's okay," he murmurs. "We're both here now, and nobody's heart is getting broken."

"Mmm," I reply, content to let him hold me for the moment. It feels so good just to know that he likes me back, as though I've won the lottery, that I can almost forget that I'm in a game.

Almost being the key word there. "Cole," I say, lifting my head up and looking him in the eye. "Where do we go from here?"

Even in the low light, his blush is visible. "I was kinda hoping that we would be able to date once we get back home," he says, rubbing the back of his neck. "I know we'd be long distance, but I'm willing to give it a shot if you are."

"I'd like that very much." I give him another kiss so he knows it's the truth. "But I meant here and now, in the game."

This time, he doesn't hesitate. "I want to go to the end with you," he says, conviction plain in his voice. "I'm not going to vote you out, no matter what happens."

"I would love for us to be the final two." Just hours before, that might have been a lie, but now that I have him, I'm not letting him go for anything. I'm sure Rhonda will be upset if I don't honor my deal with her, but I'll have to figure out a way to work around that. "I still intend to win, you know. But you're certainly welcome to try to beat me."

"I would expect nothing less," he says, laughing. "I want to win, too. But if I lose to you, then so be it." His grin fades slightly. "By the way, I hate to ask you this, but … would it be okay if we just pretend like all this didn't happen until the game is over? I can't imagine the others will just let us waltz to the end if they know we're together."

"That's fine with me." He's not wrong. In fact, if I were in the others' shoes, I would gladly get rid of one or both of us as soon as I could. "In that case, should we get back before they notice we're gone?"

"That's probably a good idea," he agrees. "But first, I need to do one more thing."

Before I can ask what it is, he pulls me into a deep kiss, his tongue brushing against mine, and I immediately melt into his arms. I can't say I'm excited about the idea of pretending that things haven't changed between us. But if this is what I have to look forward to, then I think I can handle it.

CHAPTER 20

DAY 28

The sun rises on the morning of day twenty-eight, a beautiful dawn that finds me sitting on the beach while the others sleep. I didn't think I'd be able to sleep after getting back into the shelter last night, considering how my brain was going a mile a minute with thoughts of Cole. But to my surprise, I fell asleep almost immediately, and woke up just before sunrise feeling as refreshed as I've ever been. Even now, I can't quite stop myself from grinning as I think about last night. I'm sure the rest of the game will be stressful, but it feels so much better knowing what's waiting for me when it's all over. Besides, I only have to make it through five more days, and then I'll be done. If I can go home with the million dollars *and* Cole, then I really will have won the lottery.

Of course, I still need to make it through the next few days if I want to win. The five of us go about our chores like it's any other day, which I suppose it is for the three women. Meanwhile, Cole and I try our best to pretend like everything is normal, as we agreed. Occasionally, when no one is looking, one of us will give the other a wink or a knowing smile, but for the most part, we work and eat and talk with our tribemates as we have for the last four weeks. I wish I could rush over to him and kiss him without caring who's watching, but I ignore that urge with relative ease. After all, wanting him is not exactly a new sensation. Plus, it's easier to ignore it now that I know he feels the same way. All I have to do is wait a few days, and then I can kiss him all I want.

And we both know it really is best for us to stay apart until the game ends. With only five people left, there's nowhere to hide, and if the other three found out about us, they'd almost certainly vote me or him out tonight—it's far too risky to have two people working as a unit when you're on your own. Fortunately, it seems that none of them has noticed that anything's changed, and I breathe an internal sigh of relief.

Still, just because they haven't figured it out yet doesn't mean Cole and I are guaranteed to get to the end. But I think we can pull it off with a little finesse. If Tamika doesn't win the next challenge, she's probably going home. If she *does* win, I think I can convince Rhonda to target Katie. Plus, there's a good chance Cole will win the challenge, in which case I'll play my idol for myself, ensuring we're both safe. Then, at four, Cole and I can get rid of either Katie or Tamika, depending on who goes at the next tribal council. It's far from foolproof—we still need Rhonda to vote with us tomorrow night, and there's a chance of a tie when we get down to four—but it's not a bad plan at all.

No, if I'm being honest with myself, the real problem is what happens when we get to the final three. Usually, whoever wins that immunity challenge gets to vote one of the other two out. That means if Cole and I both lose, one of us will go home no matter what. But it's not like there's much we can do, other than try to win that challenge. Hopefully, Rhonda will be in the final three with us. I love her to death, but she's not great at challenges.

Even that wouldn't be the end of it. I still want to win, for Arielle if not for myself. Despite recent events, I still think Cole will be a formidable opponent at the final tribal council. He's already won two challenges, and he probably doesn't have any enemies on the jury. Meanwhile, I'd probably lose Rhonda's vote by reneging on my deal with her, and who knows whether the rest of the jury will respect my gameplay.

On the other hand, I was the one who came up with the idea to split the votes when we got Juan out, and I convinced Tamika to flip at the merge. I may not have built the best connections with the three Sikas on the jury, but I don't think I've made any enemies, and I've got pretty good relationships with the others. So while I might not win if I'm sitting next to Cole, I at least have a good chance at beating him, and I doubt my odds would be much better against any of the other three.

That's assuming I can get to the end in the first place. There's still a lot of game to play between now and then, and in the meantime, I should focus on getting Cole and me to the end. I don't want to get ahead of myself.

But if I sometimes let my thoughts drift, and picture myself being announced as the winner of season nineteen of *Marooned*, with Cole by my side … well, lightning has already struck once. Who says it can't strike again?

DAY 29

Our next immunity challenge occurs on day twenty-nine. Just like yesterday, the weather is perfect, perhaps seventy-five degrees and without a cloud in the sky. I can't help but feel like it's a good omen, reflecting the warm feeling that's been sitting deep in my chest for the last day and a half. I glance at Cole as we get off the motorboat on our way to the challenge area, and for a moment, all I can think about is how happy I am to have found him. He sees me looking and gives me a sunny smile, and my heart soars.

But the others might be watching, so I quickly turn away and look at today's setup for the challenge area. Four small flags mark a rectangular swath of sand, perhaps ten feet by twenty feet, that looks like it's recently been dug up. Next to each flag is a simple wooden box about a foot square. Beyond that are five large slingshots spaced about ten feet apart, each about three feet tall and pointed at a group of targets. There are five targets per slingshot, so twenty-five total, and each group of five is painted a different color.

Alex waits for us to take our places on the mat, then begins his usual speech. "Welcome to your next immunity challenge," he says. "Tamika, I'll take back immunity."

Tamika walks over to Alex, who unlatches the necklace and places it on the usual podium. "You are once again playing for immunity at tonight's tribal council," he continues. "You are also playing for reward. The winner of today's challenge will have lunch delivered to them at camp: pizza, hot and fresh from the oven, with all the toppings you can think of—pepperoni, mushrooms, onions, you name it—and to drink, ice-cold soda and beer. Sound like something worth playing for?" As usual, he pauses so we can cheer and clap. "In that case, let's get to today's challenge.

"First, you'll run out to the rectangle you see marked by flags"—he gestures behind him, to the churned-up area of sand—"where you'll dig up buried sandbags. There are a hundred of them out there, and once you find a sandbag, you can claim it for yourself by putting it in your box. At any point, you can decide to stop digging and move on to the next phase of the challenge. However, once you do, you cannot return and dig up more bags.

"In the second phase, you'll use a slingshot to launch your sandbags at five targets. The first person to successfully hit all their targets wins immunity and a reward. The more sandbags you have, the better, because if you still have targets left when you run out of sandbags, you'll have to go out and collect the ones you launched before you can shoot again, which will cost you valuable time. However, if you take too long digging, you run the risk of falling behind your fellow competitors." He pauses again, this time to let it sink in. "I know it's complicated, so I'll give you a minute to prepare. Once you're all ready, we'll begin."

As promised, the cameras turn off, and Neema and Steve give us the customary walkthrough, answering all our questions. It doesn't take too long, and shortly thereafter, we're all on our mats, ready for the challenge to start.

As soon as the cameras are back on and Neema signals him, Alex raises his hand in the air. "Castaways: ready … set … GO!" he shouts.

As soon as the last word is out of his mouth, I sprint out to the sand and begin digging, trying to pick an area where there's less competition. I find one sandbag, then a second, then a third, placing them each in my box as I find them, slowly working my way towards my tribemates. At first, they're relatively easy to find, but by the time I've found ten, it becomes noticeably harder, and

I start to wonder whether I should take what I have and move on. For the moment, I keep digging, hoping to find at least a few more before I go to the next phase of the challenge.

Katie is the first one to break, picking up her box and sprinting over to the slingshots just after I've found my eighteenth bag. She's quickly followed by Tamika, who carries her own box. I speed up my search, throwing sand around like I'm a dog digging for a bone. All the while, the pressure to move on to the next phase builds, so Tamika doesn't build up too big a lead on me.

Once I've found twenty-five sandbags, I call quits, leaving Cole and Rhonda as the only ones still digging. As I run to my slingshot, I see that two of Tamika's targets have a small flag on top, which I assume means they've been hit. I pick up the pace, ignoring the spike of anxiety that pulses somewhere in the pit of my stomach. Right now, I need to forget about the others and just focus on doing my best.

As soon as I get to my slingshot, I drop my box next to it, grab a sandbag and put it into the sling. I pull it back, carefully aim, and fire … only for it to land well short of the target. For the second and third shots, I over-adjust, sending the projectiles past the target I'm aiming for. Instead of immediately taking my next shot, I pause and take a deep breath. *You can do this, Ryan.*

Now calm, or at least calmer than I was before, I step up and line up my next shot. To my surprise, this one comes much closer, and my fifth shot actually hits, causing a flag to pop out of the target. The next couple of sandbags miss, but I hit another target with my eighth shot. *Two down, three to go.*

Now that I know I can do it, I feel more confident, and over the next couple minutes, I hit my third and fourth targets, bringing me to the brink of victory. However, Tamika is tied with me, and Katie has three, so instead of resting on my laurels, I grit my teeth and pick up the pace once again.

I take shot after shot after shot, determined to win, but the final target eludes me. I foolishly left the furthest one away for last, and most of the sandbags land short, even though I'm pulling back on the slingshot almost as far as I can. My arms begin to burn, and my breathing is heavy, but I don't slow down even though I'm using up my remaining sandbags at a prodigious rate. It has to be only a matter of time before Tamika wins the challenge, sending her directly to the final four. "I have to win," I mutter to myself. "I can't let her beat me again."

And then, as I'm grabbing my second-to-last sandbag from my box, I hear a commotion off to my right. Out of the corner of my eye, I see Tamika running down towards her targets with her empty box in hand, and just like that, I find a second wind. *This is my chance*!

Slowing down a bit, I resolutely place my second-to-last sandbag in the pocket, carefully aiming and lining up with the target before I fire. At first, I think it's going to hit, but it sails a little bit, flying over the top with perhaps two inches to spare.

Grimacing, I try to clear my mind as I place the last sandbag. *This is it, Ryan.* I pull the pocket back, trying to find the same spot as my last shot, then move forward ever so slightly. Meanwhile, I hear Tamika running back to her slingshot and dropping her box to the ground. *It's now or never.*

With my heart in my throat, I let go, watching the sandbag arc into the air. It seems to move into slow motion as it rises up towards the sky, reaches its peak, and begins to fall, unerring in its flight. *Come on,* I silently will it. *Fly true.*

Seemingly an eternity later, it lands perfectly in the center of the target, causing the last of my five flags to pop up into the air. It takes a moment to sink in, but when it does, I raise my arms up in celebration, at the same time letting out a huge sigh of relief. *I did it*, I think, as the others come over to celebrate with me. *I really won.*

A short while later, after we've all gathered back on the mat and the cameras are rolling again, Alex gestures to me. "Come on over, Ryan," he says, grinning as he holds out the immunity necklace.

Feeling lighter than air, I walk over to him as the other four clap politely, turning around so he can put the necklace around my neck. "Ryan, you are safe at tonight's tribal council and are guaranteed a spot in the final four," he continues. "In addition, you've won a reward, in the form of a pizza lunch back at camp."

He gestures in the direction of the other four. "Pick one of your tribemates to join you."

Instead of responding immediately, I pause for a moment to think about who I want to pick. The smart choice would probably be Rhonda or Katie, so I can talk to them and make sure they're on board with voting out Tamika tonight. But even though I know it's not a great idea, the chance to share some one-on-one time with Cole is too tempting to pass up. We'll still be on camera, so we can't completely let our guards down, but at least I won't have to worry about the other three picking up on weird vibes.

And, I realize, *I have an excuse.* "Well, Cole picked me for a reward a few days ago," I say, deliberately addressing Alex. "So, it's only fair that I return the favor."

Alex nods and gestures to Cole, who beams at me. I return his smile, trying to give the impression that my excitement is for the pizza, rather than who I'll be sharing it with. *It's a good thing there are only four more days left,* I think, as Cole comes over and joins me next to Alex. *I don't know if I can keep this act up much longer.*

The divine scent of just-baked pizza assaults my nostrils a half an hour later as Cole and I walk up to a large picnic blanket set for two. On the blanket are three cardboard pizza boxes, just like the ones you'd find in any greasy pizza joint in the States, as well as a large bowl of salad, pitchers of drinks, and plates, utensils, and napkins. My stomach grumbles loudly in anticipation, and Cole and I waste no time getting down to business.

The pizzas—one cheese, one pepperoni, and one veggie—are amazing, with gooey cheese and thin, New York-style crusts. I'm sure there are better pies back home, but given how hungry I am, they might as well be from a three-Michelin-star restaurant. I briefly wonder how the producers managed to find a pizza oven in the middle of a deserted Samoan island before deciding that I really couldn't care less.

As I'm chowing down on my second slice, Cole turns to me, his eyes sparkling. "Thanks for picking me, Ry," he says. "I've been craving pizza for the last month, so this was perfect timing."

"No problem. I did really owe you for the spa reward." I lower my voice, conscious of the cameras around us. "Besides, I'm glad to have a chance to hang out with you."

"Well, I'm certainly not complaining," he says, giving me the barest of winks. "By the way, have you tried the veggie one yet? It's really delicious."

I haven't, so I take a slice and bite into it—he was right, it is delicious. I tell him so, and he gives me a goofy grin that makes me feel light-headed. I almost can't believe how different I feel around him now compared to just a few days ago. Before, there was this inescapable yearning, this desire to be more than just his friend or his ally, that colored all my interactions with him. Now, that sensation is gone, like the sun has banished away the clouds in my mind, replaced by a sense of utter peace and contentment. Sure, I still want to kiss him and be held by him, but I now know I *can* do those things, and that makes all the difference. And the best part is that I can tell just from the way Cole looks at me that he's feeling something similar.

While we eat, we continue to talk, at first about unimportant things—the challenge that just happened, which of our cities has better pizza, things like that. But after we've both gotten a chance to eat our fill, I turn the conversation to a heavier topic. "I really think Tamika needs to go tonight," I say. "I love her, but she's a bigger threat than Katie or Rhonda. If we don't get her out now, we might not have another chance."

"Sounds like a good idea to me," Cole agrees. "Do you think she'll target me again?"

I frown. "It wouldn't surprise me. I mean, she doesn't have many options—I'm immune, so that just leaves you, Rhonda, or Katie. But even if she does vote for you, it's not like it matters much. She's only one person."

"I know, I know." He sighs. "I just don't like the idea of my name being written down at all. I trust you, and I'm obviously not going to vote for myself, but who knows what the three of them are talking about right now? For all we know, they're going to gang up and vote me out."

I quickly weigh the risks before taking his hand and squeezing it gently. "You're not going home tonight, Cole. I'm sure Rhonda and Katie will vote with us. And if I'm wrong, and you really *are* in danger, I'll play my hidden immunity idol for you."

He raises his eyebrows. "Are you sure about that? I don't want you to waste it on me like Randy did with Ashraf."

"Why not? Tonight's the last night that I can use it, so otherwise it'll just be a souvenir."

"Well, if you insist, I'm not going to say no," he replies, giving me a warm smile that makes me want to kiss him even more. "But please, promise me you'll only use it if you think it's necessary. I'm sure Arielle or someone back home would love to have it, and I don't want you to take that away from them just because I'm freaking out."

"I promise." I don't really think it'll matter, but if it makes him feel better, I'd promise him the moon. "I'm sure everything will go just swimmingly tonight."

Cole and I finish eating and return to camp a little while later. He goes off to take a dip in the ocean, while I make my way back to the shelter. He gives me one last smile as he goes, and I almost can't believe my luck in finding him. I know that things might not work between us outside the game—dating long distance is hard, and this is an atypical situation already—but I'll get the chance to try, and that's all I can ask for.

When I get back to the shelter, Rhonda is sitting next to the fire. She's by herself, a small frown on her face, her eyes distant, as though she's lost in thought. Whatever she's thinking about, it must be intense, because she doesn't react as I sit down across the fire from her. A sudden spike of guilt hits me square in the chest. I never promised her that I would take her on the reward if I won, but we're still close allies. "Hi," I say quietly, so as not to startle her. "You okay?"

That gets her attention. She shakes her head as if coming out of a trance, her frown disappearing as her eyes focus on me. "Hey there, honey," she says. "How was the reward?"

"It was good." I mean, it was pretty awesome, but I don't want to make her more jealous than she already is. "How about you? How's your afternoon going?"

"It's ..." She sighs and looks down. "Well, I guess it's going about as well as it can in this game. You know how it is."

"I guess I do." We both sit there silently, and my anxiety grows by the second. *I better fix this before it gets worse.* "Listen, Rhonda … I'm sorry I didn't pick you for the reward. If I could have picked one more person, it would have been you for sure. I just wanted to repay Cole, that's all."

She looks up again, some of the tension leaving her expression. "Don't you worry about that, honey," she says. "I ain't upset with you. Sure, that pizza would have been nice, but I had my chance to win the challenge, just like you did."

"I'm glad to hear that." The guilty feeling in my chest lessens, and I let out a breath. "By the way, did you get a chance to talk to Katie about the vote tonight? Cole and I were thinking we should target Tamika, but I wanted to hear your thoughts before I commit to anything."

She nods, a thoughtful expression gracing her face. "I figured y'all would suggest that. Katie and I talked about it, and we're both on board."

"Really? That's great. To be honest, I thought I'd have to do some more convincing."

"Not at all." She smiles, but it doesn't quite reach her eyes. "It'll be four to one, and we'll be one step closer to the million."

I lean forward and take her hand in mine. "I know you like Tamika," I say, my voice low, "and I know it won't be easy for you to vote for her. It's like you said, we're all friends, and all the votes are going to be difficult from here on out."

"I know. I just didn't realize quite how hard it would be." She gives me another smile; this time, it looks genuine. "Don't you worry, though. I'll do what needs to be done, and so will Katie."

The rest of the time before tribal council is relatively relaxed. Just like at the final seven with Alina, everyone knows that Tamika's going home, including Tamika herself. Oh, she spends five minutes trying to persuade me to vote for Katie, but it's clear her heart isn't really in it. I'd be lying if I said I saw this coming. I definitely thought she'd want to go out fighting.

But upon reflection, maybe it does make sense. She's probably just accepted the inevitable and wants to enjoy her last day on the beach. I certainly wouldn't blame her. This game can be mentally taxing at the best of times, and it's never the best of times out here.

Meanwhile, the rest of us go about our day with a minimum of fuss. I briefly debate whether to talk to Katie about the upcoming vote before deciding against it. If Rhonda says Katie's in, then I believe her, and I don't want to overthink things—or worse, give Rhonda the impression that I don't trust her. I may be planning to go back on our deal, but I still need her for the next two tribals.

But that's only a minor issue, and by the time we walk into the tribal council set just after sundown, I'm feeling about as confident as I can. Honestly, I'm already thinking about our next tribal council. There's a chance that Rhonda and Katie might join forces and vote for Cole or me, forcing a tie, which could throw a wrench in my plans. I'll just have to do my best not to give away how closely Cole and I are working together.

As usual, Alex is waiting for us as we take our seats. "We will now bring in the members of our jury," he says, as the four of them file in. "Jenny, Ashraf, Alina, and Marina voted out at the last tribal council." The latter gives us a quick nod and a small smile before taking her seat. *Hopefully, she's not too mad at us.*

Once the jury is all set, Alex sits down across from us. "Ryan, today was your first challenge win, although you've come close before. How does it feel to have that safety tonight?"

Almost subconsciously, I reach up and touch the necklace, feeling its reassuring weight. "It feels pretty damn good," I reply. "There aren't many sure things in this game, and knowing I've got a guaranteed spot in the final four is comforting, to say the least."

Alex nods and turns to my left. "Cole, you've had that necklace before, but obviously you don't tonight. Does that make you feel vulnerable, or are you confident it won't be you?"

Cole shrugs. "I mean, any time you don't have immunity, you feel vulnerable. Like Ry said, there aren't many guarantees in this game, and anything can happen. But I'm confident that I'll still be here tomorrow."

Next up is Rhonda. "Rhonda, you said the last tribal council would be difficult for you, because you consider everyone left a friend," Alex says. "Does that still hold true? Will this tribal council be even harder?"

"Oh, of course," Rhonda replies, nodding. "I expect every vote from here on out will be harder than the last, and tonight's no different. But that's just a part of the game, and it's still better than the alternative."

Continuing down the line, Alex gestures to Katie. "Katie, do you agree with Rhonda? Or will tonight's vote be easy for you?"

Katie thinks for a moment before responding. "I don't think there is such a thing as an easy vote," she says slowly. "Especially not for the person going home, but for the rest of us too." She frowns, her gaze focused on Alex. "But sometimes you know what has to be done, and you just have to do it, even if you don't like it."

Finally, Alex turns to Tamika. "Tamika, let's say you go home tonight, and a few months from now, you're watching this with your friends and family. What would you want them to know about how you played this game?"

Like Katie, Tamika doesn't respond immediately. "I'd want them to know that I gave it my all," she eventually says. "Whether or not I end up winning, what matters is that I did my best. As long as I can say that to myself, and know in my heart that it's true, it doesn't matter what anyone else thinks."

"Excellent." Alex points at me. "And with that, it is time to vote. Ryan, you're up."

I get up and walk over to the voting booth, thinking about Katie and Rhonda's answers. I agree that there may not be any truly easy votes, but some of them are easier than others, and tonight is certainly one of those. I approach the table and write down Tamika's name on the parchment before holding it up to the camera. "Tamika, you know I love you, but I want to win, and that means you have to go. I'll see you on the other side."

Then I fold the parchment and put it into the urn before returning to my seat, already plotting the next move to bring Cole and me one step closer to the end.

While the others are voting, I think about whether to play my hidden immunity idol for Cole tonight. On the one hand, it's probably better to be safe than sorry. But on the other hand, I don't think he's in danger tonight. He might get Tamika's vote, but that's it. I did promise him I'd only use it if that was the case. He certainly seems relaxed enough right now, loosely hugging one of his knees as we wait for Alex to return, and he didn't say anything about it before we left for tribal council. Plus, I don't want to have to explain to the others why I didn't tell them about the idol before. If they find out I've kept it secret for more than a week, they might start to wonder what else I'm hiding from them, and that could be disastrous.

And there's another reason not to play it for him, I realize. If I do, it would be a glaring hint that he and I are closer than everyone thinks. As far as the others know, Cole and I are allies, but hopefully we haven't given them a reason to think we're anything more than that. But if I suddenly played the idol for him, Rhonda and Katie would definitely start to question why I'm so intent on saving Cole at their expense. I doubt they'd figure out the whole story, but it would give them a reason to target Cole or me at the next tribal council. I'd hate to go home now when I'm so close to getting everything I wanted. *What to do, what to do …*

I haven't made a decision by the time Alex rejoins us with the urn. "If anyone has a hidden immunity idol and you want to play it, now would be the time to do so," he says.

Cole turns slightly towards me, raising one eyebrow ever so minutely. It seems more like a question than a request, though, and that seals the decision for me. *Better to just hold onto it, rather than take the chance.* I shake my head a fraction of an inch, and Cole gives me the slightest of nods. I'll explain to him when we get back to camp.

After waiting for a few seconds, Alex continues with his usual script. "In that case, I'll read the votes. As always, once the votes are read, the decision is final, and the person voted out will be asked to leave immediately." He reaches into the urn, pulling out a vote and showing it to us. "First vote: Tamika.

"Cole.

"Tamika.

"Cole. We're tied, two votes Tamika, two votes Cole, one vote left."

It takes a moment for that last vote to register with me, but when it does, I frown deeply. *Who else voted for Cole?* The first one for him wasn't a surprise—we both figured Tamika would write his name down, but all the rest should be for her. Anxiety stabs into my mind as I glance at the rest of the group. *Did they really …?*

Cole turns to look at me, clearly shocked, but the other three have near-identical expressions of determination on their faces, and my heart plummets to the ground. *No. Please let it be a mistake. Please!*

In a moment that seems to last an eternity, Alex reaches into the urn and pulls out the last vote. "The fourteenth person voted out, and the fifth member of the jury …" He turns the parchment around, showing the name written upon it: "Cole. Please hand me your insignia."

For a few heartbeats, nobody moves, as though we're stuck in amber, and the only sound is that of my pulse thudding in my ears. *This can't be happening!* I wait desperately for someone to tell me that it's all a joke, or to wake me from this horrific nightmare that I've apparently fallen into.

But then Cole stands up and walks over to Alex, removing his insignia with shaking hands, and suddenly it slams into me that this is *real*, that Cole is about to go home. I want to shout at him to put his insignia back on, to sit back down with me where he belongs, but I'm frozen to the spot, my mind dominated by a single thought. *This is all my fault.*

I watch mutely as Cole gives the insignia to Alex, his hands still shaking. "Cole," Alex intones. "Your time in this game has come to an end." He snaps the token in half, my heart breaking along with it. "It's time for you to go."

Cole gives me one last, anguished glance, tears coursing down his cheeks. If my heart wasn't already broken, seeing him like this would do it. "I'm sorry," I whisper, so low I can barely even hear myself. "I should have saved you."

Then, after a few more agonizing seconds, he turns and walks down the ramp, taking all my hopes and dreams with him.

CHAPTER 21

DAY 29

The ride back to camp after tribal council is terrible, like a nightmare that I can't wake up from. *How could this have happened?* The other three must have planned this while we were on the reward, and I was too stupid, too goddamn *blind*, to see that they were lying to me. I was so sure that Cole and I would go to the end together that I ignored what was right in front of my nose.

Tears stream down my face as I remember how broken he looked right before he walked down that ramp and out of the game. And if it's this bad for me, I can't even imagine how he must be feeling right now. The thought of him sitting in the production camp, broken and devastated as he wonders how this could have happened, is almost too much for me to bear.

And the worst part is that I have no one to blame but myself, because even after the other three flipped, I still could have saved him. All I had to do was play my hidden immunity idol for him, and he'd be right here with me. Hell, I could have given it to him before tribal council and let him decide whether to play it for himself! But I was *so* sure that he wasn't in trouble, and now I'm stuck with a worthless trinket while Cole is out of the game. *I wish I'd never even found the damn thing*! I almost take it out of my pocket and hurl it overboard, but I manage to stop myself in time. *Keep it around so you remember what happens when you get too confident.*

I try to take a deep breath and calm myself, but it doesn't really work, so instead I sit there and stew in my own anger. As the motorboat skips over the waves, that anger slowly evaporates into the air, replaced by a bone-deep weariness, and by the time we get back to the beach, all I want to do is go to bed. I'm sure Tamika and Katie and Rhonda want to explain why getting rid of Cole was the right move, but I don't want to hear it now, or ever.

As soon as we hit the beach, I get off the motorboat and immediately walk towards the shelter, but as expected, Rhonda intercepts me. "I need to talk to you," she says quietly.

I shake my head. "I'm going to bed. We can talk tomorrow."

I turn to continue to the shelter, but she grabs my arm. "Ryan, I understand you're upset," she says, her tone firm. "But this was the right move. Not just for me, but for *you* too."

I bite back a comment with some difficulty. *The right move, huh*? "How can you say that?" I ask instead, my muscles quivering. "He was in your alliance!"

"He was, just like everyone else on this beach." She looks me in the eye, unfazed. "The fact of the matter is that if we didn't get Cole out tonight, while he was vulnerable, we might not have gotten another chance. I had to do what's best for *my* game. You and I both know Cole would have just waltzed right to the end if we didn't get rid of him. Sure, maybe he was gonna take you along with him. But where would that leave me?"

The fact that she's not wrong only makes me angrier. "What about Tamika? She's pretty good at challenges too, if you hadn't noticed! Isn't *she* a threat?"

"She is. And that's why she needs to go next, if she don't win immunity."

I shake my head again. *You won't fool me that easily, not a second time*. "How am I supposed to trust you after what just went down? What's to stop you from blindsiding me like you blindsided Cole?"

"Ryan, look at me." She waits until I've done as she requested, her gaze unflinching. "I never promised Cole anythin'. But you and I have a deal, and I'm not going back on that. Not now, not ever."

With that, she turns to go, and even though the rest of the tribe is no more than a few yards away, I still feel more alone than I've ever felt in my life.

DAYS 30-31

Just as the days immediately before Cole was voted out were some of the best I've had in this game, the days after are easily the worst. It's not just that he's not here, although that's certainly part of it. What really hurts is the fact that I had this plan, this perfect plan, to go to the end with him. Maybe one of us would be voted out at the final three, but if that had happened, it wouldn't have been *my* fault. The hidden immunity idol would have been useless at that point, and I wouldn't be beating myself up because I didn't play it for him.

But despite the pain, I remind myself that the game doesn't stop just because I'm upset. Even though things aren't going how I planned, I still want to win this game. I'm doing this for Arielle, and if I gave up now, I'd never forgive myself. Besides, I know Cole wouldn't want me to roll over and die just because he got voted out. I'll see him in a few days, no matter what, and until then, I need to focus on the game, no matter how much it hurts. Plus, I'd be lying if I said part of me doesn't want revenge against the others for betraying Cole.

So, I continue to talk to my tribemates, doing my best to pretend like everything is normal. There isn't much strategizing to do at this point—not with only four people left—but I do what I can. My main plan right now is to get rid of Tamika at the next tribal council, although that didn't exactly work the last time I tried. If she wins the next immunity challenge, I'll have to try to switch the vote to Katie or Rhonda. At least the latter promised she wouldn't vote for me. *Who knows if she'll change her mind, though.*

By the time we get to our next immunity challenge, on day thirty-one, I'm determined to ensure that Rhonda's loyalty doesn't get tested by winning myself. The challenge itself is a monster—the four of us have to navigate a giant maze that must have taken production a week to build, finding bags of puzzle pieces as we do, then use the pieces to complete a giant three-dimensional puzzle. In the end, Katie solves the puzzle first, winning immunity at tonight's tribal council. It's better than Tamika winning.

I'm prepared to do some more convincing, but as soon as we get back to camp, Katie pulls me aside. "I'm voting for Tamika," she says, without preamble. "I know you probably don't trust me after what happened with Cole. But I still want you around."

I still don't know if I can trust her, or Rhonda for that matter, but it's not like I have many options. If the two of them decide to team up with Tamika to vote me out, there isn't much I can do to stop them. I suppose I could preemptively flip on *them* and try to convince Tamika to vote for Rhonda, but it would still only be two against two. Plus, there's a good chance Tamika would immediately run to Rhonda and Katie, and then I'd be screwed. No, the best thing I can do is nothing, even if it feels counterintuitive.

But despite the fact that I might go home tonight, I'm actually looking forward to tribal council, for one reason and one reason only: the jury always watches the proceedings, which means Cole will be there. They're not allowed to talk to or interact with us, but I just want to see him, so I can reassure myself that he's okay. I can't imagine it's easy getting voted out, and being blindsided must make it ten times worse. At least if I go home tonight, I won't be *that* surprised. But Cole … well, he must have felt betrayed, and hopefully I can get some indication—a wink, a smile, a nod, whatever—that will let me know he's feeling better.

Once we've taken our seats, Alex signals to his right, and the jury begins to walk in. "We will now bring in the members of our jury," he says. "Jenny, Ashraf, Alina, Marina …"

The four of them parade past us, but I only have eyes for the one last in line. "And Cole," Alex continues, "voted out at the last tribal council."

I try not to stare at Cole as he walks in and takes his seat with the rest of the jury. He looks incredible, in a white button-down shirt, the top two buttons undone, and khaki shorts. His beard is gone, and he's gotten a haircut, back to the same length it was when I first met him on day one. His cheeks, which had been getting gaunt from the lack of food, are already starting to fill out again.

He glances at me, and our eyes briefly meet before he looks away. His expression is carefully neutral, and his eyes betray nothing, so I have no idea how he's feeling. That's not necessarily a bad thing. The jurors are supposed to be impartial, and he's hardly the only one who's not showing any emotion. Still, I had been hoping for *some*thing—a wink, a brief smile, anything to let me know that he doesn't blame me for what happened two nights ago.

While I'm distracted, Alex begins talking, and with some difficulty, I tear my attention away from Cole. "Rhonda," Alex begins, "I think it's safe to say the last tribal council was a blindside. What was the feeling like at camp over the last few days?"

"Well, it wasn't exactly a party," Rhonda replies, a ghost of a smile flitting across her lips for a half-second. "I don't think any of us were *happy* to see Cole go, although some of us mighta been more upset than others. But at the same time, we all know we're close to the end, and it ain't gonna be easy gettin' there. Last night was just another reminder of that."

Alex nods and turns to me. "Ryan, based on how you voted last time, I'm guessing you were one of the people who Rhonda was talking about when she said some of you were more upset than others. Was Cole's ouster a surprise?"

I hesitate before I respond. The correct answer is *yes, I had no idea he was going home*, and if this were any other situation, I'd just say that. But here, I can't afford to appear like I was completely out of the loop, or the jury might hold it against me should I make it to the end. "I didn't think Cole was going home last time," I say, studiously avoiding looking in his direction. "But there really is nowhere to hide at this point, and the only person who's safe is the person with the immunity necklace around their neck."

Alex turns to Tamika, asking her a question, then Katie, while I continue to avoid looking at Cole. I wish I could tell him that I'm sorry I didn't play the idol for him, that I still want to be with him when all this is over. But then the other competitors and the jury would know everything, not to mention the millions of people who will watch the show when it airs. Besides, even if I could figure out a coded way to say it to him, he wouldn't be allowed to respond. Better to wait until we can speak in private.

Once again, my attention snaps back to Alex as he points to Rhonda. "With that, it is time to vote," he says. "Rhonda, you're up."

Rhonda gets up to go vote, then Katie, then me. When I get to the voting booth, I write down Tamika's name once again before holding up the parchment to the camera. "This is for Cole," I say. "I just hope it's you tonight, not me."

It takes less time than usual to rearrange the votes, probably because there are only four of them. Hopefully, it's a sign that there won't be much drama tonight. That could still mean a unanimous vote against either Tamika or me.

My heart is pounding by the time Alex returns with the urn. "Once the votes are read," he repeats, "the decision is final, and the person voted out will be asked to leave immediately. I'll read the votes."

He opens the urn, pulling out a parchment and turning it to reveal a name written in my handwriting. "First vote: Tamika.

"Ryan.

"Tamika. That's two votes Tamika, one vote Ryan, one vote left."

He reaches into the urn and pulls out the last vote. "The fifteenth person voted out, and the sixth member of our jury …" He turns the parchment around. "Tamika. Please hand me your insignia."

I breathe a quiet sigh of relief as Tamika stands up and walks over to Alex, handing him her necklace.

Alex takes it from her and snaps the red token in half. "Tamika," he says, "your time in this game has come to an end. It's time for you to go."

Tamika nods and turns to face the rest of us. "It's been fun," she says. "I'm rooting for all of you."

Then she walks past Alex, down the ramp, and out of the game once and for all.

DAY 32

We make our way to the challenge area for the last time on the morning of day thirty-two, our second-to-last day in this game. The three of us file in and stand on the red mat, with Alex waiting for us, as always. I had an idea of what this challenge might be before I even got here, and what I see behind Alex, namely a pole about six feet high with the tribal immunity idol on top of it and three smaller poles surrounding it, confirms my guess. *At least I have a chance.*

"Welcome to your final immunity challenge," Alex says. "First things first, I'll take back the immunity necklace."

Katie walks over to him, and he unclips the necklace from her neck before putting it in its usual place on the podium. "For the last time, you are once again playing for immunity," he continues. "Today's challenge is exceedingly simple. Each of you will stand on one of the three footholds you see behind me and hold on to the immunity idol with one hand for as long as you can. If at any point you touch the ground or let go of the idol, you will be eliminated. The last person left standing wins immunity and a guaranteed spot in the final two, which means you'll have a chance to plead your case to the jury. You'll also get to choose who sits next to you at the final tribal council. This is probably the most consequential decision in this game, and only one of you will have the chance to make it." He pauses to let it sink in. "I'll give you a moment to prepare, and then we'll get to it."

There's no walkthrough this time—the challenge is brutally straightforward, unlike some of the others we've had—and shortly we're all in position. Neema stands behind me, just off camera, watching to see if my hand or feet slip, while Steve stands behind Rhonda, and Alex stands behind Katie.

Once everyone's ready, Neema signals to Alex, who nods. "I'll count you in, and then this challenge will officially begin," Alex says. "Three … two … one … this challenge is on."

As soon as he's done talking, there's near-complete silence, only broken by the sound of the wind rustling in the trees and the dull roar of the ocean. I do my best to ignore even those, blocking everything from my mind except the idol in front of me and the pole beneath my feet. All my focus, all my concentration, is on my feet and my hands. A single slip, an inadvertent motion, or even just reaching up to scratch my nose could lose me the game.

Time stretches on into eternity as I stand there, as still as I can, afraid to make even the slightest movement. I wouldn't know how much time has elapsed if Alex didn't occasionally let us know, each minute feeling like a full hour.

The sun beats down, making me sweat, and the pole I'm standing on is narrow and rough, eating into the soles of my feet, but I still don't move. A half-hour in, my right arm starts to hurt from holding it in an unnatural position for so long, and I carefully switch hands, making sure to grab the idol with my left hand before removing my right. Fifteen minutes later, my legs start to cramp up, then my left arm, until my limbs feel like they're all on fire. *I don't know how much longer I can do this.* I grit my teeth and force that thought away as best I can. *You* have *to do this. Arielle is counting on you.*

Just after Alex lets us know that an hour and a half has elapsed—*that can't be right, I've been up here for days*—Rhonda steps off her pole and plops down heavily in the sand. "I can't do it anymore," she groans, her voice ringing in the silence. "It's up to y'all." She goes over and sits on the bench, leaving Katie and me to battle it out.

I take my attention away from the idol for a bare second to glance over at Katie. She looks like a statue, not moving at all. It isn't going to be easy to beat her, but I have to. If I lose, there's no guarantee she'll take me to the end, and I did *not* come this far just to come in third place.

Another half-hour passes, then another, then another. My entire body is consumed by pain, like I'm burning to a crisp, but I don't move, no matter how much I want to just end this and sit down. One thought, and one thought alone, keeps me going: *Do it for Arielle.* It runs through my mind, again and again and again, in an endless loop, giving me the courage to stand there for another second, another minute, another hour, as long as it takes to win. *Do it for Arielle. Do it for Arielle. Do it for Arielle.*

And then, without warning, more than three and a half hours into the challenge, Katie groans and half steps, half falls off her pole. I wait until I hear Alex shout "Ryan! Wins individual immunity!" before I collapse onto the sand, and even though I'm in more pain than I've probably ever been in my life, a wave of relief washes over me, so strong I could cry. *I did it.*

CHAPTER 22

DAY 32

I feel like I'm walking on air as we walk up the beach toward our shelter a short time later. Not only did I just guarantee my spot at the final tribal council, but I also ensured I don't have to spend the rest of the afternoon trying to convince Rhonda or Katie to take me with them. I think I could have done it, but it would have been an incredible amount of stress to deal with over the next few hours.

Of course, the afternoon won't be *completely* stress-free, because I still have to make an incredibly tough decision—namely, who I want to sit next to in the final two. It might not matter who I pick in the end. Maybe I'm going to lose no matter which of them I choose, or maybe I'm going to win either way. But I have no way of knowing that for sure, so I have to act like this is a million-dollar decision.

The first thing I need to do is talk to Rhonda and Katie, since I'm sure they have quite a bit to say on the matter, and I'd be a fool if I didn't hear them both out. "I'd love to talk to both of you separately," I tell them as we approach the shelter. "It doesn't have to be right now, if you'd rather recover from the challenge, but preferably sooner rather than later."

Katie shrugs. "No time like the present," she says. "Rhonda, do you want to go first, or should I?"

Rhonda shakes her head. "You go ahead, dear. I'm going to go to the well and get some water. Save the best for last, I always say."

She takes our canteens and walks off while Katie and I sit on the beach in front of the shelter, joined by one of the ever-present cameramen. "First off, congratulations," Katie says, holding out her hand. "You did a great job back there."

I take her hand and shake it, grinning. "Same to you. I thought I was going to have to stand there until midnight."

"Ugh. That would have been horrible. Three and a half hours was *more* than enough." She sighs. "But I digress. What are you thinking for tonight?"

"In all honesty, I haven't decided yet. I'm betting you have some thoughts on the matter, though."

"Oh, I sure do," she agrees, giving me a hint of a smile. "I know you want to win, and I'm not going to sit here and tell you that you should take me to the end because I deserve it more than Rhonda does or whatever. That would be bullshit, and we both know it. What I *am* going to tell you is that you have a better chance against me than her." She leans back. "Honestly, once she was out of the challenge, from your perspective, it didn't really matter who won, because I was going to take you to the end no matter what. She'd crush us both."

I don't know if she's lying about taking me to the end had she won, but that's irrelevant. "Really? You think Rhonda would beat us?"

"Think about it. You love her. I love her." She spreads her arms wide. "But more importantly, the *jury* loves her. She didn't get on anybody's bad side this entire game. Well, maybe Ashley, but she's not on the jury. They'll be falling all over themselves to give Rhonda the win. Can either of us say the same?"

I lightly punch her shoulder. "Don't sell yourself short. Maybe they all think I'm a curmudgeon, but you're pretty likable."

She shakes her head. "Not like Rhonda. You and I ... well, no offense, but we can be a little standoffish at times. I mean, did either of us even say more than two words to Jenny or Ashraf?"

"I did have a conversation with Jenny," I allow. "But it was just the one time, and we voted her out the next day. So, point taken."

"Exactly. Meanwhile, right after we merged, Rhonda was doing her thing—getting to know them, making them feel at home, just like she did with everyone else."

"Really? I didn't know that." Again, she could be lying, but this time it matters. I was too preoccupied with making sure we didn't get voted out—and, yes, also with Cole—to notice whether Rhonda was building relationships with the Sikas. If she really did get close to them, they might be more willing to vote for her. "Did she really have enough time to make them love her?"

She shrugs. "Okay, maybe saying Jenny and Ashraf *love* her is an exaggeration. But they certainly have more of a reason to vote for her than they do for you or me."

"That's fair." *So many things to consider.* "Well, you've certainly given me a lot to think about."

"I should hope so." She smiles, then stands up and offers me her hand. "Come on, let's get back to camp. I'm sure Rhonda has a lot to say, too."

We head back to the camp, and Rhonda returns with the canteens a little while later. Not long after that, Rhonda and I head down to the beach, the eye of the camera once again trained on us. "I don't envy you," she says. "You got a tough decision to make tonight."

"Don't remind me," I reply, shaking my head. "I have a feeling you're not going to make it any easier."

"You're right about that." She gives me a tight smile. "I got some thoughts, and I'm gonna share 'em with you."

I laugh. "Hit me with your best shot."

"Oh, don't you worry, I will." She tilts her chin up, fixing me with a strong gaze. "There's no denying you're a smart man. But believe me, Katie's no slouch either. God's honest truth, she might even be smarter than you. No offense, of course."

"None taken." She's not wrong, from what I've seen. "Do you think it matters, though?"

"Oh, of course it does. You and whoever you sit next to are gonna have to explain your games to the jury, and that takes a lot of smarts to do well. Now, I know you're a big-city lawyer and she's still just a student, but don't underestimate her. Me, on the other hand …" She shrugs. "Well, I'm no dummy, but I'm perfectly willin' to admit I'm nowhere near y'all's level. Besides, you know she and Marina were pretty close, so that might be one vote you lose already."

I think that last part is an exaggeration, but I can't dismiss her out of hand. She might be right, and with only seven jurors, every vote counts. "What about the Sikas?" I ask. "You were closer to them than she was, except for maybe Tamika."

"Maybe I was, but that ain't saying much. I don't think the jury is gonna vote for someone just because they spent a few minutes talking to 'em on the beach. They're gonna be looking for someone who can show that they were on top of the game, from beginnin' to end. That might be you, and it might be Katie, but it ain't me."

"Don't sell yourself short," I tell her. "You were right there when we were strategizing, same as me and Katie."

She shakes her head. "Oh, I was there physically, but you two were the ones who came up with the plans. I just sat back and did what y'all told me to do."

"I still think you're underestimating yourself, but I'm not going to argue with you." I lean my head back and look up to the sky, just in case the answer is written in the clouds. "You weren't kidding when you said you weren't going to make this easy for me, huh?"

I look down just in time to see her grin. "Can't say I didn't warn you," she replies. Her grin vanishes, leaving behind a serious expression. "Listen, Ryan, I can't tell you what to do. I mean, I want you to take me along with you, but at the end of the day, the decision is yours. You just gotta trust yourself to make the right decision." She stands up, wiping sand off her legs. "And I'm sure you will."

She turns to go, but I'm not quite done yet. "How can you be sure?" I ask, genuinely curious.

She pauses and looks at me, smiling once again. "Oh, that's easy," she says. "I bet on you all the way back on day three, and I won that bet. Things may have changed since then, but I'm bettin' on you again, and I got a feelin' the outcome will be the same tonight."

I spend the next few hours lost in thought. Katie and Rhonda have each said their piece, and they're kind enough to leave me alone while I consider my choice. They've already given me more than enough to consider, and I doubt anything they'd say at this point would sway me.

The truth is that there are good reasons to keep them both, and good reasons to get rid of them both. Rhonda was less involved in the strategy aspect of the game, and the jury might not look favorably on that. Besides, we did make a deal to go to the end together, even if I didn't always intend to honor that. If I vote her out tonight, right before the final tribal council, she could hold it against me. On the other hand, she's charming as hell, and she probably has stronger personal relationships with the jury than I do, except Cole. She definitely has better connections with the former Sikas. For better or worse, I didn't really get to know them, and I bet she did.

Meanwhile, Katie isn't as much of a social threat, at least compared to Rhonda. Her main drawback is her intelligence. I'd like to think that I played a pretty strategic game, but Katie could certainly argue that she was with me every step of the way. I want to be able to take credit for all the moves that got me to the end, even if there were a few hiccups along the way, and that would be harder with Katie sitting next to me. The only question is whether her strategy outweighs Rhonda's charm. As with most things in life, there's no easy answer.

As I mull my options, it strikes me how similar this feels to right before our very first tribal council, nearly a month ago. Then, it was my vote that decided who went home, just as it will be tonight. The calculus is a little different—then, it was who could help me get to the end, and now it's who gives me the best chance of winning—but the pressure, the sense that I *have* to get this right, is the same.

Fortunately, I don't think it's going to take as long for me to decide tonight as it did with Cole and Ashley, because when I weigh up all the pros and cons, one person stands out as being a better choice to bring to the end. The more time passes, the more confident I am in my decision, and by the time we get to tribal council just after sunset, I'm ninety-nine percent sure who's going home. The remaining one percent is just in case someone says or does something at the tribal council itself that changes my mind.

Alex waits for the three of us to be seated. "We will now

bring in the members of our jury," he says. "Jenny, Ashraf, Alina, Marina, Cole, and Tamika, voted out at the last tribal council."

Once again, I only have eyes for Cole. Tonight, he's wearing a blue T-shirt that molds to his perfect body, and I have to remind myself not to stare. Like last time, his expression is carefully neutral, and I have no idea how he feels about the fact that I won immunity. All I know is that I wish he were sitting next to me right now, instead of Rhonda and Katie.

But right now, I need to focus on what's in front of me, instead of fantasizing about what could have been, so I turn my attention back to Alex. "Ryan," he says, nodding to me. "I think it's safe to say you have a big decision to make. Was it an easy decision for you, or did you have to think about it?"

I smile inwardly. "Yeah, I had to think about it a bit," I reply, a complete understatement if I've ever said one. "Rhonda and Katie both played excellent games, so it really came down to the details. I spent a good amount of time considering who I want to sit next to tomorrow night, because those details could win or lose the game for me."

Alex nods and turns to his left. "Rhonda, what was your pitch to Ryan?"

Rhonda gives Alex a restatement of what she told me earlier this afternoon. Once she's finished, at Alex's prompting, Katie does the same thing. Neither of them says anything I haven't heard before, so I briefly stop paying attention to them and glance over to the jury box, just to see if any of them react to anything. I think I see Marina nod when Rhonda says that Katie has made some good moves, and Jenny gives a little smile when Katie says that Rhonda has friends on the jury—nothing earth-shattering, but as I said, even the tiniest of details could be important.

As I'm looking at each of the jurors in turn, my eyes meet Cole's. We stare at each other for a few moments, neither of us able to look away. There's a hint of some emotion I can't quite place in his eyes, and a twinge of unease runs through me. I can't imagine it's easy for him to know that I got this far and he didn't, and I wouldn't blame him for being jealous. At least I only have one more day until I can see him again. With any luck, we'll be able to talk it out, and we can pick up where we left off.

Alex's voice shakes me out of my thoughts, just like so many times before. "Ryan, have you made your decision?"

I swallow over a lump in my throat. "I have."

"In that case, we'll get to the vote." He gestures to the women sitting on either side of me. "Rhonda, you can only vote for Katie, and Katie, you can only vote for Rhonda. That means that we're tied one-to-one, and Ryan's vote will determine which of you joins the jury, and which of you goes to the final tribal council." He points to me. "Ryan, you're up."

I stand up and walk over to the voting booth, my stomach fluttering with anxiety. Despite my nerves, when I get to the table with the parchment, I pause to savor the moment. This is the last time I'll be in here. I can't really say I love this place, or even like it, but I'm still standing, and that has to count for something.

Then, taking a deep breath, I write a name down on the parchment before holding it up to the camera. "We've come so far together, and I wish this didn't have to be the end," I say. "But I think you have a better chance of beating me, and that's the only thing that really matters."

Then I carefully fold the parchment and place it in the urn before returning to my seat.

Almost as soon as I sit down, Alex goes off to collect the urn, returning a moment later. I guess there's no need to rearrange the votes tonight, since there's only one in there.

"Once the vote is read, the decision is final," Alex intones, "and the person voted out will be asked to leave immediately." He opens the urn and places the lid on the podium next to it. "I'll read the vote."

He pulls out the parchment and opens it, staring at the name written on it for a long second. "The sixteenth person voted out, and the seventh and final member of the jury …" He turns the vote around, revealing it to us. "Katie. Please hand me your insignia."

As soon as he finishes speaking, Katie wraps her arms around me and pulls me into a hug. "Good luck," she whispers. "No hard feelings."

Then she stands up and walks over to Alex, taking off her necklace as she does. She hands it to him, and he looks at her with a grave expression. "Katie," he says. "Your time in this game has come to an end." He snaps the token on Katie's insignia in half, and with one last glance in our direction, she turns and walks past him down the ramp, the last person to be voted out of this game.

Once Katie is gone, Alex turns to address the two of us. "Rhonda, Ryan, congratulations," he says. "You have gone as far as you can in this game. Tomorrow, you'll have a chance to plead your case to the jury and explain why you should win the million-dollar prize. I recommend you spend tonight resting and tomorrow preparing your speeches." He grins, showing pearly-white teeth. "Best of luck to both of you."

Rhonda stands up and begins to walk in the opposite direction that Katie just went. With one last look at Cole, I follow her, doing my best to ignore the worry that roils somewhere deep within my mind.

CHAPTER 23
DAY 33

Heeding Alex's advice, Rhonda and I sleep late the next morning. It's not like we have to worry about chores anymore. In less than twelve hours, we'll both be in the production camp, where the jury has been staying since they got voted out. I'd be lying if I said the feeling wasn't a little bittersweet. Sure, I'm looking forward to having real food, a soft bed, and actual indoor plumbing again, but I'm surprised to find that part of me is actually going to *miss* living on the beach full-time. Maybe I've just gotten used to it over the last month. *Or maybe the lack of sleep is really getting to me.*

Once the producers verify that Rhonda and I are both awake, they begin preparations for what's become a tradition for the final two: the last day feast. Thankfully, it doesn't take long to set up, even though there's quite a spread, with eggs, bacon, bread, fruit, and, of course, champagne. It all looks delicious, and I can honestly say I've never been more excited for breakfast in my life.

After everything's ready and the camera crew has gotten some good shots of the food, Rhonda and I put a pan on the fire and start cooking the bacon and eggs, then pour ourselves drinks. "To you and me," she says, holding up her glass. "I couldn't have asked for a better final two partner."

"Same to you," I reply, grinning. "Did you ever think you'd be here?"

"Oh, I most certainly did. My momma always used to say that if you want somethin', you gotta picture yourself gettin' it. I guess you'd call it *visualizin'*. Whenever I was feelin' down, I'd imagine myself sittin' at the finale, winnin' the million dollars, until it felt like it was real. So ain't none of this a surprise to me."

"I expected nothing less." I give her shoulder a playful shove. "Does that mean you already know what you're going to say to the jury tonight?"

"Nah, but I'm sure I'll figure somethin' out." She gestures to the food. "In the meantime, I'm gonna eat. I don't know about you, but I could use some calories to help me think."

She's got the right idea, so we tear into the bread and fruit while the rest cooks. It tastes amazing, and so do the eggs and bacon once they're done frying. I don't even bother to wait for them to cool down completely. Considering I've barely eaten in the last five days, I think I can be forgiven.

As soon as I've finished eating, Neema pulls me away for one last confessional. One thing I certainly *won't* miss is being on camera all the time. It's not fun wondering if every little thing I say or do will be broadcast to millions of people and make me look stupid.

Once I'm set up on the beach, the ocean sparkling behind me, Neema nods to the cameraman, waiting for him to give her the thumbs up before she turns to me. "First off," she says, "congratulations on making it to the final two. How are you feeling?"

"I'm feeling good. And nervous, I guess. Tonight will probably be the most important night of my life, and I just hope I don't mess up."

"Do you think you have a chance to win?"

"I mean, I think I have a chance. How *big* a chance depends on what happens tonight. You can bet I'm going to do my best to make sure I walk away with the million dollars, though."

"Do you think the jury will respect your gameplay?"

"I hope they'll respect it. I think I've played a strong game, made the right moves, all that stuff. But I guess we'll find out tonight."

"Are there any jurors you're worried won't vote for you?"

I pause for a moment to think about it. "I guess I'm a little worried about Jenny and Ashraf not voting for me, since I didn't get to know them very well. And Katie might hold a grudge against me for voting her out last night. But we'll find out eventually, I guess."

"Anyone you think is a definite vote *for* you?" Neema asks.

Once again, I don't reply immediately; I need to be careful what I say here, for multiple reasons. "I really don't know," I finally say. "If I had to pick, I'd say Cole is probably the most likely to vote for me. Maybe Marina, too. But as I've said before, anything can happen."

She asks a few more questions, but I answer on autopilot, my mind already thinking about tonight. I know Rhonda said she expected to be here, but I most certainly didn't. Sure, I told myself that I had to win, that there was no other option, but I don't know if I ever really *believed* I could pull it off. But here I am, and it's exhilarating to know that I'll never be voted out. At the same time, it's incredibly nerve-wracking—what if I've come this far only to lose at the very end? Second place may sound nice, but it might as well be last when it comes to paying off Arielle's debt.

And yet, I'm a little surprised to realize that's not the only reason my nerves are frayed right now. However the final tribal council goes, once it's over, I'll finally have a chance to talk to Cole for the first time since he was voted out. I still don't know what's going through his mind, and it's driving me crazy. If I'm lucky, everything is fine, and he's just as excited as I am to continue our relationship, if you can call it that. *And if I'm not lucky* …

I shake my head minutely, hoping Neema doesn't notice. I never thought it would be possible for me to win the million dollars and still walk away unsatisfied, but here we are. *Only time will tell.*

Rhonda and I walk into the tribal council set just after the sun sinks below the horizon, having said our goodbyes to the beach and the shelter. The bittersweet feeling I had earlier intensified as we left camp a half-hour ago, but now it's been replaced by anxiety. This is it, the culmination of everything I've been building for the last thirty-three days. Soon, I'll get the chance to explain myself to the jury, and if things go right, I can finally do something for Arielle after she's done so much for me. *No pressure, right?*

We take our seats across from Alex, who waits until we're settled. "We will now bring in the members of our jury," he says. "Jenny, Ashraf, Alina, Marina, Cole, Tamika, and Katie, voted out at the last tribal council." The seven of them file in and take their seats, each with an appropriately sober expression befitting the gravity of the job they're about to perform. I do my best to ignore Cole. I'll be able to talk to him in a few hours, and for now, I need to focus.

Once the jury is in position, Alex nods to us. "Rhonda and Ryan, congratulations on making it this far," he says. "Soon, you'll each make an opening statement, which will be your main chance to plead your case to the jury. After that, each jury member will get a chance to make a statement or ask one or both of you a question about your individual games. Finally, you'll get a chance to make a closing statement." He turns to address the jury. "Jurors, for this tribal council, the power has shifted to you. At the end of the night, each of you will vote for the person you think deserves to win this game, so listen carefully and keep an open mind. Got it?" He waits for all of them to nod. "Excellent. Then we'll get started with opening statements. Ryan, you're up first."

I take a deep breath, then face the jury. *Here goes nothing.* "We all know there's a lot of luck in this game," I say. "Somebody slips in a challenge, or says the wrong thing at camp, and it changes the whole game. My strategy was to take those moments of luck, of opportunity, and turn them in my favor. When Alina and Juan swapped to Meru, and we weren't sure if one of them had the hidden immunity idol, I was the one who came up with a plan to ensure one of them would go home. When we merged and the tribes were even, it could have gone either way, but I made sure our alliance came out on top. I worked hard to make sure I'd be sitting here at the end, and that's why I deserve your vote to win."

Alex nods. "Rhonda, you're up."

Rhonda sits up straighter, a serious expression on her face.

"First of all, I wanna just thank y'all for hearin' me out," she says. "A lot of y'all probably didn't come out here to make friends, but I did." She pauses for emphasis. "I knew I was never gonna come in here and be a strategic genius or a physical threat. No, my strength is—and always has been—buildin' relationships, buildin' *trust*, with people, and if you dig down deep enough, that's what this game is about. That's why I focused on gettin' to know each and every one of you. If I hurt you, know that it hurt me too. I just did what I had to do to get to the end, and even if I'm not proud of all the backstabbin' and lyin' and deceivin'… well, I guess it worked, and that's what matters."

Alex waits for Rhonda to finish, then turns away from us. "Jurors: you've heard the opening statements. Now, it's your turn to address the final two." He points to the far end of the jury box. "Katie, you're up first."

Katie stands up and walks over to center of the set, facing Rhonda and me with a small smile on her face. "First of all, congratulations to both of you," she says. "My first question is for Ryan." She turns to look at me. "Ryan, I know we discussed it a bit, but I want to hear it in your own words. Why did you choose to sit next to Rhonda tonight instead of me?"

I figured she might ask something like that. "Honestly, in the end it came down to the fact that I thought I had a better chance of winning against Rhonda. You're an incredibly smart player, and I figured if I were sitting next to you, it would be difficult to differentiate my game. It wasn't an easy decision, and I know it sucked for you to get voted out at the last possible moment. But at the same time, I want to win, not come in second."

"Fair enough," she says, shrugging. "Rhonda, if you had won the final challenge, would you have taken me or Ryan with you?"

Rhonda thinks for a moment. "I hate to say it, but I probably woulda taken Ryan," she says. "We promised each other we'd go to the final two all the way back on day three, and I'd like to think I woulda kept that promise."

Katie nods. "Got it. Congrats again, and best of luck to both of you."

Next up is Tamika. "Like Katie said, congratulations on

making it this far," she says, her hands on her hips. "Rhonda, it seems like your strategy was to befriend all of us, and I'd say you did a pretty good job of it. But do you think that's enough to win you the game?"

Rhonda frowns. "Well, I suppose that depends on the seven of y'all," she says. "It ain't like I was completely out of the loop on the strategizin'. But, like I said, I really do believe that trust is the most important thing in this game. Sure, you can win all the challenges, and that might be enough to get you to the final two, but it ain't enough to *win*. The relationships you made are what you need for that, and I think I did a better job than Ryan at buildin' those relationships."

"Understood." Tamika turns to me, frowning lightly. "Ryan, in your opening statement, you said that at the merge, you came up with the plan for your alliance. But when you boil it down, all you really did was lie to me about Randy so I would vote with you. Do you regret manipulating me like that?"

A shard of guilt stabs in my gut. "Of course I regret it," I reply. "You're a good person, and I hate that I had to lie to you to make it further in this game." I look her directly in the eye. "But if I had to go back and do it again, I wouldn't change a single thing. Our backs were up against the wall, and there were no good options. I just picked the least bad one that would still give me a good chance of getting to the end."

Tamika considers me silently for a moment. Then she says, "Thanks, guys. I'll be listening carefully, so make sure you answer the rest of the questions honestly and fully." She resumes her seat, her expression inscrutable.

It's Ashraf's turn next, and he asks us what we think our best move was from before the merge. Rhonda says hers was getting Ashley out on day three, since that set the tone for the entire game, and I say mine was coming up with the plan to split the votes after the tribe swap and get Juan out. He seems satisfied with our responses, nodding to himself as he sits back down.

After Ashraf is Jenny, who doesn't ask either of us a question. Instead, she tells us that she wishes she'd gotten more time to get to know us, and that she'll be keeping an open mind.

Next is Alina, followed by Marina, both of whom ask us questions about our specific gameplay. The former nods along with Rhonda's answer but frowns at mine, while the latter gives us both a wide smile as she congratulates us and wishes us the best of luck.

Last is Cole, who looks as amazing as ever in a dark purple T-shirt and white shorts. My stomach flutters as he gets up and walks over to the center of the set. This is the first time I'll get to actually hear from him since he got voted out, and I still have no idea what he's thinking. I wouldn't be surprised if he throws me a bit of a curveball with his question, but if I'm lucky, he'll just lob up a nice softball for me to hit out of the park.

He takes his spot, then turns slightly to face Alex. "I just have one question," he says. "For Ryan."

My heart immediately drops upon hearing the last word. That was the first time he's ever used my full name, and it can't be a good sign. The fluttering sensation in my stomach is gone, replaced by a pit that seems to weigh a hundred pounds. *Please, let it just be for the cameras.*

Cole turns to face me, his eyes as hard as diamonds. "Ryan," he says, his voice trembling ever-so-slightly on the second syllable. "The conversation we had the night after Marina was voted out—did you mean *any* of the things you said to me? Or were you just lying to get yourself further in the game, like you did with Tamika?"

My heart immediately plummets to the ground and stays there. I knew he might be upset about being blindsided, but this clearly goes deeper than that. "I meant every single word," I reply, struggling to hold back tears. "And, just for the record, I had no idea you were going to be voted out. That was all Tamika, Rhonda, and Katie." I want to say more, but I can't, not in front of everyone. *Please, you have to believe me.*

Cole's eyes glisten, and his expression softens slightly. I want him to tell me that he believes me, that he forgives me, even if he can't be very specific while the cameras are on him. *Please, Cole,* I silently will him. *Just give me some indication you still want to be with me.*

But then he shakes his head, and when he looks up again, his eyes are hard once more. "Thanks, Ryan," he says, his tone as cold as winter. "That's all I wanted to know."

Then he returns to his seat, while I hang my head, trying not to cry. What kind of monster would I have to be to even *consider* pretending to have feelings for him just to get myself a bit further in this game? *Does he really think I'm that bad a person*? Sure, I may have lied to Tamika about Randy wanting to get her out, but that's completely different! My feelings for Cole transcended this game, and I thought he understood that. Maybe I was wrong.

I barely pay attention as Rhonda makes her closing statement, unable to move on from thoughts of Cole, and when it's my turn, I stumble through on autopilot, even though I should be paying attention. I just have to hope that there's been some misunderstanding, some miscommunication that I can clear up easily. Maybe Tamika told him that getting him out was my idea, or maybe something I said just now made him think I was in on it. If only I can get through the rest of the tribal council, then I can talk to him privately and reassure him that my feelings for him are real.

At least, that's what I tell myself. I try my hardest to believe it, because if I don't, I might just break down in front of everyone.

Once Rhonda and I have finished our closing statements, Alex tells the jury that it's time for them to vote for a winner. One by one, they stand up and make their way to the voting booth. I do my best to put on a neutral expression, even though my mind is roiling like a storm-tossed motorboat. If they see me looking nervous, they might think I have reason to *be* nervous, and I need to project confidence right now. Each of them seems to move in slow motion, and I silently urge them to move faster so we can get this over with and I can talk to Cole.

Finally, after what feels like an eternity, the last juror returns to their seat, and Alex goes to retrieve the votes. He brings the urn to the podium, but unlike previous tribal councils, he doesn't open it. "Jury, thank you for your service," he says. "Rhonda, Ryan, I'm sure you're anxious to find out who won. But you're going to have to wait until the live finale in a few months." He gives us one last grin. "I'll see you back in the States."

With that, the final tribal council and this portion of the game is over. The cameras turn off, their job done. Meanwhile, Neema directs me, Rhonda, and the jury back to the production camp. I force myself to slow down and take a deep breath as we walk in a single file down the ramp and along a trail lit with torches, Rhonda and I taking the rear. *It'll be okay, Ryan. You just need to talk to him and explain what really happened.*

After a few minutes of walking, we reach a clearing with a large outdoor space and two squat buildings lit by spotlights and strings of bulbs hanging from palm trees. Neema points out bedrooms for Rhonda and me in one of the buildings before leading us into the courtyard, which has two large tables under a wooden roof, one set with chairs and the other holding trays of food. With a considerable force of will, I ignore the buffet, instead squaring my shoulders and making a beeline directly towards Cole, reaching him just before he picks up a plate. "Can I talk to you?" I ask, my voice low. "In private, preferably."

He stares at me for a moment silently, then nods. My heart in my throat, I lead him to my new bedroom. It's rather spartan, just a bed, a night table, and a small dresser, with a door on one wall that I assume leads to a bathroom—in other words, basically a five-star hotel compared to where I've been living for the last month.

Once we're both inside, he closes the door behind him and turns to me, crossing his arms in front of his chest. "Well?" he asks, his voice breaking just the tiniest bit. "What did you want to talk about?"

For a moment, I just stare at him. "Cole, please don't play dumb with me," I say. "What the hell was that at tribal council? Do you *really* think I was lying to you?"

His eyes hold mine for a second longer, but then he looks away. "I'm not sure what to think anymore," he mutters. "I *thought* you and I had something real." He looks up at me again, his eyes glistening with unshed tears. "But just when everything was going perfectly, I got blindsided. Can you even begin to understand how much it hurt to have everything ripped away from me like that?"

I take a cautious step forward. "Of course I understand," I

reply, my tone low and soothing. "But it was hard for me, too. I wanted to sit next to you at the final two, and I would have given anything to make that happen."

"How can you expect me to believe that when you had a chance to stop it and didn't? You told me not to worry, 'cause you'd play the idol for me. And then, right when I needed it, you kept it in your pocket. How am I *supposed* to feel when you betrayed me?"

A feeling of emptiness settles deep within my chest, like there's a black hole where my heart used to be. "I didn't betray you!" I nearly shout. "I did what you told me to do! *You* were the one who made me promise that I'd only play it if you were in danger, remember?!"

"And obviously I *was* in danger, since I got voted out!" He stops and takes a deep breath, visibly attempting to calm down. "Look, just *try* to see it from my perspective, okay? You just spent the last hour doing your level best to convince the jury that you played this amazing strategic game, that you were on top of everything from beginning to end, right? And now you're telling me the exact opposite, that you had no idea I was going home. What am I supposed to believe?"

My vision goes blurry. "You're supposed to believe the truth," I say, blinking away a tear. "You're right. I should have played my idol for you. If I could go back and do it differently, I gladly would. But holding onto it was a *mistake*, not some nefarious plot to send you home. My feelings for you are real, and I would never, *ever* do that to you."

Tears begin to fall down his face, and he looks away again. "My feelings were real too," he says, his voice quivering. "But that doesn't change the fact that you could have saved me and didn't."

I step closer to him, gently cupping his face with both hands. "Please, Cole," I whisper into the canyon that separates us. "I'm begging you, don't throw away everything we have because of one mistake."

For a second that feels like a lifetime, he just stands there silently, unmoving as a statue. Then he sighs and pulls away from me. "I'm sorry," he says, his eyes not quite meeting mine. "I think

… I think I just need some time."

Without giving me a chance to respond, he turns away and leaves the room. His footsteps echo in the caverns of my mind, and even though I might have just won the game, it feels like I've lost everything.

CHAPTER 24

I'm woken the next morning from a fitful sleep by a knock on my door. I almost don't answer it. Even though I just slept in a real bed for only the second time in the last month, I'm more tired than I ever have been in my entire life. I spent the rest of last night in self-imposed isolation, only leaving my room to sneak out for just long enough to fill up a plate with food and bring it back. I should have been celebrating with my fellow contestants, but I couldn't stand the thought of pretending like everything was okay when all I wanted to do was break down and cry. More importantly, I couldn't take the chance that Cole would be out there, too. If I saw him, that might have pushed me over the edge.

Now, as I struggle to get out of bed and put on clothes, I wonder if it's him at my door, here to apologize to me and try to make up with me. I'm honestly not sure what I'll do if that's the case. I want to slam the door in his face, to hurt him like he hurt me last night, and I also want to run into his arms and never let him go.

But when I answer the door, it's only Neema waiting for me, and part of me can't help but be disappointed. She looks as dapper as ever, her attention absorbed by a clipboard that holds a few papers. "Ryan, good to see you. I just wanted to—" She glances up, her voice cutting off abruptly as she frowns. "Are you okay? You look like shit."

"I'm fine," I reply, ignoring the pang of pain that flares in my chest. *What would you even say if it were him*? "What do you need?"

Her frown deepens. It's obvious she doesn't really believe me, but thankfully, she doesn't press the issue any further. "I need to go over a couple of things with you before you go home. Do you mind if I come in?"

I wave her into the room, and she steps in, taking off her

sunglasses. "For starters, congratulations on making it to the final two," she says, her tone as professional as ever, like we're in a conference room in some nondescript office building rather than on a tropical island. "Like Alex said last night, you'll find out whether you won at the live finale in a few months. We'll email you an invitation a couple of weeks before. It'll let you know where and when to show up, and how many guests you can bring. I think last year we allowed everyone to bring four family members, but if you really need more than that, contact me, and I'll see if we can get you some extra tickets."

Arielle is probably the only person I'll want to be there, so that shouldn't be a problem. "Sounds good," I reply. "Anything else?"

She nods. "I know you're a lawyer, so you probably read the contestant agreement we had you sign before the game in full, but I'm still going to remind you of a few provisions just to be certain." She holds up a finger. "First, don't spill any details of the game, especially your placement. We don't want any spoilers floating around the internet. That includes not showing off your insignias or any other souvenirs you're bringing back." Another finger. "Second, while you are free to exchange contact information with your fellow contestants, we ask that you try to avoid being seen together in public. *Definitely* don't post on social media with any of the other contestants until after the finale." A third finger joins the other two. "Finally, don't speak to any reporters or media about your time on the island unless you get explicit approval from me or another producer. Got it?"

Those rules sound a bit excessive, but I'm sure they'd rather be safe than sorry. "I understand."

"I figured you would. Of course, those rules only last until the finale airs. After that, feel free to publicly hang out with the others or do interviews to your heart's content."

"Got it. Thanks, Neema."

"No problem." She turns to go, but right before she reaches the door, she faces me once more, and when she speaks again, there's a note of warmth in her voice. "And, Ryan … look, I don't want to step on anyone's toes, but I think I know what's bothering you. I've watched you play for the last thirty-three days, and I've seen how resilient you are. I know it hurts now, but you'll get over it soon enough."

I spend a good portion of the day pondering what Neema said. *Does she really know what happened between Cole and me?* I know the producers watch the film pretty much in real time, but I feel like we were pretty circumspect, and our big conversation on the beach the night after Marina was voted out wasn't filmed at all. At least, I *think* it wasn't. Cole could have mentioned something about it in one of his confessionals, but that seems unlikely when he was so concerned about coming out on TV. Maybe she heard us arguing yesterday, remembered his question to me at tribal, and put two and two together. I wouldn't put it past her.

I haven't solved the mystery by the time a bus comes by to take us to the airport a few hours later, and with some effort, I push it to the back of my mind as I load up my luggage. *It's not like it really matters anymore.* But it niggles at the back of my mind, like a rock in my shoe that I can't quite get out.

For better or worse, the ride to the airport is long, and eventually I let my mind turn to other topics. I'm excited to see Arielle after so long apart, and I can't wait to sleep in my own bed and order from my favorite restaurants whenever I feel hungry. But at the same time, as we get further from our own little portion of the island, an ache builds within my chest, as though I'm leaving a little piece of myself behind.

That ache only intensifies as we arrive at the airport, but thankfully, I'm able to put it out of my mind in the commotion of unpacking and checking in for our flight. The airport is fairly small—I can't imagine they get too many visitors, given how remote it is—and some of the production crew will be flying back with us, making our group even larger. The good news is that it's easier to avoid Cole; every time I think I see him, I look away as quickly as I can. I really don't think this is a good place to have a mental breakdown.

Thankfully, we only have to wait a little while before we all get on a flight to Honolulu, and my seat on the plane is nowhere near Cole's. I spend most of the ride with my earbuds in, listening to music while I stare out the window, trying to think about anything other than him. I'm mostly successful, and when we touch down five-and-a-half hours later, I hurry off the plane and to my next gate, so I don't even have to look at him.

As my final plane touches down in northern Virginia nearly twelve hours later, the noonday sun high in the sky, all I can think about is how it feels like a lifetime since I took off in the opposite direction, bright-eyed and excited, with no idea of what was coming my way. *If only I could go back and tell myself not to fuck it up.*

Once I've collected my bags and made my way through customs, all that's left to do is take the Metro to my one-bedroom apartment in Logan Circle, and I finally stumble through the door after more than twenty-four hours of traveling, jet-lagged to hell, ready to collapse into my bed and sleep forever.

But to my surprise, Arielle is waiting for me in my living room, curled up under a blanket on my couch, with a steaming cup of something in her hands. Her dark brown hair reaches down to her shoulder; it was quite a bit longer before the chemo, but even in the last month, it's grown out a bit. She's skinny, but nowhere near as gaunt as she was right after the treatment ended, and her eyes sparkle as she looks at me. In short, even if she's not fully back to the way she was before the cancer, she's clearly on the upswing, and some—but not all—of the guilt I felt at leaving her evaporates.

As soon as I walk into the room, she sets down her mug and gets up to greet me, wrapping me in a tight embrace. "Hey there, little bro," she says, gently rubbing my back. "It's good to see you."

"Hey to you too," I reply, giving her a tired grin. "Aren't you supposed to be at work? I didn't expect to see you until tonight or tomorrow."

"I told the principal you were coming back today, and she basically insisted that I take the day off. Didn't even have to use one of my vacation days." She squeezes me once more, then moves back to the couch, patting the seat next to her. "Anyway, I'm here now, so come sit and tell me all about your exciting journey! I want to hear everything."

I open my mouth, ready to regale her with tales of my time on the island. But before any words come out, it finally sinks in that I'm home, that it's done, and suddenly all the emotions that I've been barely holding back for the last two days, all the memories of Cole, both happy and sad, slam into me. *Why? Why did I have to fall for him when I* knew *it would end badly*? Before I know it, I'm sobbing, great heaving wracks that seem to start deep in the pit of my stomach and work their way up to my eyes and nose and mouth.

In a flash, Arielle is wrapping me in her arms again, guiding me to the couch while I continue to cry. "It's okay," she whispers, her voice full of love. "It's all right. I'm here for you."

She holds me while I let it all out, allowing the pain and sadness and regret to wash over and through me. I know there's no use in fighting it, so I just ride the wave, and after a while it recedes, slowly at first and then quicker, as my sobs turn to tears, then hiccups. In a weird way, it feels good to get all of it out, and when my tears are finally dry, I feel like a new man.

Apparently deciding that I'm in the clear—for the moment, at least—Arielle lessens her hold on me just enough to lean back, so I can see her face. "Do you want to talk about it?" she asks, her eyebrows raised.

I nod, wiping a stray tear away from my cheek. I know Neema told me not to spoil anything, but I trust Arielle not to spread it around. Besides, if I don't get all this out, I think I might burst. "Yeah, I do. Just give me one second." I close my eyes and take a deep breath, trying to calm myself a bit more, then open my eyes again and look at her. "Okay, I should probably start at the beginning. There was this guy named Cole on my tribe, and he …"

I continue my story, telling her absolutely everything: how I fell for Cole even though I tried my best not to, how I eventually found out that he felt the same way for me, how I feel like I lost everything even though I might have won the grand prize. Just like when I was crying before, it hurts to remember everything, much less put it into words. But at the same time, it also feels cleansing, like my memories were venom flowing through my blood that's now being purged.

When I finally get to the end, we're both quiet for a few moments. "Ryan, I'm so sorry," she eventually says, her voice low. "I can't begin to imagine what that must have been like."

"It was terrible," I reply, my throat scratchy. "But if I end up winning, it was worth it."

She frowns. "Do you really mean that, or are you just saying it?"

"I mean it. I'm not saying there's nothing I would change, but if it makes your life better, then I'm happy."

She just rolls her eyes at that. We had this debate several times before I left, and I don't think either of us really wants to re-litigate it now. "We'll find out whether you won soon enough," she says, gently poking me in the stomach. "In the meantime, how about we get an early dinner? You look like you haven't eaten in a month."

I laugh despite myself. "I mean, yeah, that's pretty much exactly what happened."

"I know, that's why I said it." She grins at me. "Pizza or Chinese?"

Over the next few months, I gradually slip back into my normal routine. At first, it's more difficult than I expected, because in some ways, my mind is still out there on the island. I eat far more than I usually do those first few weeks, partially to replace the weight I lost, but also because each time I sit down for a meal, some animal instinct the back of my head worries that it could be days until I eat again. And when I go back to work, I have to stop myself from analyzing every little thing my coworkers say, just in case they're planning to vote me out.

Thankfully, as time passes, I find it easier and easier to unlearn those habits, and my time in Samoa seems to fade into a distant, hazy memory. Of course, I can recall details if I stop to think, or if someone asks me what it was like. But I no longer have a moment of confusion when I wake up in the morning, wondering why I can't see the sky through palm fronds or hear the roar of the waves on the sand.

Meanwhile, I hear from a few of my fellow contestants, mostly through social media. Marina and Katie both follow me on Instagram; the former posts pictures of delicious Cuban food pretty much every day, while the latter and I incessantly trade the nerdiest memes we can find. Tamika reaches out through email, and I give her Arielle's contact information—with Arielle's permission, of course—in case she has any questions about becoming a teacher. It'll be nice to see them in person once the show airs, but for now I'm content to keep in touch online.

Early on, part of me hopes that I might hear from Cole, too. After all, he did say he needed time rather than rejecting me outright. But I hear absolutely nothing from him, and as time goes on, the tiny spark of hope in my chest grows dimmer and dimmer, until one day I wake up and realize it's gone. I'm not sure what hurts more: the fact that he hasn't even *tried* to contact me, or that I've apparently accepted that he doesn't want me. But after a few days of agonizing, I manage to convince myself that it's better this way. At least now I can move on.

It doesn't take long for that conclusion to be tested, because I have a few first dates in the months after I get back, and not a single one of them goes anywhere. It's not that the guys I meet are bad, or anything as easy as that. No, the problem is that my heart isn't in it. Every time I start to wonder if maybe *this* one will work out, I inevitably start comparing them to Cole, and none of them match up. Eventually, I stop going on dates altogether. It's not fair to waste their time when there's a Cole-shaped hole in my heart.

I feel like I've almost gotten back to normal by the time the first episode of my season of *Marooned* airs, about four months after I got back from Samoa. Arielle plans a watch party at a bar near Dupont, and my friends and I watch as I meet the rest of the Merus on the very first day. They cheer during the first immunity challenge, groan when Meru loses, and debate whether the tribe should vote out Cole or Ashley. I cheer and groan and debate along with them, even though it hurts to see Cole when I know what's coming. Fortunately, he doesn't get a ton of screen time, not when there are seventeen other contestants still in the game, so I'm mostly able to sit back and enjoy watching myself stumble through the first three days.

We do the same thing the next week, and the week after that. To my mild surprise, the show hews pretty faithfully to what actually happened, albeit with a few changes. The editors seem determined to present me as some sort of strategic mastermind, which I personally find hilarious. Sure, I think I played a good game, but in reality, it was much more luck than skill. Meanwhile, it's fun to find out what was happening on the Sika tribe those first few weeks. Tamika told us some of it, but it's one thing to hear about it and another to actually see it.

As a fan of the show, I'm happy to see that the first few episodes are actually pretty good, and they only get stronger as the season goes on. The merge episode is my personal favorite: Randy is portrayed as an over-the-top villain, Tamika as his unwilling victim, and me and the Meru alliance as the plucky underdogs who flip the tables on him and use his own cockiness to bring him down. Somehow, the editors manage to make it feel even more satisfying than it was in real time, and I give them a lot of credit for that.

Early in the season, Cole and I don't get much screentime together. Of course, they had to show the reward in the pirate ship after the second immunity challenge, but that's about it. In fact, in the first episode, they even make it seem like I was set on voting for Ashley from the beginning, and present *Katie*, of all people, as being the swing vote.

That all changes after the merge, though, when it seems like Cole and I have a scene or two together in every episode. I almost can't watch the episode with the reward at the spa. It's just too painful to watch when I know how it's going to end.

At least now I have Arielle with me. When the scene with the spa reward finally ends and the show cuts to commercial, she leans over and takes my hand, squeezing it gently. "I see why you fell for him," she says quietly. "You'll get over him. I promise. All you need is time."

I try to give her a grin in return, but it feels fake, even to me. *If only it were that easy*. Still, I power through, and as the days go by, the pain lessens, and I can almost start to believe that things might go back to normal someday. Sure, I still think about him all the time, but at least when I do it's a dull ache, like an echo of remembered pain, rather than a knife to the chest.

The upturn in my mental health only lasts a few weeks, though, because as the live finale draws closer and closer, I begin to feel a rising sense of dread. I could lie to myself and say that I'm worried about finding out whether I won or lost—and, to be fair, that is a rather large part of it. But deeper down, I can't deny that part of the reason I'm ready to tear my hair out is that I'll have to see Cole again. Part of me wonders if I'll ever truly be able to get over him, and seeing him now, just when I was beginning to heal, feels like it could make everything worse.

The reality is that I don't have a choice. I can't skip the finale—even if I wanted to, I'm contractually obligated to do so unless I'm on my deathbed or something equally ridiculous—and I doubt Cole will miss it. The least I can hope for is that he'll avoid me, and I won't have to talk to him.

And yet, something tells me that's not going to happen. Maybe it's a premonition, or perhaps it's just pure pessimism, but somehow I know beyond a shadow of a doubt that I'm not done with Cole.

But, as bad as that is, it's not even the worst part. The part that really scares me is that I don't even know if I *want* to be done with him.

CHAPTER 25

My heart pounds as I walk into the studio building on the night of the live finale. Tonight I'll find out whether I'm going home with the million-dollar prize or empty-handed.

But first, I'm supposed to attend a reception with the other seventeen contestants, and to say I'm nervous would be an understatement. This episode will show everything from the final five on, which means I'll have to relive my heart breaking all over again. And that's not even considering that Cole will be here, whether or not I want to see him.

Arielle glances at me as we walk up to the front desk and frowns, as though she can read my mind. "Don't worry," she says quietly. "Just ignore him and think about how happy you'll be when you win the million."

I glance at her and give her a quick smile. "Is it that obvious that I'm freaking out?"

"You're about as subtle as a bull in a china shop," she says, rolling her eyes at me. "Now, come on. I know you can do this."

I nod, feeling slightly better. We step up to the security desk, where a suited guard gives us both badges and directs us deeper into the building. Tonight's schedule is, unsurprisingly, quite packed. According to the invitation Neema emailed me, first up is the aforementioned reception for the contestants and their families. Then, the guests take their seats in the auditorium while the eighteen of us go to our dressing rooms and get our hair and makeup done. After we're suitably coiffed, we'll gather in a private room to watch the first part of the episode together, while the guests watch on a big screen. Once it gets to the final tribal council, Rhonda, the jury, and I will move to the auditorium stage so Alex can reveal the winner on live TV. Honestly, I wish they could just tell me and Rhonda who won now, but that wouldn't make for good entertainment, so it's not going to happen.

To my surprise, when I scan the room, I don't see Cole, even though it's clear that just about everyone else is already here. *Did he get delayed?* Maybe he just went to the bathroom or something. Whatever the reason, I'm not going to look a gift horse in the mouth, so I stride into the room before my brain can tell me to stop. *Worry about him later.*

Rhonda spots me almost immediately and comes up with a huge grin on her face. "Ryan!" she exclaims, giving me a warm hug. "I missed you, honey."

"I missed you, too," I tell her. It's the truth; hopefully, now that the show is ending, we can actually see each other once in a while. "How have you been?"

"Oh, you know. Same old, same old." She turns to Arielle and gives her a hug, too. "And you must be Arielle. I'm glad we finally get to meet in person. I've heard so much about you."

"Is that so?" Arielle gently pokes me in the side. "I don't know what this one said about me, but I'm sure it was all positive."

Rhonda laughs. "Of course it was," she says, winking at me. "Why don't you both come over and meet my family?" She motions us to follow her, heading deeper into the mass of people.

I look at Arielle, who nods, and we catch up to Rhonda in short order. "By the way," I say to the latter, "have you seen Cole? I didn't see him when we came in."

Rhonda turns to look at me, her eyebrows slightly furrowed. "Can't say I have, but I'll let you know if I do."

I nod silently and continue to follow her, trying to keep my expression normal despite the fact that my thoughts are roiling. *What is he waiting for?* I don't really *want* to see him, but if I have to, I might as well get it over with now, so I don't have to worry about it anymore. If I'm going to have to see him, I'd at least like a little bit of a warning. I don't want to have him come out of nowhere and surprise me when I'm not expecting it.

It's for that reason that I keep one eye on the entrance as Rhonda introduces me to her husband and son, although I try my best to seem engaged and outgoing. I continue to watch the door even after Rhonda and I finish our conversation, and I go say hello to the other contestants. But Cole doesn't show up, and with each minute that passes, I grow more and more confused. *Where is he?*

By the time production lets us know that we need to make our way to the dressing rooms, Cole still hasn't arrived. As I bid Arielle goodbye and follow the other contestants deeper into the studio, I'm starting to wonder if he's going to be here at all.

Having my hair and makeup done takes less time than I expected, and before I know it, I'm in the green room with the other contestants. There are plush chairs facing a big-screen TV showing the local news, which usually airs in the hour before the show comes on. Most of the others are here already, either seated in one of the chairs or filling up a plate at a buffet table in the back of the room, but Cole isn't among them. For a brief moment, I consider getting some food, but my appetite is completely gone. Instead, I just take a seat between Tamika and Rhonda, wondering why the hell Cole is doing this to me. I try to make small talk with the two women as we wait for the show to start, but I'm just too nervous to focus, so after a little while we just sit in silence. Hopefully, they'll chalk any awkwardness on my part up to anxiety about the winner reveal, rather than anything to do with Cole.

Then, just as the clock hits eight, there's a commotion at the entrance. Cole walks in, looking incredible despite appearing harried, wearing a blue button-down shirt that matches his eyes and white chino pants. I quickly look away before he catches me staring, my ears hot. A pulse of pain beats somewhere down low in my chest, and now that he's here, I almost wish he wasn't. *At least I don't have to talk to him.*

Thankfully, the episode begins just then, and I let myself get lost in the spectacle of watching myself on the big screen. Instead of getting straight to the action, the first few minutes are spent recapping the season up to this point, interspersed with confessionals from each of the final five, where we talk about our strategies and how we got here. Next, they show us at camp the night after we voted out Marina, with a voice-over from Cole saying how he's happy it wasn't him, and Rhonda explaining why we targeted Marina over Cole. Then the editors cut to the next morning for a quick scene with all of us sitting around the fire, and a confessional from Tamika where she says how important it is for her to win the next challenge.

After that, they cut to the challenge itself, and I watch as I run around on screen, collecting sandbags and shooting them at the targets. My heart pangs as screen-me picks Cole to share the pizza reward, and it gets even worse when the editors show us digging into our pizza, laughing and smiling like everything's fine. *If only I knew what was coming.*

After a minute or so of torture, the show cuts away from the reward to a shot of Tamika, Rhonda, and Katie walking back into camp, followed by another confessional from Tamika. "I *really* needed to win immunity today, and I came up short," screen-Tamika says, her shoulders slumped. "Lucky for me, there's one person out here who's a bigger threat, and my only chance is to convince the others to get rid of him instead."

Next is a shot of Tamika talking to Rhonda and Katie around the fire. "How would you two feel about getting rid of Cole?" she asks, her voice betraying only the tiniest hint of the desperation she must have been feeling. "He's a huge challenge threat, and he's likeable, too. If any of us are sitting next to him at the end, it's basically a guaranteed loss."

Cut to Rhonda doing a confessional, leaning up against a tree not too far from the ocean. "Tamika asked me and Katie what we think about getting rid of Cole," she says, tapping her finger against her lip. "At first, I thought there ain't no way I'm gonna do that. Cole's my ally, and I'd like to think I've built a pretty good bond with him." She frowns, clearly torn. "But then I realized that she's right, that he *is* a threat. And for all I know, this could be the last chance for us to get him out." She shakes her head. "But at the same time, there's one glarin' problem that we gotta fix before we can pull this off."

Back to the women sitting around the fire. "I might be interested," Rhonda says, while Katie nods. "But only on one condition."

Tamika lets out a long sigh. "What is it?"

Rhonda looks Tamika in the eye, her expression dead serious. "We can*not* let Ryan find out about this," she says. "Not even a whisper. If he gets the slightest hint o' what we're thinkin', he'll try to stop it. We gotta make sure he thinks it's you goin' home tonight, Tamika."

A feeling of mounting anguish rises in my brain as I begin to get the full picture. I knew they had lied to me, but actually *seeing* it happen—the effort to keep me from finding out, the way they strung me along like a lovestruck fool—makes me feel even worse. I glance at the real Rhonda, and she gives me a shrug and a guilty smile. *I can't believe they tricked me.*

I look back at the screen just in time to see the editors return to Rhonda's confessional. "I don't know what's goin' on between them boys," screen-Rhonda continues, her chin held high, "but all of a sudden they're like two peas in a pod." Shots of Cole and me enjoying ourselves at the reward are shown while Rhonda continues to speak. "I'm afraid they're gonna take each other to the end, and that leaves me high and dry."

Then it moves back to the three women sitting around the fire again, where they begin to hash out the details of their plan, strategizing how to keep me from finding out they're targeting Cole. Meanwhile, I put my head in my hands, the anguish I'm feeling now tinged with bitterness. I knew I was telling the truth when I told Cole I didn't betray him when we talked after the final tribal council, but I had no way to prove it. All I had was my own word, and that clearly wasn't enough for him.

Now the evidence is right in front of me, on a giant TV screen, being broadcast for the whole world to see. I still should have played my idol for Cole or just given it to him and let him decide whether to play it, and I regret not doing that. But this proves that I had no reason to think he was in danger, because Rhonda was telling me exactly what I wanted to hear. *He broke up with me for nothing.*

It's all too much to handle, and an overwhelming desire to flee, to be somewhere, *anywhere* else, takes over me. I jump up from my seat and all but run out of the room, not caring what the others think. *How could he do that to me*? I stumble down the hall towards my dressing room, blindly grasping for the handle, barely able to see where I'm going through my tears.

But just as I reach the door, I hear a voice behind me, from the very last person I want to talk to right now.

"Ry, wait!"

I turn to see Cole running up to me, his face flushed. "What do you want?" I ask, my muscles quivering and my voice taut. "Come to kick me while I'm down?"

He skids to a stop in front of me, slightly out of breath. "I just wanted to talk to you," he says, the words tumbling out like he's been holding them in for months. "Privately, I mean."

I narrow my eyes at him, my heart pounding like a drum. How dare he try this shit after what he did to me? "You want to *talk*?" I hiss. "What is there to talk about? I have nothing to say to you."

"Please, Ry." He steps forward; unlike his voice, his movements are slow, as though he's afraid I'll get spooked if he moves too fast. "Just for a moment. That's all I ask. If you don't like what I have to say, then I'll leave."

I consider him silently, then jerk my head towards the door, pushing down on my anger as best I can. I have a feeling he's not going to give up easily, and I might as well get this over with. Besides, it's not like this whole situation can get any worse than it is right now.

He follows me into the dressing room, carefully closing the door behind him. The episode is playing on a small TV in one corner, but I don't bother to turn it off. I want him to see just how wrong he was.

Cole turns to me, blinking rapidly. "Listen," he continues, his voice low. "I understand that you're furious with me right now, and I don't blame you. I guess I just …" He sighs and runs a hand through his blond hair. "I wanted to tell you I'm sorry."

My vision goes red, and I take a step towards him. Despite the fact that he outweighs me by at least twenty-five pounds, he flinches. "You're *sorry*?" I say, my voice heated. "We haven't talked in *months*, and that's all you have to say to me? The last time I saw you, you accused me of betraying you! Now you know the truth, and all you can say is *I'm sorry*?!"

At least he has the decency to *look* abashed. "You're right," he mutters, rubbing the back of his neck. "I fucked up big time. I realized as soon as I got home that you would never do that to me. It's just … well, when I saw you sitting next to Rhonda at the end, all I could think was that it should have been *me* sitting next to you, not her. And then when we talked right after, I let my paranoia get the better of me. You didn't deserve that, and I should never have reacted the way I did. I've been beating myself up about it for the last eight months."

If anything, his apology only makes me angrier. "You're damn right that I didn't deserve it. But why are you only telling me this *now*, when you apparently figured it out *several fucking months ago*?"

"I wanted to tell you before. But I wasn't sure *you'd* want to talk to *me*." He makes a sound that's somewhere between a laugh and a sniffle. "I was so nervous about seeing you tonight that I almost made myself sick. That's why I was late getting here in the first place. Besides, I knew if I was going to apologize, it had to be in person, and I was afraid that if I showed up at your apartment out of nowhere, you'd just slam the door in my face. I think that might have broken me for good."

He sounds so sincere, like he actually would've been hurt if I'd ignored him. That, plus the undertone of raw grief I hear in his voice, dispels my anger, leaving only emptiness behind. "What do you want, Cole?" I repeat, my voice leaden. "Just tell me already so I can go back to the green room."

He steps forward, stopping barely a few inches away from me, and I let him take my hand in his. "I want to be with you," he says, his voice as soft as his touch. "I pushed you away, and it was the biggest mistake of my life. You're still the most amazing, wonderful man I've ever met, and I was a fool to forget it. If you don't want to be with me, then just say the word, and I'll leave you alone. But I'm not going to leave here without at least *trying* to make things right."

I thought I was done crying, but apparently I was wrong, because tears once again come to my eyes. His words have given me something I thought was impossible: hope. *He wants to be with me?* Even though I tried to move on, I can't deny that part of me still wants him almost as badly as I did the day I first saw him, if not more.

But another, larger part is wary, because I've felt this same hope before. "I want to be with you too," I say, my voice shaky, barely above a whisper. "But first, I need you to promise me you truly mean it. You really hurt me, and I can't—I *won't*—go through that again. If you aren't absolutely, *positively* certain, then tell me now, so I can save myself the heartbreak."

"I mean it, Ry. I can't promise that I'll be a perfect boyfriend, or that dating me will be completely smooth sailing one hundred percent of the time." He lifts my hand up to his lips, lightly kissing my knuckles. "But I *can* promise you that I'll give it my best shot, and that I'll never hurt you like that ever again."

He falls silent, clearly waiting for me to respond, but for once in my life, I have no idea what to say. I want to believe he's telling the truth so badly it hurts. But if he was so willing to throw me away because of a misunderstanding, who's to say it won't happen the next time we hit a bump? I'd be the world's biggest idiot if I allowed myself to walk into that trap. On the other hand, if I let him go now, will I regret it forever?

I'm still undecided when I hear my own name coming from behind me. I turn to see the finale episode playing on the small TV in the corner, and wince when I see that it's showing the tribal council where Cole was voted out. If only I had just played my idol for him, I could have avoided all of this.

I move to look away, but Cole places a gentle hand on my shoulder. "Please watch it," he says softly. "I think you'll want to see what comes next."

I nod silently and focus on the TV, not trusting myself to speak right now, even though I'm incredibly curious.

On the screen, Alex finishes asking questions, and the five of us go up to cast our votes. It hurts to watch knowing what's about to happen, and when Alex comes back with the urn and asks if anyone wants to play an idol, I almost have to turn away again. But I power through, steeling myself as he reads the votes, announces that Cole has been voted off, and takes Cole's insignia and snaps it in half. The camera lingers on my face as Cole walks down the ramp, an expression of pure devastation reflecting the heartbreak I felt inside.

Then the camera cuts to Cole, sitting by himself in an area surrounded by torches. This must be his last words—everyone who's voted out gets to say a sentence or two right after they leave, and the editors usually play it over the end credits. I look at him questioningly, the real him, and he just nods to the TV.

Screen-Cole looks ragged, his face puffy, like he's been crying. "I didn't see that coming at all," he says, his voice trembling. "I'm sad that I won't win, but I'm even more sad that I'm leaving Ry behind, because …" He takes a breath and leans toward the camera, his jaw set. "Ry, if you're watching this, I want you to know that I love you. I'll miss you so much, and I can't wait to hang out with you once all this is over."

I turn back to the real Cole, tears in my eyes again. "Did you really mean it?" I ask, my voice uneven. "*Do* you really mean it?"

"I did, and I do." His eyes are locked onto mine, leaving no room for doubt. "I love you, Ry, and I always will."

All remaining shreds of resistance in my mind dissipate, and I gather him into my arms and kiss him deeply before pulling away again. "Oh, Cole," I breathe. "I love you too."

This time when he kisses me, his lips as soft as moonlight reflecting off the ocean, and it feels incredible. More than that, it feels *right*, like we were always meant to be together. *I've missed him so much.*

After a few seconds, he leans back again, although his body is still pressed up against mine. "Does this mean you'll give me a chance?" he whispers, grinning and tilting his head slightly.

I laugh despite my tears. "Yes, you big dummy. I want to be your boyfriend." My good mood fades slightly. "What happened to wanting to come out to your friends and family first? If they didn't already know, that was a pretty big giveaway."

He shrugs. "I've told everyone who matters. And even if I missed someone, it's not important. All I care about is getting to be with you."

Something warm and comforting alights deep within my chest, as though I've swallowed a tiny piece of the Samoan sun, and I give Cole a gentle smile. "In that case, count me in."

Then I'm kissing him again, slower this time, but no less sweet. He kisses me back, again and again, softly at first and then deeper, his body hot against mine. I grow flushed, like I'm standing in front of an oven with the door open, but it feels good, and I want *more.* I push him backwards until he's up against the wall, cupping his face in one hand. Still kissing him deeply, I slowly move my other hand down his back, feeling him pressed against me, and—

Just then, there's a knock at my door, and I jump away from Cole like a kid who's been caught with his hand in the cookie jar. A muffled voice comes through the door. "Ryan, are you in there?"

I motion for Cole to get behind me, holding a finger to my lips. Then I quickly attempt to fix my hair and clothes—unsuccessfully, for the most part—before opening the door a crack, revealing Neema's concerned face. "Everything all right?" she asks, frowning. "You're missing the show."

"I'm fine." My voice sounds higher than usual, but hopefully she just thinks I'm nervous about the upcoming reveal. "I spilled some soda on my shirt, and I came here to see if I could get the stain out."

She raises one eyebrow, giving me the distinct impression that she can see through that lie like glass. But all she says is, "Well, make it quick. You're supposed to be on stage in less than an hour."

"Understood. I'll be back in a minute or two."

"Awesome." She moves to go, but before she can get more than a step away, she turns around. "By the way," she says, the corners of her mouth turned up ever-so-slightly, "if you happen to see Cole, let him know that he needs to be back soon, too."

Doing my best not to blush, I assure her that I will, and she walks away again, for real this time. I wait until she turns the corner before I close the door, letting my head rest against the wood. *That was close.*

Cole's arms wrap around me from behind, and he kisses my neck, making me shiver. "Good thinking," he murmurs. "That would have been super awkward."

"Agreed." I turn to face him again and press my lips against his. "We should probably get back, shouldn't we?"

"We should." He kisses me once more, then grins. "After all, we still have to find out if you're leaving here with a million dollars in addition to a new boyfriend."

After a quick check to make sure we don't look *too* disheveled, Cole and I head back to the green room. I resume my seat, feeling as though a hundred-pound weight has been lifted from my shoulders. Rhonda gives me a questioning look as I sit down, but I just wave a hand to let her know I'm okay, and she nods and turns her attention back to the TV. I'm sure she, and everyone else, will find out about Cole and me soon enough, assuming they didn't already figure it out from his last words. For now, I just want to focus on the finale. I may have solved one problem, but there's still the little issue of the million dollars remaining.

I watch silently as the episode continues, showing Tamika's ouster, then me winning immunity at final three. As screen-Alex puts the immunity necklace around my neck, I can't stop myself from glancing at Cole, who smiles at me. I return his smile, even though I'm starting to feel very nervous again. *Less than half an hour left.*

After a little bit of on-screen deliberating and confessionals from me, Katie, and Rhonda, the show cuts to the final three tribal council. The editors keep this one relatively short, and before I know it, screen-Alex is snapping Katie's insignia in half, leaving Rhonda and me as the final two. Katie's last words play, and she talks about how proud she is to have made it this far, even if she didn't win.

As soon as Katie finishes talking, the episode cuts to commercial and Neema pokes her head into the green room less than five seconds after. "All right, everyone, time to get on stage," she says. "Follow me, please."

My heartbeat, which had calmed down a bit in the last hour or so, starts to pick up again as Neema leads the eighteen of us down a hallway, through a door, and onto the main studio stage. *It's now or never.* The stage is set up like a smaller version of the tribal council set, with stools for me and Rhonda on one side, the jury on the other, and a podium in between. The other nine contestants who were voted off before the jury phase get their own seats next to the stage, but off-camera.

The audience hushes as we all take our seats, presumably excited for the upcoming reveal. I search the crowd for Arielle and spot her in the front row, sitting next to Rhonda's family with a wide smile on her face. I do my best to smile back at her, although it's difficult considering how anxious I'm feeling right now. It's one thing to be on camera and know you're being watched by the viewing public, and another to actually *experience* it, especially when I might be about to lose to Rhonda.

But then I look over at the jury and see Cole, who winks at me and gives me a wide grin, and some of my nerves melt away. *Even if I lose, at least I'll still have him.*

Meanwhile, the episode continues to play on large screens surrounding the stage. I watch as screen-Rhonda and I eat breakfast together, interspersed with confessionals from each of us explaining why we should win the million. Then it's off to the final tribal council, where we make our opening statements before the jury grills us in turn. Hearing Cole's question and seeing his anger still hurts, even with all that's happened since then, but it's a mere shadow of what I felt at the time. I'm sure I can find a way for him to make it up to me.

Finally, screen-Alex makes his little speech about reading the votes at the live finale, and walks off-screen with the urn in hand. Almost seamlessly, the real Alex walks onto the stage holding the urn, while the audience claps and cheers. He's wearing the same clothing he was at the final tribal council, as though he's just stepped off the set in Samoa and been instantly transported to New York.

He takes the urn over to the podium and waves at the audience, giving them a chance to express their appreciation, while my heart rate somehow increases even more. *Come on, hurry up and tell me if I won already*!

Alex gives the audience a few more moments to run out of steam, then addresses them. "Thank you all for coming," he says, his voice booming, "and welcome to the live finale of season nineteen of *Marooned!*" More clapping and cheering from the audience. "Really," he continues, "thank you from the bottom of my heart. None of this would be possible without the fans. It's been an exciting season, but there's still one thing left to do." He turns to the two of us. "Ryan and Rhonda, are you ready to find out which one of you will win the million?"

I nod, feeling faintly nauseous, and Rhonda does the same, taking my hand in hers and squeezing it. *Here goes nothing.*

Alex grins. "In that case, I'll read the votes." He opens the urn and places the lid to one side, then pulls out one of the parchments and reveals it to us. "First vote: Rhonda.

"Ryan.

"Rhonda.

"Ryan.

"Rhonda.

"Ryan. We're tied: three votes Rhonda, three votes Ryan, one vote left."

Rhonda squeezes my hand tighter, and my heart thrums in my chest like a hummingbird. It all comes down to this.

Alex reaches into the urn for the last vote and pulls it out, moving as slowly as he can for maximum dramatic effect. "The winner of season nineteen of *Marooned* is ..." He turns to reveal the vote to us as the audience begins to cheer in anticipation. "Ryan!"

For a moment, I'm stunned, not quite believing what I heard. *Did he just say* ...?

Then the audience reaches a crescendo, and it all comes crashing into me. *I won*! Suddenly I'm crying again, for the second time in as many hours, but this time they're tears of joy. Rhonda hugs me, and I hug her back. *I really did it!* Arielle's going to be so proud of me. *Wait until she sees this*! I'll have to—

And then I remember that I'm not in Samoa anymore, and I

gently disengage myself from Rhonda before making my way off the stage, where Arielle waits with a huge grin. She hugs me tight, applying enough pressure to crack a rib. "Congrats, little bro," she says, almost shouting into my ear in order to be heard. "I never doubted you for a second."

I can't help but laugh at that. "Well, that's good, because *I* sure did."

"Trust me, I know." She laughs too, then unwraps her arms from around me. "Go celebrate with the others. I'm sure they want to congratulate you, too."

I do as she said, still grinning like I've just won the lottery, which I suppose I have. The other contestants, all seventeen of them, are waiting to greet me as I step back onto stage and I gladly accept their hugs and handshakes.

But even though there are more than a dozen people around me, I only have eyes for one. Cole hangs back, a big grin on his handsome face, and I slowly but surely make my way over to him, my smile matching his.

When I get close, he throws his arms around me and pulls me to him, crushing me into a hug almost as tight as Arielle's. "I knew you could do it!" he exclaims, his voice sending goosebumps down my spine. "I'm so proud of you."

"Thank you," I reply, my voice somewhat muffled since my mouth is pressed against his chest. "I couldn't have done it without you."

"I don't know about that." He leans back so I can see his face; he's still grinning, but his eyes are serious. "You would have won no matter what. You're incredible, Ry. That's why I love you so much."

If I thought my heart was full before, I was wrong, but it surely is now. "I love you too, Cole," I whisper.

I look up into his beautiful eyes, and he must see the question written in mine, because he nods, grinning even wider. I close the distance between us and kiss him, and he kisses me back, neither of us caring that there are millions of people watching. His lips taste sweet, like triumph, and when it's over, I rest my forehead against his, the two of us in our own little bubble, surrounded by and yet separate from the other contestants and the cheering crowd. *This is what I really won*, I realize, a sense of wonder dawning over me. *Not just the million dollars, but Cole, too.*

And if I had to choose, I'd take him over the money every single time.

ABOUT THE AUTHOR

Ben Chalfin is an intellectual property lawyer by day and a romance writer by night, skillfully bridging the gap between the precision of patent law and the emotional depth of storytelling. Hailing from Maryland with a loyal allegiance to the Ravens, Ben's academic journey took him from Virginia to North Carolina, culminating in a career in Philadelphia—a city that reflects his own blend of innovation and historical richness. Whether drafting patent applications or exploring the complexities of love and loss in their novels, Ben brings a unique perspective to both the legal and literary worlds, celebrating the power of creativity and the human spirit.

LOOKING FOR MORE ROMANCE?

Sergio Durand, renowned photographer and playboy extraordinaire, plans to welcome the New Year in style. Along with his brother Adrien, they're off to the winter wonderland of Lake Placid, ready for a holiday filled with skiing, laughter, and good company. Their group includes best friend Holden, his wife Rose, and their charming son Henry—a perfect celebration... until it isn't.

The festive spirit turns sour when Sergio crosses paths with Jeremy Owens, the one who got away. After a series of blunders leaves everyone around him fuming, Sergio finds himself caught in a bizarre twist of fate: a time loop forcing him to relive New Year's Eve repeatedly. With each reset, Sergio scrambles to mend broken bonds with his brother, pacify a disgruntled Rose, and perhaps, rekindle a lost love with Jeremy.

Can Sergio navigate through his mistakes and salvage the relationships most important to him, or is he doomed to spend eternity making the same missteps on the last night of the year? Dive into 300 New Year's Eves to find out if Sergio can discover the true meaning of the holiday spirit and secure a second chance at love.

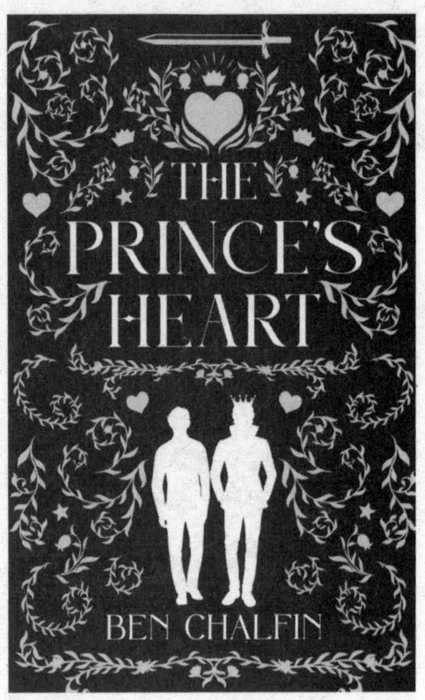

In the heart of Soeria, where royal bloodlines carve the paths of destiny, Prince Darien Garros, the kingdom's beloved second son, faces the age-old clash between duty and desire. For years, Darien has dodged the court's expectations to find a suitable match, yearning instead for a love that values the man behind the crown. His longing seems answered in Tag Leara, whose charm and genuine affection ignite a hope Darien dared not admit.

Yet, fate is a fickle master. A sudden tragedy propels Darien into a role he never sought, challenging his deepest convictions. As the weight of legacy and the whispers of power threaten to suffocate him, Darien confronts the ultimate test. Torn between the call of his blood and the pull of his heart, he stands at a crossroads that could reshape the future of Soeria itself.

With every choice comes a price, and Darien must decide: Will he follow the stringent demands of royalty, or will he choose the perilous path of love? In a world where allegiance and affection collide, Prince Darien's story is a testament to the enduring battle between the crowns we bear and the hearts we hold dear.

Abigail Meyer and Freya Jonsson can't stand one another.
But could their severe hatred be masking something else entirely?

From the moment they locked eyes in high school, Abby and Freya have been at each other's throats. Fifteen years later, when Abby and Freya cross paths again, their old rivalry doesn't take more than a few minutes to begin anew.

And now Naomi, Abby's best friend, is falling for Freya's producer and close pal, Will. Both women are thrilled to see their friends in a happy relationship – except they are now only a few degrees of separation from the person they claim to despise… and they can't seem to avoid seeing one another.

After their encounters repeatedly devolve into warfare, Abby and Freya's friends decide their age-old rivalry can only mean one thing: true love. Will their friends bring them together? Or will Freya's refusal to admit who she is keep them from discovering their underlying passion?

Chicago hairstylist Bastian Russo has only three things to his name: a pair of $1,200 shears, a Boystown studio apartment, and a list of men's names written on his closet wall. His constant worry that he's not good enough and his chronic inability to trust are what leaves him heartbroken time and again.

After he adds the latest name, he turns to his best friend, Andres Wood, for solace. But instead of treating Bastian to dinner, drinks, and the usual effortless banter, Andres makes an interesting suggestion: that Bastian should get over the breakup by dating ... Andres.

Sure, Andres is successful and attractive, but he also knows everything there is to know about Bastian—including what an insecure pain in the ass he is. Meanwhile, everyone in Bastian's life, from his mother to his co-workers, thinks he's an idiot for not having dated Andres already. So, what could go wrong? Everything.

Now Bastian has to sort out his inadequacy and trust issues to prove he's worthy of transitioning from Andres' best friend to his lover. Otherwise, it's a matter of time before one or both of them end up on Bastian's list of Boystown Heartbreakers.